"WE'RE TALKING A RELIGIOUS COUP OF INCOMPREHENSIBLE PROPORTIONS."

"Do I smell a change in plans, then?" McCarter asked Price.

"Not for you," she replied. "But we wanted you to have a better idea of what you're up against. We'll be taking care of the rest of this through Able Team."

"And how exactly do you plan to do *that*, if I might be so bold as to inquire?"

"We're sending them to Tehran to handle the matter personally," Price said.

"Wait. Let me make sure I just heard you correctly. You're sending Able Team into Iran?"

"Yes."

"Oh, bloody hell," McCarter said. "I don't think that's such a good idea."

"Well, the decision's already been made by the President, and Hal's in complete agreement. I had my own reservations, but it didn't seem like the issue was up for debate. Not now anyway."

"Have you told Able Team yet?"

DON PENDLETON'S

STONY

AMERICA'S ULTRA-COVERT INTELLIGENCE AGENCY

MAN®

CLOSE QUARTERS

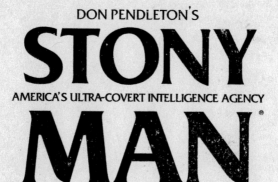

A GOLD EAGLE BOOK FROM

WORLDWIDE®

TORONTO • NEW YORK • LONDON
AMSTERDAM • PARIS • SYDNEY • HAMBURG
STOCKHOLM • ATHENS • TOKYO • MILAN
MADRID • WARSAW • BUDAPEST • AUCKLAND

Recycling programs
for this product may
not exist in your area.

First edition June 2012

ISBN-13: 978-0-373-80433-7

CLOSE QUARTERS

Special thanks and acknowledgment to
Jon Guenther for his contribution to this work.

Printed in U.S.A.

CLOSE QUARTERS

CHAPTER ONE

Paraguay, South America

Sweat stung his eyes.

The collar of a khaki shirt chafed his sunburned neck.

The stifling, oppressive heat of the jungle threatened to overtake him.

His lungs burned and his legs ached with every stride.

Christopher Harland had been running through the dense jungle for the past half hour as if his life depended on it—because it did. He didn't know the identity of his pursuers, but there was no doubt about what would happen if they caught him. That was all the incentive he needed to run this race —giving up was tantamount to a prolonged and painful death. Or worse, even, as his pursuers might actually subject Harland to the same things to which they had subjected his trusted colleagues, his friends, even a woman he loved.

Who the hell knew about their fates? He couldn't even be sure of his own at this point.

Harland's lungs threatened to give out on him. He heard the crash of the small armed unit as they closed the distance. He couldn't keep this pace forever. No amount of track and field at Rutgers could have prepared him for it. He could only thank his coaches now for the training, although the repeated wind sprints at the time hadn't seemed all that useful to most of the members on his team.

Harland's flagging endurance ceased to be a concern as he felt something snag his ankle. He stopped and turned to see what it was, but got no further in his inspection—the sensation of his body leaving the ground proved as distracting as it was disconcerting. The world around him seemed to swirl in a haze of reds and blacks, stars popping in front of his eyes from the abrupt change in orientation.

Harland coughed as he fought for air. It felt as if his heart might explode in his chest. Would that be such a bad way to go? Not as bad as the way he'd exit this world at the hands of the figures who emerged from the jungle shadows. Most of them were dark-skinned but not in a mestizo way. These faces implied a more exotic place of origin, most likely somewhere in the Middle East or northern Africa. Harland had learned quite a bit from his ethnic studies in college.

Harland's head hammered as he dangled helplessly from the tree. As he spun he could see that at least a dozen men had been chasing him. Why? Was he really a target of that importance or was it merely that they didn't want him to get away? Clearly these men were operating in secret here, although Harland couldn't imagine who they were or why they'd be interested in him. He'd heard the stories of Americans being kidnapped and held for ransom or missionaries murdered for proselytizing, but this situation seemed much different.

Harland opened his mouth and gulped air. He thought about speaking to them, but before he could decide his body suddenly plummeted to the ground.

He cursed as putting out a hand to break his fall sent shooting pains up his wrist, resulting in what was more likely a sprain than a fracture. Either way, it hurt and he wished these men would either kill him outright or let him go instead of toying with him.

It wasn't to be.

In a minute that seemed more like an hour, two men grabbed Harland and hauled him to his feet. They shoved him against the gnarled trunk of a giant tree, the surface biting into his skin like sandpaper. They pinned his arms behind him, and then Harland felt something thick and smooth being inserted under his right armpit and drawn across his back until it extended out the opposite side under his other armpit. The men then jerked Harland's arms down, causing a fresh wave of searing pain to travel up his arm from his injured wrist. They bound the stick to him with thick cord at shoulders and forearms and then spun him.

"Why are you doing this?" he asked, first in English and then in Spanish.

That bought him a slap across the mouth. "Shut up!"

Harland's face stung and he surmised the striker had left a red welt.

Without another word his captors each grabbed one end of the stick and lifted just enough that Harland had to walk almost on his tiptoes to accompany them. He'd probably managed to make it at least a couple of miles from the Peace Corps encampment—walking all that distance back in this fashion would not be pleasant. Then again, what was pleasant about any of this?

His forced march turned out to be even more grueling than he'd suspected it would be, and Harland was exhausted by the time they reached the volunteer camp. Or what was left of it. The wooden buildings that had been home for the past three months were now smoldering hulks, their insides gutted by fire and the exteriors little more than charred, smoking frames. Only the concrete pads on which they'd been built had managed to survive. Harland noticed an odd, thick haze—a mix of orange and green in the late-afternoon sunlight filtering through the jungle canopy overhead—had fallen on the camp. It wasn't caused by the smoke. This was some sort of natural phenomenon he'd never experienced before and he wondered if it had something to do with the fire.

The men half dragged, half walked Harland across the remains of the encampment until they reached the one building that had remained untouched: the camp mess. A man stood there, dressed in camouflage khakis like the others. A belt with a mixture of shotgun shells and high-velocity rounds encircled his waist in some kind of military webbing. His boots were highly polished and muscular arms bulged taut against the rolled-up sleeves of his uniform shirt. While the other men wore black berets, this one wore a blocked utility cap with gold wreaths braided along the brim and some kind of circular emblem on its crown.

The man turned and studied Harland for a time, his eyes indiscernible behind his sunglasses. A scar ran along his meaty jaw, very faint but evident. It was thin and looked as if it might have been caused by a razor blade or very sharp knife. His breath stank of cigarettes as he leaned in and studied Harland with a steady gaze.

"What is your name?" he asked in English.

That accent! Where the hell had Harland heard it before? He couldn't remember and it was driving him nuts because it sounded nearly identical to the accent of the one who'd yelled at him. Harland knew it didn't really matter, however, since his chances of getting out of here were slim. And even if he did manage to escape or they decided to let him go, who would he tell?

"I asked you your name!" the leader said. He tapped Harland's forehead and said, "Are you stupid, American?"

"Harland," he said. "My name is Christopher Harland. What've you done with my friends?"

"You should be worried for your own future," the man said with a smile that lacked any warmth.

"Where are you from?" Harland asked. He looked around him at the men busily emptying the trays and silverware and other materials from the camp mess and then affixed his gaze on the man. "You're not part of any guerrilla outfit I've ever seen. And I should tell you that we're a U.S. Peace Corps group. If we're out of contact long, you can bet your ass someone will know about it soon enough. They'll come looking."

The military leader favored Harland with another flat smile as he removed a pack of cigarettes from his pocket, put one in his mouth and turned his head to the side. An aide immediately stepped forward and lit it. The man took a deep drag, let out the smoke slowly through his nostrils and studied Harland, nodding steadily.

"Yes, yes…I'm sure you're correct. And that is exactly why you have been chosen among your people to walk out of here alive."

"What? What are you talking about?"

"I'm saying as long as you do what I tell you, your friends will remain alive. Otherwise, they are all dead and so are you."

Harland considered this for a time, finally realizing he didn't have any choice. If Dee and the rest of his entourage were to survive then he would have to do exactly as the man said. He couldn't very well risk their lives. He'd never wanted this responsibility anyway—never asked to be responsible for the safety and welfare of others—so it didn't make cooperating with this man seem so bad. Whoever he was, it made little difference. Harland was going to come out of this breathing and save a lot of lives in the process. How could that be bad?

"All right, I'll play the game your way. What do you want me to do?"

And so the man issued Christopher Harland detailed instructions.

CHAPTER TWO

Little Havana, Florida

The stifling humidity had put Carl "Ironman" Lyons in a foul mood.

Only the ice-cold beer served by a smoking-hot waitress with wild brunette hair kept his temper in check. The sweat from the frosty bottle dribbled across Lyons's left hand and pooled onto the table. Once in a while, he'd wipe the cool water against his forehead but it didn't help much. Lyons couldn't remember the humidity being this bad during his time in Los Angeles when he was a cop with the LAPD.

Watching his Able Team partners stuff their faces with jalapeño nachos washed down by copious amounts of Malta Hatuey soft drinks didn't improve his disposition. Lyons, leader of the elite covert-action team, sighed as he took in their surroundings for the tenth time in the past half hour. "Once more we've been relegated to doing a job that should be assigned to the federal boys."

"You know what I think?" Hermann "Gadgets" Schwarz managed to ask around a giant bite, cheese and sour cream running down his chin. "I think we should order another one of these."

Rosario "Politician" Blancanales made a concerted effort to chew and swallow his own decadent mouthful before saying, "Cheer up, Ironman. You should make the most of this. Try to think of it as a vacation."

"A vacation."

"Sure," Blancanales said, drawing the word out like a man tempting his grandchildren with a story. "I mean, there are much worse places the Farm could've sent us."

"Oh, yeah? Like where?"

"Well, I—"

"Alaska," Schwarz said.

Blancanales jerked a thumb at his companion. "There you have it! Alaska. It's cold there."

"They also have some of the best fishing this time of year," Lyons countered.

"They also have polar bears," Schwarz mused. "You could get eaten alive."

Blancanales feigned a conspiratorial whisper, cupping his hand to his mouth as he said, "I don't think they'd find Ironman too palatable."

Lyons ignored the gibes from his friends as two men escorted a third across the street. They headed straight for Able Team's table in the cabana-style exterior setting of the lounge. Lyons scowled at them, wondering how they'd managed to escort the guy this far without getting him wasted. Their charge wore khaki shorts and a Hawaiian-style silk shirt; sandals adorned his feet. He had light red hair that protruded in clumpy tufts from beneath his Marlins baseball cap. The man's dress perfectly blended with the styles worn by the Able Team warriors, but his escorts stood out like highway cones in their government suits.

They stopped at the table, and the taller one in serge blue removed his sunglasses. He looked around, then said, "You Irons?"

"Yeah," Lyons confirmed. He gestured to Blancanales and Schwarz respectively. "This is Rose and Black."

"Here's your man," they said.

Without a word the pair whirled and made distance back the way they had come.

The man stood there with a somewhat beleaguered expression. Lyons felt a bit of empathy for the guy. The two FBI agents assigned to bring him here were obviously intent on more important things, and Lyons couldn't imagine what he'd been through. The wrist brace on his right arm and deep scratches on his legs made it obvious he'd been in a recent tussle. Lyons had no doubt this was Christopher Harland.

"Have a seat," he said, waving Harland into the one vacant chair at their table.

The young man stuck his hands in his pockets and studied their faces in turn—almost as if sizing them up—before he sat.

"You hungry?" Blancanales asked.

Harland inclined his head at the disappearing agents and said, "They got me something when we landed. I'm good." After a pause he added, "Thanks."

"How about something to drink? You must be thirsty."

He nodded and Blancanales signaled the waitress. The young man ordered a beer—a Tecate—and watched the waitress with obvious appreciation as she jiggled away with his order.

Lyons smiled at his two companions. Okay, so maybe he could learn to like the kid, after all.

"How was your flight?" Schwarz asked to break the silence.

"It was okay."

"Those guys, they treat you okay?" Lyons asked.

"I suppose."

"You go by Chris?" Blancanales asked.

"I prefer Christopher."

"Fair enough."

Schwarz went back to shoveling food into his mouth while Blancanales took another pull at his malt-based soda.

Lyons looked around. He saw only a couple of people nearby, nobody within earshot. Midafternoon and the lunch crowd was gone. It was too early for happy hour. "We've been briefed on what happened to you."

"Okay," Harland said.

"Anything you want to add?"

"It's pretty much like I told them." Harland clammed up as the waitress dropped a napkin on the table, followed by his beer.

Lyons handed her enough cash to cover the entire tab plus a tip that was generous enough to imply they wouldn't need her again.

Once she'd left, Harland continued. "I barely managed to escape with my life. Those bastards are holding my friends hostage, including a woman I care about."

"What do they want with your team?" Blancanales asked.

Lyons eyed Harland. "And especially why would they keep the others and release just you?"

Harland pulled off his sunglasses to expose a fresh black eye. Something in his expression seemed hardened, more mature and empowered than the average twenty-eight-year-old college grad. His expression bore witness to untold brutalities and hardships, and Lyons felt a measure of regret.

"I didn't make any deals, if that's what you think," Harland said.

Lyons leaned close. "Hey, asshole, take it easy. We're on your side."

Blancanales quickly intervened in a way that had earned him the "Politician" nickname. "Listen, Christopher, we're not trying to give you a hard time. You can relax with us. Our job's to keep you alive, but in order to do that we need to know everything. You shoot straight with us and we'll do the same, no bull. Just tell us everything you can remember about these men."

Able Team had, of course, already been thoroughly briefed by Stony Man Farm. As soon as word came from channels—specifically a SIGINT analyst from the American embassy in the Paraguayan capital of Asunción—mission controller Barbara Price had called the Stony Man teams into action. The situation, as Harland had laid it out, was that seventeen members from a U.S. Peace Corps contingent along with three missionaries had been brutally assaulted and taken hostage by parties unknown. After they razed the camp and brutalized several of the women, they took them all except Harland. He'd been fortunate or maybe unfortunate enough to get the crap beaten out of him and sent to Asunción with a message: don't attempt to interfere or the hostages would be slaughtered.

"What were you doing there exactly?" Schwarz asked.

"I was there on a Peace Corps mission," Harland said.

Lyons said, "We understand that, but what kind of mission? Humanitarian aid, education, what?"

"Take your pick. After I left Rutgers I got selected to go down there and help try to bring modern facilities to their indigenous tribal populations. In some respects, these people have chosen a self-imposed exile.

Mostly it's a social and cultural isolationism but there's a political play to it, too."

"What kind of play?" Blancanales asked.

Harland took a long swallow from his bottle and wiped his mouth with the back of his hand. "More than sixty percent of the population of Paraguay is urbanized. The rest are content to retire to farming life, particularly since they have the sixth largest soy production in the world. A very small percentage have made their homes deeper in the jungle, traveling to the farms like sharecroppers and then back again at the end of the workday. It's almost a migratory existence. It's those people we were sent there to help."

"So these military men," Lyons said. "What can you tell us about them specifically?"

"Nothing. I was told that if I so much as breathed a word about what I saw they'd kill my friends. I took a risk just leaving the country. I'm sure they'll figure I've talked." Harland's voice cracked when he added, "They're probably all dead by now and I killed them."

"You can't think like that, man," Schwarz said.

"That's right, Christopher," Blancanales added in a gentle tone, squeezing Harland's shoulder. "We're not going to let anything happen to you. And if we can help it, we're not going to let anything happen to your friends, either."

"Get real, dude," Harland said as he wiped his bloodshot, swollen eyes. "You don't have any control over what's going on down there."

"We have more control than you might think," Lyons said.

Indeed, even as Harland's tough facade melted, the Able Team warriors knew something perhaps less than a dozen people in the world knew. Five of the toughest and bravest men alive were touching down in Paraguay at that moment. Few knew their names or places of origin, but the exploits of Phoenix Force were no less mythical than the fiery bird from which they drew their namesake.

"You haven't seen what these men are capable of," Harland said.

Blancanales smiled. "They haven't seen what we're capable of."

"Why don't you go ahead and drink up," Lyons said. "Sitting here with our derrieres hanging out for just anybody to take a shot at is starting to make me nervous."

"Remember," Schwarz quipped. "We were going to try to look at this as a vacation?"

Lyons's cold blue eyes glinted wickedly in the sunlight as he expressed alert like a terrier on a rabbit's scent. "I think it just got cut short."

Even as Schwarz and Blancanales turned to see what had Lyons's attention, the Able Team warrior was rolling out of his seat and grabbing hold of Harland's shirtsleeve. He yanked backward as he warned his two companions to take cover, although it seemed pointless since Blancanales and Schwarz were already in motion with the practiced reaction of combat veterans. The four men ate the decorative tile of the patio as young Arab types exited a black sedan, leveled SMGs and opened up on their position.

The report from the weapons drowned a shout of pain from Harland, who got slammed onto his shoulder with some significant force. He wouldn't realize until later it was a small price to pay in consideration that Lyons had kept his promise to save Harland's ass. Lyons ordered his charge to stay where he was, then whirled on one knee and reached beneath his loose-fitting shirt. In his fist rode a 6-inch Colt Anaconda, its silver finish brilliant in the afternoon sun. A successor to Lyons's .357 Colt Python, the pistol had been qualified by Lyons with six rounds in a one-inch shot grouping using 240-grain XTPs at 30 yards—a champion marksman's score. The Anaconda was deadly in the hands of the Able Team leader.

Lyons snap-aimed the pistol, going for the opponent who had experienced a gun jam, and squeezed the trigger twice. A pair of 300-grain jacketed hollowpoints crossed the gap in milliseconds and caught the intended target as if Lyons had fired point-blank. The first busted the gunner's chest open and exploded his heart, while the second ripped out a good portion of the left side of his neck. The man did a pirouette as the jammed SMG fell from his fingers and then he toppled to the pavement, bright blood springing from his neck in a geyser.

Lyons went low and pressed his back to the waist-high brick wall lining the dining patio even as a fresh maelstrom of rounds buzzed the air around them. The street and sidewalks had erupted in complete pandemonium, and the few diners who'd been sitting outside had either hit the ground and crawled for cover into the restaurant or simply beaten feet out of there.

Schwarz and Blancanales had produced their own sidearms, a Beretta 92-DS and a SIG-Sauer P-239, respectively. The pair found relatively decent concealment behind a set of potted rubber trees just ahead of the patio wall to the left of where they'd been seated. They took up positions and began dishing out some of what they'd been served.

Lyons took the moment to inspect Harland and make

sure the young man was still alive, and then risked breaking cover to assist his companions.

Two of the remaining gunners made a beeline for the cover of an old, beat-up SUV while a third apparently thought he was Superman and tried to take out his quarry single-handedly. For his troubles he got three of Schwarz's 9 mm slugs to the belly, followed by a head shot courtesy of Blancanales.

The other two opened up from the cover of the SUV parked at the curb, but they didn't have great position and their attack proved mostly ineffective.

Lyons considered their options and realized they had a better chance of squaring off with the opposition if they didn't have Harland to worry about. After all, chances were good he was the real target, and their enemy probably considered Able Team little more than collateral damage. They hadn't obviously thought it through, figuring they had surprise on their side, and now it had cost them half their team.

During a lull in the firing, Lyons said, "It would seem discretion being the better part of valor would apply in these circumstances."

"Agreed," Blancanales said. "You have a plan?"

"An idea. Give me covering fire. I'm going to get our lucky boy out of here."

Schwarz and Blancanales nodded in unison and returned their attention to their attackers. Lyons waited until they started pouring on the heat and then jumped to his feet, ran to Harland and hauled him to his feet. They continued on to the entrance in the restaurant, where Lyons quickly located the waitress.

"You got a freezer?"

She swallowed hard but an impatient scowl from Lyons shook her back to reality. She nodded and jabbed her finger toward a swinging door at the back. Lyons, one hand clamped on Harland's good arm, made the door in three strides and pushed it open with the muzzle of the Anaconda. He followed the weapon, his eyes tracking where he pointed the muzzle, ready for any sign of trouble. They reached the freezer door unmolested and Lyons yanked it open.

"Inside, little man."

"What? You ain't sticking me in no freezer…big man."

"They always want to argue," Lyons said before he hurled Harland through the doorway and slammed it shut behind him. He located a mop handle, wedged it against the bar so it couldn't be opened from the inside and then yelled, "Stay toward the back and keep down! I'll be back in a minute!"

The Able Team warrior then whirled and began searching the kitchen diligently for what he knew had to be close. It took what seemed like hours but was only actually a few minutes to locate several Sterno cans, the oversize kind designed for catering large parties. Lyons nodded in satisfaction and spun on his heel. He headed through the kitchen and returned to the main restaurant.

"One more thing, miss," Lyons said calmly amid the continuous exchanges of gunfire echoing on the air. "Any high-content alcohol? Preferably clear?"

Without leaving her position tucked behind the bar, the waitress turned, withdrew a bottle filled with clear liquor from a cabinet nearby and tossed it to him. Lyons set the cans on the counter, quickly inspected the contents and then nodded with satisfaction. He broke away the cap, snatched a wad of paper napkins off the bar and stuffed them into the top.

"Hey, buddy!"

Lyons turned in time to see something small and silver fly through the air. He reached out and snatched it, then noted it was a Zippo lighter with the symbol of the U.S. Army 82nd Airborne, Vietnam era. Lyons looked at the dark-skinned man whose salt-and-pepper beard stood out starkly against that face. The man sat on the floor against a booth and gave Lyons a double thumbs-up. Lyons offered him a wicked grin as he flipped back the lid with a metallic zing and fired up the napkins. He closed the lighter and tossed it back to the man with a nod.

"Airborne," Lyons said.

"All the way!" the man declared.

Lyons stepped through door and into the courtyard. Blancanales had just opened up with a fresh volley, while Schwarz was slamming home his last cartridge. He noticed Lyons approach and said, "Well, it's about time. You stop for a potty break or something?"

"Figured we could use a little help," Lyons replied as he tossed the Sterno cans at his friend.

Lyons then stepped into the clear and tossed the Molotov cocktail. Even as the bottle sailed toward the pair of gunners, they had noticed him and were fixing to turn their weapons in his direction.

That single mistake cost them the end game.

As Lyons dived for cover, the bottle clipped the edge of the SUV and broke open. Flaming liquor doused the two men and immediately ignited their facial hair. They stepped from cover, dropping their weapons as they tried to beat out the flames, but there would be no reprieve. Lyons turned to see Blancanales and Schwarz had the Sterno cans open and ready. Simultaneously, the pair rose and tossed their homemade grenades with unerring accuracy.

The gel substance clung to the pair of terrorists like goo and in moments their clothes had ignited. While it didn't really burn their skin, the highly flammable gel acting as a mild ignition point, the distraction proved fatal. No longer in danger of taking fire from the SMGs, Able Team doled out justice in a variety of calibers. Their two opponents fell under the heavy fire, and when the smoke cleared there were only two bloodied bodies remaining, the clothes still smoldering from the remnants of the liquor and chafing gel.

"Well, that's going to make identification a problem," Blancanales pointed out as sirens wailed in the distance. "You suppose we should stick around?"

"No, we better get scarce," Lyons said. He looked at Schwarz and said, "Still feel like a vacation to you?"

Schwarz shrugged. "At least we got nachos."

CHAPTER THREE

Tehran, Iran

Farzad Hemmati made his way through the alleys and back streets of his hometown with practiced ease.

It wasn't difficult given the fact the route tended toward desertion this time of morning—the Tehran police didn't feel any particular inclination to enforce the curfew unless someone appeared suspicious. A few of the citizens had work visas to be out during these hours, and Hemmati's forged papers were enough to pass all but forensic scrutiny.

That's if anyone bothered to check.

Hemmati had a cover story and had been schooled thoroughly in deception, first by the American CIA and then by his cleric masters. In fact, the head of the Pasdaran had ordered this meeting, summoning him to attend them at their hideaway nestled in the heart of the city's worst ghetto—as if there could be a worst ghetto. Hemmati didn't want to break it to his masters, but the fact remained this part of town didn't exactly have the market cornered on poverty. To call it a ghetto could've described about three-quarters of Tehran.

Still, this had been Hemmati's home for the past thirty years and it had seem him through the toughest times. It had also cost him the lives of his parents when he was ten, turning Hemmati into an orphan since none of his living relatives had either the interest or the money to take care of a growing boy. Hemmati might have ended up another street urchin or dead or even slaving away for the glory of the regime's war machine. The Pasdaran had spared him that fate, taken him under its wing.

They'd fed him, clothed him, educated and trained him.

And then they'd turned him loose on society and made him earn his way, gaining him the experience he would need to survive. Now he knew in his heart and mind that it was time to repay all he owed them. Hemmati welcomed whatever tasks might befall him with all of the obedience and respect due his masters.

Hemmati reached the rendezvous point and made his way along a very narrow alley that stank of urine and garbage mixed with the occasional whiff of hashish on the air. In the predawn gloom he could make out the hump of a displaced person—there were many throughout the capital—hunkered down and wrapped in whatever tattered cloth they could find to keep warm against the icy nights the prevailed that time of year.

Hemmati reached what appeared to be a wooden door, although it was lined with two inches of lead. He rapped twice—a simple knock, so simple that few would think to duplicate it. A moment later a plate slid aside, a pair of white eyes peered out and then the see-through slammed closed with a thud. The door opened a minute later just enough to allow Hemmati to slide past.

The man attending the door said, "Go right in, Master Hemmati. They await you."

Hemmati nodded and proceeded down a hallway about half the width of the alley. Only candles provided light. The place had no electricity and for very many good reasons that Hemmati opted not to consider at that moment. There'd be time for daydreaming later. Right now he would need his every wit about him for the task ahead. Hemmati continued to the end of the hallway and then turned to his left. He rapped once on the door before opening it and stepping into a room that was so familiar to him he almost felt as if he were a youth again, kneeling at his master's knees, studying the Koran and memorizing the fatwas, principles of the jihad.

"Come, Farzad," a voice called from the shadows on the far side of the room. "You are most welcome."

"It is good to see you again, Mullah," Hemmati said as he crossed the room and took a seat on the pillow at the edge of an ornate scarlet carpet covering the wooden floor.

Hemmati heard the rasp of a match against a striker and then a flame flared to life. The flash looked like lightning against the worn, haggard features of his master, but a moment later the wick of the oil lantern the cleric lit cast a glow to his countenance.

Hemmati had no idea how old Hooshmand Shahbazi actually was, as it would've been disrespectful to ever inquire of such matters, but the man seemed ancient to his ward. Among Shahbazi's other students the subject had never been broached, even in private; not that privacy was something they'd ever known. Hemmati and his adopted brothers had eaten together, slept together and defecated alongside each other without shame. They'd never gone anywhere in public, such ventures being rare occasions indeed, without being in the company of at least two others. Shahbazi had insisted on this so they would maintain their purity and not fall victim to the temptations offered by a city out of control.

When they were of age, Shahbazi had brought women into their midst and observed them as they practiced the arts of sexuality. Every part of their lives had been controlled but never by coercion or threat of violence. Hemmati had never seen his master, a man whom he really viewed as his true and only father, lose his temper or even raise his voice. Even his commands were in the softest manner but with an implied imperative that dare not speak of the consequences for disobedience. It just simply was what it was, it always had been, and Hemmati knew fealty and honor to this one man.

"Where are my brothers, Mullah?" Hemmati inquired.

"They are preparing, Farzad," Shahbazi replied. "The time's now at hand for us to enact our plans. You're to lead the way."

Hemmati's heart beat a little faster. "Me? I don't understand."

"You do," Shahbazi countered. "You've been trained all your life for this. Although I loved each of you in equal portions, it was in you I saw the most promise. You excelled among your brothers, never revealing your superior intellect and skill when you could have flaunted it. This is the mark of a humble man and it's this humility that makes you the strongest. Do you understand?"

"I think so, Mullah."

"Then it is well." Shahbazi smiled, his face wrinkling more. "So now let us talk of what you must do. Are you still in contact with the CIA agents the Americans claim they don't have operating in the city?"

"I am."

"You can contact them?"

"I can."

"You must go to them and tell them you have knowledge of what's happening in South America."

"You want me to tell them the truth?"

"It is imperative you do this," Shahbazi said. "President Ahmadinejad has made a critical error, a misstep in judgment really. We can no longer afford to support him. I've spoken with my other brothers in the government, and they agree that the Pasdaran must take control of the city before the president undermines the efforts of our brother Khamenei."

That didn't sit well with Hemmati. He'd never trusted Seyyed Ali Khamenei—head of Ahmadinejad's elite paramilitary forces—despite the fact Khamenei claimed roots as a Basij Islamist. Khamenei had never lifted a finger to help Shahbazi or any of his father's brothers in government. When Ahmadinejad dismissed a number of high-ranking officials within the Revolutionary Guard for being too "extreme" in their religious views, Khamenei had remained silent, almost stoic, in fact. The thought still burned in Hemmati's gut.

"Forgive me, Mullah, but I don't see how revealing our operations in Paraguay will help our cause," Hemmati said. "Aren't they still many months from completing the training of the Hezbollah contingent?"

"I received a recent report from Jahanshah," the cleric said. "If I understood him correctly, they've already been discovered. It's only a matter of time before the Americans learn what's happened. Jahanshah has bought us some time but it isn't much. We must act quickly if our plans can succeed."

"You are planning a diversion."

Shahbazi emitted a titter of amusement, what passed as the closest thing Hemmati could judge a laugh. "That's exactly what I'm planning. I'm hoping you can be convincing enough that the Americans will come running here. The local men with the CIA won't make a move until they've consulted with their superiors. Given the unrest in this entire region, the uprisings by our brothers in Egypt and Libya, they'll see capitulation as only in their best interests. Their leadership is weak and I plan to seize that advantage. I'm confident I can depend on you."

Hemmati scratched his chin and considered the request, although he already knew he could refuse his mullah nothing. This was an opportunity he'd not considered before, and Hemmati realized that Shahbazi had a side to his personality that hadn't surfaced until now. Hemmati could only call it as he saw it: his mullah was as devious a bastard as he was wise.

"You can depend on me, Mullah."

"It's settled, then. Now I need to discuss with you another matter. One of *great* importance."

HIS PARENTS NAMED HIM Ronald but to his few friends in the Company he went by Jester.

It had little to do with Ron Abney's sense of humor, as most might have thought; rather it was his way of behaving around others when he felt uncomfortable. As one of his companions at Langley attested, "You start pulling that court-jester routine." So the name stuck and in some small way Abney didn't really mind. He only afforded the moniker to others within the Company, however, and they never spoke it in the company of outsiders since it ended up being his code name among the CIA walls of power in Wonderland.

"Hey, Jester," Stephen Poppas said as he walked through the door of their run-down apartment on Tehran's west side.

The place didn't really qualify for the name, being more of a shithole than much else, but it was what Abney and Poppas liked to call home. Both of them had arrived in Tehran about the same time and fast developed a friendship that could only evolve naturally being all but stranded together in a very inhospitable, if somewhat exotic, locale. Abney was new to fieldwork, having only spent about two years abroad, but Poppas—who had to be somewhere on the order of fifteen years Abney's senior—had been country hopping for the Company since he was "out of diapers" was the expression Poppas favored.

"Yo, Pops," Abney called back, using Poppas's nickname, "find anything decent to eat?"

Poppas dropped a greasy paper bag on the small counter that adjoined the kitchenette and replied, "Look for yourself, bro. I ain't your mother."

Abney grunted and got up from his position in front of what appeared to be a shortwave radio. The antiquated box was actually a high-tech frequency receiver and transmitter capable of sending encoded voice and data messages to an orbiting Joint Intelligence Task Force satellite. It provided the sole means of communication between the men and their contact they referred to simply as Mother.

"You weren't followed?" Abney asked as he peeked in the bag and withdrew two paper cartons filled with squared portions of fried dough ladled with a local concoction that was half sweet, half spicy. Really it amounted to little more than a box of greasy bread, but it was better than much of the food served by the vendors on this side of town and a damn sight tastier. It also didn't have any of the more popular spices in much of the local cuisine.

"You ask me that every time, Jester, and every time I give you the same answer."

"Okay, don't be a grump-ass," Abney said. "You know I have to ask. There's a system of checks and balances in this business. You taught me that. Remember?"

"That's only one-way, plebe," Poppas said. While his expression soured, his tone implied he was doing nothing more than some good-natured ribbing. "We ain't the frigging Congress here."

The banter dispensed with, the pair sat at the small table near the silent radio and dug into the food. They ate silently, mechanically, only taking breaks between bites to wash down the Iranian dumplings with bottled water. Nothing but bottled water—that was the rule, and at least one bottle from every grouping had to be sampled for poisons. It was quite a life case officers had to live, particularly in Middle Eastern and African countries, where for the most part they were unwanted. Abney had once asked Poppas, a happily married man of twenty years, if he'd ever told his wife about his experiences, to which Poppas had replied, "Fuck no."

That had put an end to the conversation and Abney never asked him another personal question.

"So what's the plan for today, Jester?"

Around a cheek filled with chewy dough, Abney replied, "I haven't actually checked the book yet but I think—"

A soft rap sounded at the door.

The two men looked at the door, each other and back again before they got to their feet simultaneously and withdrew their pistols. Neither of them said a word. They weren't accustomed to talking loudly and Abney hoped whoever stood on the other side hadn't heard them conversing. It wasn't the landlord. The guy worked a day job and he tended to mind his own business, especially with two Americans who paid rent four times the rate. Frankly, the pair could have been making bombs and the landlord couldn't have cared less.

Another rap came, this one a bit more insistent.

Poppas made a couple of standard gestures, held his pistol high and level, and then nodded for Abney to open the door. As soon as he did, Poppas reached out, hauled the dark-skinned man inside and tossed him practically the length of the room—not difficult given the size of the place. Before the visitor knew it, he had two pistols trained on him a few inches from his face. He looked frightened at first, holding his hands high, but eventually he smiled and produced a chuckle.

"Damn it, Farzad!" Poppas said. "How many times have I told you never to come here?"

"Sorry, sorry…but it was important."

"Important enough to break protocol?" Abney said.

"Screw protocol," Poppas interjected. He waved the muzzle of his pistol skyward and said to Hemmati, "Was it important enough for you to risk getting your head blown off?"

"It may very well be that important, yes."

Poppas and Abney exchanged surprised glances for the second time that day, then helped Hemmati to his feet. They pushed him onto a dirty, disused couch. It wasn't outside the rules of the playbook for the Company to recruit local informants if the need arose, and Hemmati had proved useful in the past. If he'd risk coming here, there had to be a pretty good reason for it.

"All right," Poppas said, taking a chair and fishing a cigarette from his pocket. He offered Hemmati one, who declined. "Sorry. I forgot you're one of the few Iranians I know who doesn't smoke."

While Poppas lit a smoke, Abney asked, "Okay, so what's going on?"

"I've come by information that I think will be of great value to you."

"It better be," Poppas said. "Now quit trying to build suspense and spill it already."

"Recently you had an incident that took place in Paraguay."

"There a lot of incidents in Paraguay, Farzad, in fact, all over the world. You want to be more specific?"

"I don't have many details but it's something about Peace Corps volunteers taken hostage by armed men who could not be identified."

Poppas looked at Abney, who shrugged. He didn't have any information about it. In fact, this was first he'd heard of it and the same was true for Poppas, given the older man's expression. It could've been Hemmati was simply looking to dangle a carrot that might not pan out to be anything, but then it might also be the biggest thing to hit the intelligence community since the end of the Cold War. Case officers got junk information all the time from operators on the payroll—many of them working as double agents—which they usually referred to as "soap flakes." Every so often, however, they hit a gem.

"So what about it?" Poppas said, not willing to let on they knew nothing about what Hemmati was telling them.

Internally, Poppas's textbook approach amused Abney.

"I know who these men are."

Poppas took a drag of his smoke before saying, "Who?"

"They are members of the Hezbollah, men being trained by officers in our Guard Corps."

"You're full of it!" Abney said. "There's no way you could possibly know that."

"There is a way I could know it," Hemmati said. "I haven't told you something until now because I needed it as leverage."

"Why would you need leverage against us?"

"I don't need leverage *against* you. I need leverage to get out of Iran, to go to America and never to return this country."

"That's a tall order, Farzad," Poppas said.

"It is something you can do," Hemmati replied. "Do not pretend that you don't have the ear of the highest powers in your Washington. I know enough about you to know who you are and who you work for. Let us not pretend that I'm stupid. I went to college in Europe, remember? To be trained to work in the military. I have contacts close to Seyyed Ali Khamenei, you could even call them family. Only because of my bad eyes was I not able to do this. I have told you all this, so I would think my request comes as no surprise to you. Or my price."

"Your price?" Poppas said.

"Oh, so you not only want us to spend a whole bundle of cash getting you out of here, but you want us to finance your life in the U.S., too," Abney added.

"You're a wackadoo if you think this tidbit of gossip you're handing us is going to buy you a free ride across the pond, joker."

"I have more," Hemmati said.

Through a gust of smoke Poppas said, "Okay, tell us your more."

"A faction within President Ahmadinejad's officer corps is planning a coup. They plan to move on him soon and establish a new power within Iran. They are seeking the support of the Americans and they've sent me to make the offer."

"Jumping jeebus," Abney whispered.

Poppas looked at his companion and said, "I think it's time to call Mother."

CHAPTER FOUR

Atlantic Ocean

David McCarter stared at the blue-white horizon, the kind that could only look this pure and clean at an altitude of eight thousand feet. The sight liberated him inside, freed his soul and imagination from the cares of the day. Very soon, McCarter knew that feeling would dissipate to be replaced by a range of dangers that most men never experienced.

David McCarter had experienced enough to fill a thousand lives.

The other five men who accompanied him aboard the Stony Man jet could claim very similar circumstances, although none would have boasted about them if given a chance.

McCarter realized the time for introspection was nearly over. According to Jack Grimaldi—Stony Man's ace pilot—they'd be touching down in Asunción in about ten minutes. McCarter had to consider all the angles of their present mission. Stony Man's intelligence had been unusually scant. Between the powerful computers overseen by Aaron Kurtzman and the keen intellect of Barbara Price, sending either of the teams into a situation with little intelligence was an exception—a very disconcerting exception at that.

As leader of Phoenix Force, McCarter didn't like

unknowns and he certainly wasn't big on winging it when it came to missions where vast numbers of angry, armed men were involved. Nevertheless, Phoenix Force was only alerted when the situation was serious, and the absence of hard intel was never reason enough to prevent their deployment.

"You'll be going in with your eyes wide shut," Hal Brognola, head of Stony Man Farm, had told them during their briefing nearly fourteen hours earlier.

"It wouldn't be the first time," McCarter had replied.

"THE INFORMATION IS sketchy because it's all we have," Price said. "Three days ago the American embassy in Asunción, Paraguay, received a request for sanctuary by a volunteer with the U.S. Peace Corps. The man's name was Christopher Harland. Harland told a story so absurd that at first the secretary to the U.S. Ambassador didn't believe him. Apparently they had an NSA analyst with the Signal Intelligence Group on staff."

"They turned him over to the analyst, who immediately realized there may be a bigger problem brewing in Paraguay," Brognola added.

"A crazy story by this one man has the White House jumping?" asked Gary Manning, disbelief evident in his tone.

"Not just one man," Brognola told the Canadian demolitions expert.

"There are sixteen other U.S. Peace Corps members who have gone missing," Price confirmed, "and the atrocities Harland claims to have witnessed against them were confirmed by an investigative team sent to their camp. Or what was left of it."

"What do mean, what was left of it?" T. J. Hawkins asked.

A native of Texas and the youngest, newest member of the team, Hawkins had served with Delta Force before joining Stony Man. Hawkins may have been a bit unconventional at times and was still an occasional hothead, but he was a good fit with the highly disciplined Phoenix Force operatives. He'd become an integral part of the tight-knit field unit and all of his companions were glad to have him along when the going got tough, which was most of the time in Phoenix Force missions.

"They burned the thing to the ground after plundering everything they could get their hands on that might have had value." Price replied.

"Word has it they even stole the silverware from the camp mess hall," Brognola added.

Rafael Encizo, former Cuban refugee and unarmed-combat expert, said, "Mess hall? I thought most Peace Corps volunteers stayed in the homes of native families, not only for safety but translation purposes."

"This particular mission was somewhat special according to Christopher Harland," Price said. "A fact we confirmed with their main offices after the initial reports came in from the U.S. Embassy via the State Department."

"What about the NSA's investigation?" Calvin James asked. "Did that reveal anything useful?"

Calvin James was a former Navy corpsman and SEAL, who served as the team's chief medic—and a chief badass, as well.

"It didn't reveal any identity but we're guessing they aren't local dissidents," Price replied.

"Did you say guessing?" McCarter said. "You, luv?"

"I know," replied a booming voice from the door of the War Room. "Isn't it a shocker?"

Though the man who came through the doorway

was in a wheelchair, nobody would mistake that for weakness. Aaron "the Bear" Kurtzman didn't just fill the role of technical wizard for Stony Man; his intelligence and prowess had literally saved the lives of every team member more times than anybody could count. Kurtzman had a way of pulling off technical feats like a magician pulled a live rabbit out of a hat, and that had paid off many times over.

"You can blame me for our lack of information," Kurtzman replied. He looked at Price and added, "Sorry I'm late."

Price nodded. "Did you learn anything else?"

"Nothing definite but some patterns emerged from a software algorithm Akira and I wrote to scan travel documents into and out of South America, particularly around Paraguay. It seems there's been an increasing number of Muslim visitors. Now supposedly they came in and later left, but there were some inconsistencies we didn't really like so we're digging deeper into those patterns. They're complex, however, so it's going to take time. For now we can conclude that this paramilitary force, if nothing else, is not comprised of native South Americans."

"You're suggesting Muslim terrorists?" Manning asked.

As a former member of the Canadian RCMP and recipient of training with GSG 9—the federal antiterrorist police unit in Germany—Manning boasted expertise on the many terrorist groups in the world. He also had a clear grasp of their various methods of operation, something that resulted in an almost bloodhound instinct for global terrorist activity.

"We think it's possible," Price said.

"And the President agrees with our assessment,

which is why we're sending you down to Paraguay immediately," Brognola said. "We don't have much, I know, but we think it's enough that we want to get in front of this thing. I'd hate to be caught with our pants down because we weren't being as proactive as we could have been."

"It surprises me the Man wants to send us this soon," McCarter said. "But I agree. I'd rather be prepared than wait for further incidents to prove your theory."

"Do we have any idea which terrorist group might be operating there?" Encizo asked.

"If I had to venture a guess, I'd say either Hezbollah or New Islamic Front," Manning said.

"Which in any case spells al Qaeda," Hawkins remarked.

James sighed. "Doesn't it always seem to spell al Qaeda?"

"Not always," Hawkins said with a shrug. "Occasionally we get some terrorists who like to be original. Remember the IUA?"

Indeed they did. The Intiqam ut Allah, or Revenge of Allah, had stolen the plans to a new U.S. fast-attack nuclear submarine and built duplicates right under the noses of Americans. The battle to stop them had stretched from South Carolina to Africa and nearly cost the lives of every member on the team.

"Whoever they are, they're obviously dangerous and whether an Islamic terrorist force or simply a band of Islamic fanatics getting support from other organized groups, they have to be stopped," Brognola said.

"Your mission is to pick up where the NSA investigation left off," Price told them. "Your contact in Asunción will be Brad Russell, the SIGINT analyst who conducted the initial inquiry. He's been instructed to give you his full cooperation and not to ask questions."

"Hopefully not just another run-of-the-mill spook ruined by political bureaucracy," McCarter said.

"I've spoken with my contacts at the NSA and they tell me he's top shelf." Price smiled. "Just be your usually charming and cordial self. Russell's a hard-line patriot who'll give you the shirt off his back. He's also a one-man geekfest so you'll have every technical advantage at your disposal." She glanced at Kurtzman with a wink and said, "Present company excluded, of course."

"Back at you, girlfriend," Kurtzman said, the reply very uncharacteristic when matched against the masculine bass in his voice.

McCARTER SMILED IN RECOLLECTION at Kurtzman's droll retort before the sudden waver as the engines revved in preparation for landing at a small airfield near Asunción.

"Prepare for landing, boys," Grimaldi's voice called over the cabin intercom. "Tray tables up, seat backs in their locked and upright positions…blah, blah, blah."

This brought a chuckle or two from the roused Phoenix Force members.

They could've landed at one of the major airports, but McCarter had opted to go in using more covert means. Any public display would have attracted unwanted attention. Grimaldi had filed a flight plan with the Paraguayan government with a request from the U.S. Embassy to not pay much attention to the flight, a request that they'd chosen to honor in light of the recent events. The last thing they needed was for seventeen missing Peace Corps volunteers, possibly seized by a terrorist group, to leak. The press would eat it up—the situation would turn overnight from a private nightmare into a very public one.

That was the reason they'd decided to keep Harland under the spotlight, as well.

The Gulfstream C-38 had just rolled to a stop when the onboard phone next to McCarter's seat signaled for attention. The engines whined down even as he picked it up. "Yeah."

"David," Price's voice replied. "We just got notification from Able Team. Somebody tried to kill Harland."

"Oh, that's lovely," McCarter said. "I take it Ironman and friends pulled his bacon out of the fire?"

"Barely, but yes. We also just got word from the Man and his morning CIA briefing. Somebody has apparently come forward and identified our mysterious paramilitary group. Looks like Bear's theory panned out."

"Who're we dealing with?" McCarter asked.

"It's a training contingent of Hezbollah under the leadership of an elite paramilitary unit inside of Iran... the Iranian Revolutionary Guard Corps."

"Bloody hell," McCarter mumbled. "Why would the IRGC have any interest training terrorists in South America?"

"For one thing, they've had economic and soft power in the region for quite some time. Due to Paraguay's large production of soybeans, these food exports are vitally important to Iran's stability more than ever after the embargos, injunctions and other economic sanctions the UN's leveled against them."

"Yeah, Ahmadinejad's not known for his working and playing well with others."

"That's only half the news," Price said. "The other half is that this individual who approached some agents in Tehran indicated the Muslim cleric group of power in Iran, known commonly as Pasdaran, plans to make their move against Ahmadinejad soon. We're talking a religious coup inside the country of incomprehensible proportions."

"Do I smell a change in plans?"

"Not for you. Your mission is the same as before but we wanted you to have a better idea of what you're up against. We'll be taking care of the rest of this through Able Team."

"And how exactly do you plan to do that, if I might be so bold as to inquire?"

"We're sending them to Tehran to handle the matter personally." Price replied.

"Wait. Let me make sure I just heard you correctly. You're sending Able Team into Iran?"

"Yes."

"Oh, bloody hell," McCarter said. "I don't think that's such a good idea."

"Well, the decision's already been made by the President, and Hal's in complete agreement with it. I had my own reservations but it didn't seem like the issue was up for debate so I'm going along with it. For now anyway."

"Have you told them yet?"

"No, we're still trying to sort out the details regarding Harland and who to hand him off to. This just isn't a contingency we saw coming until now."

"All right, then, thanks for keeping me in the loop. And, Barb?"

"Yes, David."

"Tell Ironman I told him to bring his ass home in one piece. I don't want to hear about anything like what happened a few years ago aboard the USS *Stennis*."

"Will do."

"Out here."

McCarter broke the connection and then assembled his gear with the other members of Phoenix Force. Once they were settled in whatever temporary quarters had been arranged, he'd brief the team while they cleaned and double-checked their equipment. This news wouldn't sit well with his teammates, but there wasn't anything they could do about it. Phoenix Force had its mission and now Able Team had theirs. The stakes had gone way up and they couldn't police everything at once, although they may have liked to.

A fresh-faced man met them outside the Gulfstream C-38. He had dark hair and skin, which would have made him fit in well among the local population save for the blue-gray eyes, which implied a European background. He wore tan slacks, loafers and a midnight-blue silk shirt with a crop collar. The figure looked almost athletic and although he might have been hired by the NSA due to his brains, McCarter could easily identify between men who couldn't handle themselves versus those who could, and clearly Brad Russell fell into the latter category.

Russell offered McCarter a strong handshake and broad smile. "Mr. Brown, I presume?"

"You presume right."

"I'm Brad Russell."

McCarter grinned. "I know that, chap."

"And I'm sure you know that I know your name isn't really Brown, but I wasn't supposed to ask questions, so Brown it is."

"Touché."

Russell acknowledged in turn the other Phoenix Force warriors ranged around McCarter's flanks. "And these are Misters Gray, Gold, Green and White," he said, referring to Manning, Encizo, Hawkins and James.

"Though not necessarily in that order," Hawkins said with a laugh.

Russell returned the jest with a good-natured chuckle of his own before saying, "If you'll come this way, gents, your chariot awaits."

They hauled their tired butts across the tarmac as a muggy morning wind tugged at their exposed skin and flattened their hair. McCarter hoped they'd get the opportunity to clean up, although no guarantees had been made. Russell led them to what looked like an old airport shuttle converted into a private-use vehicle. The vehicle was beat up and unobtrusive—a good thing since it was similar to most of the vehicles in Paraguay. But thankfully it had air-conditioning and provided a surprisingly decent ride.

As they got under way, the vehicle driven by a man Russell assured them spoke about half a dozen words of English, McCarter said, "You've arranged accommodations?"

"Yes, a small place just outside the city as requested by your people. Completely out of the way. This is actually the off-season for tourists so you should have plenty of privacy there."

"And the staff?"

"Every one of them cleared by my people," Russell said. "Don't worry, Brown, I've done my homework. I don't know who exactly it is you work for but I do know how to secure an op. Lots of experience in that area."

"I understand you're also quite technically adept."

Russell smiled. "You could say that."

"That's excellent. We'll need your assistance getting everything set up at our new digs. My people have a decent comprehension of the technical aspects, but we could your expertise to fill in the high-level bit."

"And leave the fighting to you?"

It was McCarter's turn to grin. "That's typically the way we like it."

"I've already informed my people that you'll have my full cooperation. I'm here to assist you in any way I can. Consider your wish as my command. I'm at your beck and call."

"I got the picture, thanks." McCarter fired up a cigarette and said, "What can you tell us about this camp that got overrun?"

"I can tell you a lot about the camp," Russell said. "It's the identity of the people that hit it I can't seem to put my finger on, which is odd."

"Why odd?" Manning asked.

Russell looked Manning in the eye. "I've spent most of my adult life using technology to detect and identify paramilitary and terrorist groups of every make and color. That's one of the reasons the NSA hired me. I started as a crypto-analyst for the U.S. Navy and that eventually landed me this gig."

"So you think this is odd because you've found a group that can stump you?"

"You've heard about the pattern-analyses programs being evaluated in both the commercial and defense contractor sectors that use fractal patterns and algorithms to identify patterns in terrorist activities." Russell got five blank stares. "Okay look, there have been lots of studies done that prove with the right programming languages and algorithms we can derive detectable patterns in the way terrorists and other paramilitary groups operate based on historical data. We use things like what groups claim credit for what incidents, weapons signatures, explosives and ordnance composition and so forth."

"So if a bomb gets detonated in someplace like Israel or Afghanistan or even Europe, you can predict with a fair amount of accuracy who might be responsible," Encizo said.

"I can go one better than that, sir," Russell said with an exuberant wave. "I can predict it *before* it happens, potentially help to save lives and avert a full-blown disaster."

"Sounds fascinating," Manning said.

"Agreed," Hawkins added.

"So we can assume that this pattern you've seen is odd because you couldn't find a predictive analysis capable of identifying the doers," McCarter said.

"In this case, yes," Russell said. "It's almost like the perpetrators did it purposely, as if they knew we had this technology and would try to use it."

"Maybe they did," Hawkins said.

Russell expressed puzzlement. "What do you mean?"

"We've got some new intelligence just as we landed," McCarter said. "It looks like—"

The road ahead suddenly lit up like the sun and the windshield of the shuttle bus splintered and fragmented. A heartbeat later a storm of metal, wood, glass and plastic blasted through the forward interior, the driver—whose chair backed against a wide metal panel—took the brunt of the impact. The vehicle shimmied as the explosion shredded both front tires. Another moment and the shuttle bus rode only on its front rims.

"Hang on!" McCarter warned even as the rear end of the vehicle swung around.

With a bang and high-pitched squeal, the shuttle bus flipped onto its left side and continued down the gravel road for a hundred feet before it finally ground to a halt.

CHAPTER FIVE

A cloud of dust—acrid and lung searing with explosive residue—rolled through the interior of the shuttle bus.

Gary Manning knew that scent. The expended cordite stung his nostrils as he worked to extricate his body from beneath the legs tangled with his own. He did a quick physical inventory as he wriggled to freedom; he hadn't suffered more than a few bumps and bruises. The Phoenix warrior turned to the nearest motionless figure. A quick check of the pulse at Rafael Encizo's neck revealed a strong and steady rhythm. Manning confirmed rise and fall of the Cuban's chest before producing a relieved sigh of his own.

"Roll call!" McCarter shouted in a raspy voice.

"Check," Manning said. "Rafe's out cold but stable."

An all-clear came back from the remaining Phoenix Force members, including a quip from Hawkins about who got the license number of the truck. It seemed to take Russell a little longer but eventually he sounded off to indicate he was conscious and mostly in one piece. Even as they began to shift and attempt to right themselves inside the capsized shuttle bus, the first metallic pings against the body of the vehicle reached their ears.

"We're taking fire!" Manning said.

"Un-ass this AO!" McCarter shouted.

Fortunately the Phoenix warriors had debarked from

the plane with concealed pistols so they weren't entirely unarmed. Hawkins ordered Russell to help him wrestle Encizo from beneath the overturned bags while Mc-Carter, James and Manning broke free of their confines and crawled to the rear and a shattered back window. Manning removed the jagged shards at the edge of the frame with a few swift kicks of his boot before lurching through it feet first, propelled by grabbing the cross-bar typically used for standees. Clear of the wreckage, Manning took one knee and produced a .45-caliber Colt Government Model pistol from shoulder leather. He panned the rear flanks with the muzzle of the pistol but didn't detect any muzzle-flashes. Either the enemy had taken concealment or they were positioned on the opposite side. Their stopping point with the nose of the shuttle bus facing the leeward edge of the road may have well been their only saving grace, and Manning thought it made good sense to take maximum advantage of such good fortune.

James and McCarter followed him out and Manning briefed them.

"You two cut around and head toward those trees," McCarter directed. "See if you can draw their fire."

The pair nodded and left the position of safety without hesitation.

The chatter of full-auto reports—some kind of light squad weapon, Manning and James guessed—reached their ears as they dashed for the tree line. Rounds bit at the ground just ahead of their path, churning dust and stone chips from the gravel road as the enemy gunner tried to gauge an appropriate lead. They reached the trees unharmed and dived into the cover of deep grass and thick, gnarled tree trunks.

"That was too close!" James observed.

Manning nodded in agreement and said, "We're not dealing with novices."

The Canadian risked a glance through a gap in two ground vines and spotted the winks of flame from the muzzle of the machine gun just a heartbeat before it stopped. Manning pointed in that direction and James nodded. The pair raised their pistols, Manning leveling his .45 and James wielding a 9 mm H&K P-2000. They opened up hot on the enemy position, pumping as much lead as they could downrange. Maybe they wouldn't hit their target but at least they could keep the heat off their friends long enough to buy them time to get clear of the vehicle.

As soon as Manning and James took off, McCarter turned and headed in the opposite direction with a Browning Hi-Power in hand.

As he ran along the road, hunched to minimize his profile, the Phoenix Force leader listened for the direction of the fire. The targets his friends presented had obviously commanded the full attention of the enemy gunner because McCarter didn't detect any rounds buzzing over his head or chewing the ground at his feet. He ran toward a large rock near a copse of trees and dived for cover. McCarter grinned when he peered around the rock and got his first look at the enemy position. He had a clear line of sight, and even through the shadows provided by the tree line he could see two of his opponents.

McCarter took careful aim on one of his targets, estimating the distance at fifty yards, and waited until his friends opened up from their position. He stroked the trigger twice. Both 9 mm Parabellums hit their mark and McCarter detected just the faintest hint of spray, confirming once more the reason he'd taken home prize after prize for his pistol marksmanship. The hits took their enemy by surprise, obviously, because McCarter perceived a bit of scrambling among those trees and heard a shout.

Maybe they no longer had the advantage of surprise, but McCarter figured at least this one time he'd made it count for something.

T. J. HAWKINS PANTED, the muscles in his shoulders bunched like knotted cords as he dragged the unconscious Rafael Encizo through the opening and down the shallow slope of the road that provided a defilade. Russell followed on his heels and dropped to his belly in a cloud of dust.

"You. Stay here and watch him," Hawkins ordered. He handed Russell his pistol and said, "You don't leave his side for any reason. Got it?"

Russell took the weapon with unflinching resolve and nodded, his lips pressed into a thin set.

Hawkins slapped his shoulder, then dashed back to the shuttle bus and dived inside. He quickly located the duffel bag he sought. He unsnapped the clips with practiced efficiency, reached inside and came away with exactly what he'd hoped. The M-4 A1/M-203 A1 was the perfect small-arms weapon in Hawkins's mind. Not only had the weapon proved itself through its parent model, the M-16 A2, but its lighter weight and compact profile made it perfect as a tactical operations alternative to the full-size deal. Hawkins reached into the bag again and withdrew two readied 30-round magazines, one of which he inserted into the well.

A yank of the charging handle brought the weapon into battery. Hawkins searched the wrecked vehicle like a dog mad on a scent until he found the hard box that contained 40 mm HE grenades. He loaded one into the breech of the M-203 A1—a special military variant of the M-203 designed specifically for the M-4 A1—and stuffed two more into the pocket of his khaki trousers.

Hawkins cleared out and rounded the corner of the shuttle bus. He immediately flattened to the ground, avoiding a volley of high-velocity rounds that burned the air just above him. Hawkins had the leaf sight up and in position. He estimated his distance at sixty yards max, settled the stock of the M-4 A1 tight against his shoulder and squeezed the trigger. The pop and kick from the grenade launcher mimicked that of about a 12-gauge shotgun but the results were much more spectacular. The high-explosive blew on impact, blowing the machine gun position and its owner apart in a fifteen-foot tower of flame.

Hawkins pressed the attack by following with a second grenade before charging the position and triggering short bursts on the run. He looked to his flanks and saw McCarter, James and Manning leave their own positions to provide covering fire. Hawkins produced a rebel war cry as he continued to advance on the enemy's position—or what was left it—his M-4 A1 spitting 5.56 mm rounds at anything that appeared to move. The four warriors converged on the tree line simultaneously with weapons blazing, more intent on keeping heads down and shocking the enemy into panic or retreat than on taking viable targets. Hawkins had expended his first magazine by the time they breached the position, and rammed the second one home as he knelt and gestured for the others to continue forward while he provided cover.

The other three Phoenix Force warriors crashed

through the trees, careful to circumvent the immediate area seared by superheated gases and what was left in the wake of the twin grenades. They expanded their search and found three bodies. McCarter was certain one of them was the one he'd shot, while the other two were close to one another just behind the smoking, broken shell of a machine gun wedged in the mud.

"The gunner and his spotter, more than likely," Manning said.

"You think this was it?" Hawkins asked.

"No bloody way to tell, mate. But I'm guessing if there were any others they're moving away from here as fast as possible."

James stared into the darkened jungle and said, "That's okay. We'll catch up with them later."

"Bet on it," McCarter agreed.

The four men retreated to the vehicle and James immediately began to work his magic on Encizo, performing a full assessment and breaking out smelling salts and water. Hawkins and Manning provided a loose perimeter while Russell helped McCarter salvage whatever equipment and weapons they could find. McCarter only had to look at the body of the driver for a moment to know the guy was long gone.

Yeah, they *would* catch up to whoever had done this.

And there'll be bloody hell to pay when we do, David McCarter thought.

Miami, Florida

THE WINDOW AIR-CONDITIONING unit produced a drone as it blasted ice-cold air into the hotel room. Able Team hadn't picked the choicest place in town to stay but it was large, clean and comfortable. They'd immediately changed their plans with Harland including switching vehicles, accommodations and wardrobe. They now sat ranged around the small coffee table of the suite.

Schwarz sat back on the couch and propped his feet on the table. "Ah, now this is more like a vacation."

Blancanales had just returned from the kitchen and handed a bottle of water to Harland before cracking the top on his own. As he plopped next to Schwarz on the couch, his friend asked, "Where's mine?"

"In the fridge," Blancanales said as he took a long pull and smacked his lips. "Ah, very refreshing."

"I can't believe you didn't get me one."

"I'm not your mother."

"Shape it up, you two," Lyons said, rubbing vigorously at his blond hair, wet from the shower. "We have weapons to clean and decisions to make."

The cell phone at Lyons's belt signaled for attention with the theme from *Mission Impossible.*

"Really?" Schwarz said. "Really, Ironman?"

Lyons's waggled his eyebrows before he answered, "It's your nickel."

He turned and left after listening a moment, retreating to the bedroom and closing the door behind him.

"Must be a new girlfriend," Blancanales said, although he knew otherwise.

"He's been so mysterious lately," Schwarz quipped.

The pair sat and watched television with Harland for about five minutes before Lyons emerged from the bedroom. His face had colored a dark hue. Blancanales and Schwarz realized he hadn't liked whatever he'd heard, a fact that became even more evident when Lyons stormed across the living area, grabbed Harland by the shirt and hauled the young man out of the overstuffed chair. Lyons dragged Harland into the center of the room, yanked his arm behind his back and shoved him to his knees.

"Ironman, what the hell—" Blancanales began.

"Stay out of this!" Lyons exclaimed with a new flush to his face. He leaned close to Harland's ear before continuing. "Now listen to me and listen good, you little son of a bitch. I don't know what sort of game you're playing but whatever it is you've got about five seconds to come clean or I swear I'll snap your arm in two."

"What is happening here?" Schwarz said.

Lyons looked at him and replied, "You want to know what's happening? Our friends down in Paraguay just got hit by Hezbollah terrorists and nearly all of them bought the farm. One of them was injured."

Lyons turned his attention back to Harland, who could barely talk fast enough, his voice little more than a high-pitched squeal of outrage mixed with pain. "Let…me…go!"

"I'll let you go," Lyons said. "I'll let you go right out that window if you don't talk and talk now!"

"Hezbollah?" Blancanales inquired.

"Yeah. And there's a lot more to the story, but I'll fill you in on the rest of it later. For now our orders are to turn two-face here over to the U.S. Marshals as soon as they arrive. But they weren't very specific about what condition he has to be in. Only that he's still breathing." Lyons directed the last statement to Harland. "And if he doesn't fess up here in the next few seconds he's going to be breathing through a straw."

"Okay! Let me go— You're breaking my arm!" Harland wailed, and then began sobbing. "Please…"

Lyons released his hold, got Harland to his feet and tossed him into the chair he'd occupied a minute earlier. He then folded his arms. "We're listening. Spill it, shithead."

"Yeah, Harland," Schwarz said. "What's this all about?"

"I swear I didn't want to do it!" Harland said, rubbing his arm as he stared daggers at Lyons. The ice-cold blue eyes staring back caused Harland to look at the floor. "They told me if I didn't play along they'd kill me."

"Who told you that?" Blancanales asked.

"Those...those bastards," Harland confessed. He looked at Lyons. "You're right, they are terrorists. They didn't tell me which group they were with. The guy who talked to me spoke English but he had an accent. I couldn't figure it out at first but after talking to him awhile I deduced he had to be Arab, Muslim or something. Somewhere from the Middle East, I was pretty sure of that."

"How could you tell?" Lyons demanded.

"I hold a Masters Degree in liberal arts. I've been to many countries. I know Middle Easterners when I see them."

"And this story you gave the Embassy about you being blindfolded," Schwarz said. "About not seeing anything other than the camp and the two men who captured you. Was all of that just bullshit?"

"It was a lie. Part of the story they told me to tell."

"Oh, Christopher," Blancanales said in a voice heavy with disappointment. He shook his head. "You should've told us the truth from the beginning. This has only made things much more complicated."

"They said if I didn't cooperate they'd kill my friends!"

"Your friends may already be dead, genius," Lyons

replied. "Did you ever think about that? Terrorists aren't typically interested in taking hostages unless it's distinctly advantageous to their goals."

"So you're being tracked?" Schwarz asked.

Harland kept his eyes to the floor as he nodded slowly.

"How?"

Harland reached slowly to the watch on his wrist and removed it. He handed it to Blancanales, who then passed it immediately to Schwarz after a cursory glance. Schwarz reached into his shirt pocket and retrieved a small leather case. He flipped open the soft lid and after a moment carefully selected a miniature flat-tip screwdriver. He carefully pried the lid off the back and inspected the contents. After a minute and a grunt of satisfaction, Schwarz replaced the screwdriver, withdrew another implement and began working at the innards. He soon came away with a small chip held between the tiny three-pronged extractor.

"Very interesting," Schwarz said, staring at the chip.

"What is it?" Blancanales asked.

"Microtransmitter, I'd guess. Hard to tell for certain without the proper testing equipment here, but I'd say it probably has about a ten-mile range if it transmits low-band. More likely it's GPS-enabled, in which case it has an almost limitless range."

"So they know where we're at?" Lyons asked.

"Hard to tell," Schwarz replied. "But I can tell you this is advanced electronics. High-grade stuff, amigo, not something you can get just anywhere."

"Grand," Lyons replied.

"What else do you know?" Blancanales asked. "You need to tell us everything you heard and saw. There are other men risking their lives to help your friends. You owe them that much."

Harland nodded and began to spill it all to them. He told them about how they first encountered the terrorists, described the leader's mode of dress and the other things he saw. He included every nuance of the conversation he had with the leader and some of the foreign words he'd heard used between the leader and his men. He also gave them the details of the story they had forced him to memorize several times over. When he'd finished, he sat back in the chair with utter exhaustion, the tears streaming down his cheeks unabated.

While Blancanales rose to get Harland a rag for his face, Lyons considered the information. He would wait until they'd dumped Harland on the U.S. Marshals Service before he told them of their new mission parameters.

Lyons had cringed when Price and Brognola informed him Able Team would be taking a trip out of the country. He'd listened with rising anger as they'd relayed the story of how a man named Hemmati had contacted the CIA with an incredible tale of a possible coup at the highest levels of Iranian government. He could remember the anger reaching the boiling point when they'd revealed McCarter and the rest had been ambushed while meeting their NSA contact, and how Rafael Encizo had been injured—although Lyons understood the tough Cuban would be okay.

"I'd normally send Phoenix Force on this," Brognola had said, "but with what they're juggling down there, I don't think it's tactically sound."

"I get it," Lyons had said. "I may not like it but we're the better choice for this kind of mission. We're also smaller and better suited for the urban environment."

Price had directed, "You'll take a civilian hop to the city of Sulaimaniyah, near the Iran-Iraq border. From there, you'll have a CIA contact who'll arrange for a HALO jump into the Elburz Mountains. There's a deep-cover ops team that will pick you up there and get you into the city."

"Once you reach Tehran you'll coordinate with Hemmati," Brognola'd told him. "He'll be your guide and sole contact outside of the two Company men. Your job is to take custody, help Hemmati's people and then get your collective asses out of there with Hemmati in one piece."

"You know what?" Lyons had replied. "Pol and Gadgets were right. Florida's looking better all the time."

CHAPTER SIX

Asunción, Paraguay

Rafael Encizo sat surrounded by his friends at the medical facility attached to the U.S. Embassy. The staff physician had given him a clean bill of health, save for a mild concussion. He'd agreed to waive the standard twenty-four-hour observation window with McCarter's solemn promise Encizo wouldn't engage in any "excitement or strenuous physical activity" for the next three days. McCarter hated to be short a team member but it was a promise he intended to keep.

"I feel fine," Encizo protested after the doctor left the group to arrange for the Cuban's release.

"You're grounded, mate," McCarter said. "Simple as that and we're not going to argue about it. I can't bloody well have you suddenly go down in the middle of a hot zone, then we got two more that have to carry you out. It's too dangerous."

"I suppose it's pointless trying to get you to change your mind."

"It is."

"Fine, we'll do it your way," Encizo said with a frown. "But I don't know what I can bring to the table sitting around the hotel room."

"I'm sure Russell could use your help," Hawkins offered.

"Yeah," Encizo said. "Great."

"Cheer up, Rafe," Manning said. "It could've been much worse."

"Like how?"

"Like we could be standing here around your dead body for one thing," McCarter replied. "But that's enough of the chitchat. The subject's closed. Let's get out of here so he can get dressed."

The Phoenix Force warriors vacated the room and five minutes later Encizo emerged attired in a fresh change of clothes. The five men left the Embassy and headed straight to the garage where Russell had managed to acquire a staff van that would transport them to their original quarters outside the city. Every man remained vigilant during their twenty-minute commute, their eyes roving every street corner and building top for potential trouble. Each of them had resolved to be on high alert until they could figure out how the op had gotten blown so soon after they arrived.

As they climbed from the van at their destination, Hawkins whistled at the sweeping courtyard that doubled as entryway into the resort. "Nice digs!"

"It would appear they spared no expense this time," James added.

The men proceeded inside, each toting the equipment bags salvaged from the shuttle bus. They practically had the place to themselves, true to Russell's word. Encizo and Russell shared one suite, which they declared to be their makeshift operations center given Russell could set up the high-tech equipment there, while McCarter and James shared a second and Manning and Hawkins the last. Their suites adjoined the ops center on either side.

They would have liked to take a dip in the pool but

this wasn't a vacation and McCarter ordered them to get cleaned up. He did arrange to have dinner catered to the ops center; at least they could share a meal together while they discussed strategy. It was a feast to behold with garlic-roasted prime rib, boiled potatoes and salad. They also enjoyed bowls filled with a variety of tropical fruits, cinnamon pudding, coffee and a well-stocked bar compliments of the management.

When they finished, McCarter said, "All right, chums, we've got a lot to talk about. The first thing we should discuss is the latest news from the Farm. You already know about Ironman, the friends and their new mission. Apparently this Christopher Harland bloke confessed that the terrorists had coerced him into duping Russell here with that cockamamie story."

"I hope they're planning to lock that piece of crap behind bars," Russell interjected.

"They'll do whatever's in the best interests of the U.S.," Manning replied. "And it's good protocol not to interrupt the team leader during the briefing."

Russell tendered the expression of a puppy who'd just been chided, but he clammed up. Nobody could fault the guy. He'd operated with almost pure autonomy while working the embassy in Paraguay and wasn't used to being on a team. According to the dossier Price had run down for McCarter, Russell had pretty much kept to himself. That type of introversion wasn't unusual in people with high IQ levels and technical skills—Kurtzman being an exception to the rule—so McCarter couldn't fault Russell too much for not observing Phoenix Force protocols.

"No worries, Russell," McCarter said. "So now we're certain that the terrorists operating here are probably Hezbollah. We're also pretty sure that they're being trained by a contingent of the Islamic Revolutionary Guard Corps. What we don't know is *where,* and that's going to be our primary objective. Questions?"

Russell raised his hand and McCarter acknowledged him with a nod.

"I'm happy to help set up a technical station here for you, that we can easily tie into our B-Sat signal intelligence system, as well as allowing you to coordinate with whomever you work for," Russell said. "But do we have any more intelligence we might be able to use to actually pinpoint these guys? I mean, I'm good, but I'm not clairvoyant."

"That's a valid question," James added.

McCarter scratched his chin and considered it. "I think our first and best option is to get you tied into our systems first. Our man back in the States can guide you on that. Once we have that uplink established, he may be able to send us something you can use."

"At least Harland's betrayal explains how we were compromised so soon after being in country," Encizo said.

"I'm not entirely sure that it does," Manning countered.

"What do you mean?"

"Well, we know they were tracking Harland but that doesn't explain how they knew *we* were coming here. Harland didn't even know that and I'm sure our counterparts in the States didn't tell him."

"Or if they did, they wouldn't have given any specifics," James observed.

"That's a good point," Encizo replied.

"Yeah, it's obvious there's a leak somewhere within the Embassy or among one of their contacts," McCarter said. He looked at Russell and asked, "How many people knew the details of our mission here?"

"Three," Russell replied. "The ambassador, his first assistant and me. We're also the only ones who knew the details of Christopher Harland's encounter with the local IRGC leadership."

"Any of that end up in your computer systems?"

Harland shook his head. "Absolutely not. We have a pretty solid security system in place, but it would be insane to have put that kind of sensitive information into computers not hardened against intrusion by NSA standards."

"Emails or phone calls from the others?" Hawkins asked.

"Nope." Russell shook his head emphatically. "At least not to my knowledge. I personally monitor all electronic traffic in or out of there to make sure that any information that must be encrypted *is* encrypted. I didn't note any references in the content to Harland or his transfer."

"If he was being tracked electronically," Manning said, "maybe they somehow used that to get their information."

"Maybe, but that still doesn't explain how they knew we were here, which is the real question at hand," McCarter said. "How about the guy who drove us?"

Russell frowned. "I don't think that's feasible. He didn't know the details of our route until after we'd left the Embassy. I can't see how he would have had an opportunity to inform them far enough in advance to coordinate such an elaborate ambush. I mean, road bombs? That takes some real planning."

"He makes an awfully good point," Hawkins said.

"Well, we're not going to find out sitting around here

on our bloody arses chewing the fat about it," McCarter said. "Mr. Gold will help you get your electronic systems into place as quickly as possible."

Encizo and Russell looked at each other with mutual nods.

"The rest of us need to do a little recon."

"Where?" Manning asked with a furrowed brow.

"The Peace Corps west of here," McCarter replied. "Bring your waterproof bags and mosquito repellent, blokes. We're taking a trip up the Rio Negro."

IT WOULDN'T HAVE BEEN anybody's first choice to navigate the winding, narrow road that snaked along the Rio Negro in the dead of night, but Phoenix Force had never been known for taking the easy route.

It bothered David McCarter being one man short but he understood all too well the importance of giving the body time to rest after trauma. Besides, Encizo wouldn't lack things to do back at the hotel if things continued on the course they had to this point.

This mission could've been classified as anything but easy, and yet McCarter could only think about the challenges facing Phoenix Force. McCarter had told the Farm in no uncertain terms that he thought sending Able Team into the heart of Iran wasn't the hottest idea. After all, this was the CIA's screwup. Why couldn't they clean up their own messes? Still, he knew orders were orders; they went where they had to and did what they had to. It was this kind of professional ethic that had guided the field teams of Stony Man all of these years, and McCarter wouldn't have changed it for anything.

It took nearly two hours to reach the destination of the destroyed Peace Corps camp. As Phoenix Force bailed from the SUV—a loaner from the American Embassy—McCarter ordered them to scout the perimeter. It wouldn't do to get ambushed again. Until they could figure out how the Hezbollah trainees had managed to track their movements, McCarter had told them to assume their every step remained under observation. Manning had also ensured they weren't followed and during their entire trip to the site he could have counted on one hand the number of vehicles they encountered traveling in the opposite direction.

Once they cleared the perimeter, they began to search the scorched remains of the encampment. Manning and Hawkins teamed up and took one half of the camp while McCarter and James scoured the other side.

As they moved through what remained of the camp mess, the beams from their flashlights sweeping the interior, James said, "So you never really told us what we're looking for."

"That's because I'm not sure myself, mate," McCarter replied. "I just have a gut instinct that something here could help us."

"I suppose it's possible." James squinted as he searched the gloom and said, "I don't mind saying, though, this place gives me the creeps. It smells like… death."

That forced a chuckle from McCarter. "You've been watching too many horror movies."

"Nah, that doesn't bother me," James said. "Besides, it's always the white chick who—"

Something caught James's eye as it glinted in the flashlight beam. James peered at it for a bit, cocked his head and said, "Well, I'll be damned."

McCarter stopped searching and turned toward the direction of his friend. "What is it?"

"Come look for yourself."

McCarter advanced on James's position and shortly the pair stood directly over a small, tubular object several inches in diameter and a half foot tall. At first it looked like a miniature coffee urn but on closer inspection they could see the remains of what appeared to be an advanced electronic gauge set into its face. The most telling thing about the object was that despite the fire the majority of it had appeared to survive the blaze. One thing was certain, it wasn't any sort of equipment that would be in possession of a Peace Corps contingent and it sure as hell looked out of place in this environment.

McCarter keyed his radio and ordered the others to join them in the wrecked building. Manning and Hawkins arrived less than a minute later.

"What'd you find?" Hawkins asked. "Buried treasure?"

McCarter pointed at the odd-looking device. "Ever see anything like this before?"

Hawkins gave it a cursory glance and shrugged, but Manning knelt to gain a more detailed appraisal. A few times they heard him grunt to himself as he brushed gently as the soot and ash around the electronic inset. He then looked around the area with his flashlight. After a time, he rose and dusted his hands off.

"It's not an explosive device—I'm sure of that much," he told his compatriots.

Hawkins appeared to let off a sigh of relief.

"You think it's some kind of food processor or something?" James asked.

"Definitely not," McCarter said. "And definitely not any sort of luxury afforded most Peace Corps volunteers. A lot of them travel with only the most basic necessities because they want to fit in with the natives, as it were."

"So what are we looking at?" Hawkins asked.

"Well, I'm not expert but I'd say it's some sort of homing device," Manning said.

"Pretty odd thing for a bunch of Peace Corps volunteers to have," James replied.

"There's no identifying marks on its exterior, but I'm betting if we take it back to HQ for a closer inspection Russell can probably determine exactly what it is," McCarter observed.

"And likely even who made it," Manning said.

"Well, it's not exactly the X-marks-the-spot you were looking for, boss, but it's a start."

"Indeed it is, chum," David McCarter replied.

"WELL, IT LOOKS LIKE you were right on the money, pal," Brad Russell told Manning. "It's definitely a homing beacon."

Phoenix Force had returned with the device and after a couple of tense hours, Russell and Encizo had managed to get enough of their communications system up that the NSA expert could then turn his attention to their prize. Russell made short work of it, figuring out how to disassemble the device and determining its purpose in no time flat. Whatever else Russell might have been, Price had pegged him well when she'd told McCarter that he was an electronics genius to rival some of the best in the business.

"A homing beacon inside a Peace Corps camp," James said. "Doesn't make any sense."

They had Aaron Kurtzman on speakerphone and it was he who replied, "It does if you consider this in light of what we learned from Christopher Harland."

"Meaning?" Hawkins said.

"Meaning that they didn't stumble onto those Peace Corps blokes by accident," McCarter replied. He scratched at the stubble already forming on his chin. "They had this whole thing planned out. They stalked them and they planned their attack."

"And they also managed to get someone to plant that beacon inside the camp," Russell said.

"But who?" James inquired.

"One of the locals. Had to be," Encizo declared.

"What makes you think so?" Manning said.

"There's little doubt in my mind now they have folks on the inside working for them. I think they have a lot of natives on the payroll, in fact."

"Paraguayan citizens helping Hezbollah terrorists?" Russell asked in disbelief. "But why?"

"Maybe the money's good," Hawkins said.

"That's one possibility," Encizo said. "But the more likely scenario is that they've agreed to leave the locals alone. The economy here isn't exactly stable and since the fact one of this country's strongest revenue streams comes from farming, it's not impossible that the Hezbollah might be offering security in exchange for people to look the other way."

"I don't know," McCarter said. "That sounds a bit far-fetched, mate."

"Not really if you consider the possibility," Encizo said. "How else can you explain their ability to get this beacon inside the camp without being seen? Hezbollah terrorists couldn't just waltz in and out unobserved, but local natives were around them constantly. That's the people they were serving, remember? And let's consider that the attack on this Peace Corps contingent was obviously part of a larger plan. The terrorists didn't have to reveal themselves but they chose to risk doing so. Doesn't that make you stop and ask yourselves why? It sure does me."

"That's a good point," Hawkins said.

"I have to admit that he may be on to something," Manning agreed.

"Ditto," James said.

With all of the opinions voiced, McCarter had to consider that majority opinion had merit; it was possible Encizo had just cracked the mystery wide open. "Okay, so let's just say we're right and they have the locals helping them. How does exposing their operation help them? I mean, I don't know about the rest of you but I don't see how revealing the secret training operation in the middle of bloody South America helps the Hezbollah. Or the people training them, for that matter."

"What if it's a diversion?" Russell offered.

"Okay," Kurtzman interjected via speakerphone, "but a diversion from what?"

"Well, didn't you say that they found a homing beacon on Harland that had advanced electronics?"

"Yeah, that's right," Kurtzman replied.

"And now we find this homing beacon—it also has advanced electronics. From what I've seen so far, I'd say much of the guts were manufactured in Europe somewhere."

Kurtzman said in a faraway tone, "If I'm correct in my recollection, Gadgets said the same thing."

"Gadgets?"

"Don't ask," Manning told Russell with a smile.

"So let's look at what we have," McCarter said. "Hezbollah terrorists being trained by members of the Islamic Revolutionary Guard Corps, and using highly advanced technology to spin whatever plans they have. They've also committed several coordinated strikes, and now we suddenly have Ironman and friends headed into the heart of Tehran to assist some no-name CIA informant who claims all of this part of a plan by a mysterious group high up in Ahmadinejad's political ranks to overthrow the Iranian government."

"Well, I don't know what the hell all of that means, exactly," Russell said, "but it doesn't sound good."

"It sounds like terrorists on the verge of implementing a high-tech threat against Americans is what it sounds like," Manning said.

"Great!" Hawkins said. When they all looked at him in surprise he added sheepishly, "I just mean…it'll be business as usual."

CHAPTER SEVEN

Stony Man Farm, Virginia

Harold Brognola and Barbara Price sat in the Operations Center of the Annex.

They'd been reviewing the intelligence provided by Stony Man repeatedly for the past twelve hours without a break. Word had just come in from Lyons that Able Team had left and would reach Iraq within the next sixteen hours. There hadn't been any word from Phoenix Force but Kurtzman had been working with Russell without ceasing, and he'd promised to have something very soon.

"It feels like we're being played, Hal," Price finally said. "Almost as if someone knows our every move."

"I'll admit that this has me stumped, as well," Brognola replied. "I'm also very troubled by what Phoenix Force found in South America. That's the second piece of high-tech equipment being used by the IRGC we've stumbled on in the past twenty-four hours."

"Don't you get the feeling that perhaps we've been duped, that the IRGC knew how we would respond?"

Brognola scratched at the two-day growth on his chin. "I don't know that I buy they knew exactly what we'd do in a situation like this, although I'll agree they seem to have predicted our response pretty well thus far. No, there's something more sinister at the heart of this thing. I just can't put my finger on it."

Price managed a smile. "Don't beat yourself up, Hal. We're all tired. We've been working around the clock. How about some coffee?"

"No way," Brognola said, raising a hand. "I don't think I can take another cup of that battery acid that Bear slurps all day."

"And here I thought you enjoyed my coffee," said Kurtzman, wheeling into the room. He headed directly to the central access terminal recessed in the table. An LCD monitor rose with the push of a button from out of the tabletop and exposed a keyboard beneath it.

"I completed my analysis of the device that Phoenix found," Kurtzman said as he pecked furiously at the keys. A moment later the massive HD screen at the end of the conference room flickered to life and a picture of the device appeared. "This is the closest approximation Akira could come up with based on my secondhand descriptions and the digital photos of what was left that he sent to us."

Akira Tokaido was a member of the Stony Man cyberteam led by Kurtzman. His exploits in the world of software engineering and programming were legendary. He specialized in programs designed to run on sensitive electronic devices, programs that handled everything from flashing EPROM to enabling secure and encrypted traffic on communications equipment. In recent years, he'd become significantly advanced with data-based graphics and 3D rendering engines. It was one of his programs that had obviously reconstructed the device displayed in front of them now.

"Looks like a coffee urn," Brognola remarked.

"That's exactly what our boys thought until they

took a closer look," Kurtzman said. "In fact, though, this thing is a highly advanced homing beacon. Certainly nothing you'd find as standard equipment in Tehran, even among their intelligence people. No...this thing is very high-tech."

"Source of origin?" Price asked.

"We ran it through every recognition program we could think of, but no hits. I walked Brad Russell through disassembling the thing one piece at a time over our high-res video feed. Most of the guts were still intact—it had obviously been built to withstand heat."

"Sounds like maybe whoever planted it didn't know that," Brognola said.

Kurtzman nodded. "Exactly. Otherwise they wouldn't have left it to be found."

"Unless they wanted us to find it," Price said.

"You're sounding a little paranoid, Barb, if you'll forgive me saying so."

"Um, Bear...probably should leave that where it's at right now," Brognola said helpfully.

Kurtzman looked at Price, who didn't meet his glance, shrugged it off and continued. "So since none of the internal parts had identifying marks, I finally decided to take my best guess. There's little doubt this thing came out of China."

"What makes you think so?" Price asked.

"We had Russell overnight a package with two of the chip boards inside," Kurtzman said. "Based on a materials analysis, quantitative architecture of the electronics and a few other telltale signs, we have a strong enough amount of evidence to draw a conclusion it originated in China—at least the parts we examined."

"That's interesting," Brognola said. "After careful analysis in Florida, Gadgets swore up and down that the watch found on Harland's person was indisputably made in Switzerland."

"So the IRGC is obtaining high-tech equipment from all over Europe and Asia?" Kurtzman said.

"It would appear that way," Price replied. "And I think I just may have a theory as to what's going on."

"I'd be happy to entertain any notions at this point, Barb," Brognola said. "Go on."

"What's the most important resource for any terrorist organization?"

Kurtzman clapped his hands together. "Even I know that. Money!"

Price smiled. "Exactly. Without ready cash, terrorists have a very difficult time getting cooperation. They need it for weapons, equipment, clothing and training. They can't use credit cards, obviously, so they need currency and they need large quantities."

"Okay," Brognola interjected. "I still don't see what you're getting at."

"Well, we're pretty certain they don't know much about the equipment they're using," Price said. "That kind of unfamiliarity makes me think their decisions to use it were improvised."

"So...you don't think they intended to use it but in a pinch they would?"

"Right." Price snapped her fingers. "Just like that, they have this equipment but they use it in unnatural ways. My guess is that they're actually stockpiling high-tech equipment to sell on the black market."

"Terrorists smuggling high-tech equipment into foreign countries for cash," Kurtzman said. "I can see that."

"Me, too," Brognola said. "Very lucrative and carries a low risk, since it's obviously been rendered untraceable except by the most advanced methods of analysis."

"It also provides them with a source of local cash wherever they are," Price added. "Consider this for a moment. The IRGC sends a group of their elite members into the heart of an impoverished nation. They need cash to train a terrorist group, whether it's Hezbollah or not, and that means they need money. Money for weapons or smuggling operations or whatever.

"Now suppose that things start to heat up, so they need to put the focus on something else to prevent their smuggling operations from being exposed. So they nab a group of American Peace Corps volunteers, rig up some cockamamie story that they pass along through U.S. political channels and then disappear into thin air while we scramble around the world chasing phantoms."

"Okay, but what about Farzad Hemmati and his story?" Brognola asked.

"I think Hemmati's legit," Price said. "But I also happen to think that he's as intent on keeping the eyes off their smuggling operations as the IRGC contingent in South America."

"So if these two things are still related and this is all about high-tech smuggling," Kurtzman said, "how do you expect to stop them?"

"I'm glad you asked, my friend," Price said. "In a country like Paraguay, there aren't many who could afford this type of equipment. You need to go right to the source of the cash, and that source can usually be found with conglomerate corporations that are in the high-tech business. Most of those are technical futures traders and finance corporations willing to bankroll such goods and not ask too many questions."

"It's a heck of a good place to start," Brognola agreed. "Nice thinking, Barb!"

"I can start digging into those right away," Kurtzman said.

"I'll work with you to get a profile," Price said. "Even among the majority of the lot, I think we'll only find a likely few."

"What about the volunteers, though?" Brognola said. "If there's any chance they're still alive, the President is going to ask us to do everything we can to save them."

"I couldn't agree more. And I fully intend to make sure that we do everything to meet those ends," Price said. "Although we have nowhere for Phoenix Force to start looking, so this is the next best thing. I'm hoping maybe we can get Encizo to work the angles posing as an inside trader, perhaps even a local confidence guy."

"Good idea," Brognola said. "He's the right physical profile for the area and he's also on light duty. I'm sure he'll be keen to the idea."

"Agreed," Price said. "Rafe's never been one for sitting idle long."

"As soon as you have the information together on your most probable leads, make contact with them," Brognola said as he rose. "I need to shave and get ready to leave. I have a meeting with the President in less than two hours."

"He's called a meeting?"

Brognola nodded. "Ever since the information got leaked to the press, he's been on pins and needles. This is an election year."

"Ah, politics," Kurtzman said wistfully. "There's always an election to think of."

"Tell me about it," Hal Brognola replied.

Asunción, Paraguay

"SOLO MISSION?" RAFAEL Encizo sat back, folded his arms and stared at the screen.

Price smiled. "We figured this might interest you, give you a chance to get out and stretch your legs instead of being cooped up."

"How best to say hell yeah," he replied.

Encizo turned to glance at McCarter, who nodded his approval. "It sounds perfect for your talents. You'll hear no objections from me. Beside, we'll be bloody close enough to pull your arse out of the fryer should anything go south."

Encizo sighed deeply and batted his eyelashes at him. "My hero."

McCarter made a face and then turned and walked toward the door, twirling his finger at Hawkins and Manning. "Time for another recon, blokes."

The pair obediently checked the actions on their pistols before stowing them beneath their shirts and following McCarter out the door of their makeshift headquarters. Russell had finished hooking up the direct, secure-feed satellite that would boost communications speed between their crude technical facilities and Stony Man's powerful computer systems. James, who had been assisting with some of the cabling, now sat in front of an oscillating fan with a tall glass of iced tea.

He sipped at the cool drink and said, "If it weren't for the terrorists, I could sure get used to this life."

"I don't know," Encizo said. The Cuban rose and shoved his hands into his pockets. "I'll be glad for a mission, any mission, even if it is rubbing elbows with a snobbish tech runner."

"So the Farm's convinced we'll actually be able to

locate the terrorists through this businessman?" James said. "I don't know. Sounds like a long shot."

"Not as long as you might think," Russell said.

"Come again?"

Russell had been focused on the keyboard and computer screen in front of him, but now he turned his full attention to James and Encizo. "I overheard your people mention the guy's name. Lazario Giménez is no small potatoes. He runs one of the most successful companies in Paraguay, and he has business contacts all over the continent."

"That doesn't necessarily mean he's into high-tech smuggling," James replied.

Russell shook his head. "No, but it does mean he's one of the few who could finance such an operation. He'd have access to resources that most others operating in Asunción wouldn't."

"Well, whatever his deal, we'll know soon enough if he's in bed with the Hezbollah or their IRGC trainers," Encizo said. He rose. "I'd better get changed."

Five minutes passed before McCarter returned. "Looks like we've got the all-clear out there."

"Where are the others?" James asked.

"Waiting in the SUV," McCarter replied.

Encizo emerged from the door of the adjoining suite in cream-colored slacks, a jade silk shirt, chinos and a sport coat to match. He'd also added a bit of styling gel and slicked his black hair. Actually, it looked like he'd stepped out of an episode of *Miami Vice* but nobody commented to that effect.

"Very good, Mr. Gold," James remarked. "You most definitely look the part of the slick wheeler and dealer."

"Your chariot awaits," McCarter said.

The three men said goodbye to Russell before heading out to the SUV. When they were all aboard, Manning drove into the city. It took no time to locate the offices of Lazario Giménez thanks to the GPS unit installed in their loaner from the embassy. Manning circled the block twice and then parked directly across from the office building. As Manning got out to feed the meter, McCarter turned in the front passenger seat to look at the other three in back.

"Okay, here's the deal. You'll go inside and make contact by whatever means you can. Hawkins, you'll go along with him as muscle. Cal, you'll post yourself around the elevators or wherever you can be discreet. We'll wait here as soft backup. Questions?"

The men shook their heads and then went EVA.

They crossed the street and within a minute they were standing in front of a broad semicircular reception desk. Behind the exotic-looking woman manning the desk was Mercury Investments, Ltd. in bright red lettering with silver trim backed by lighted glass. The logo of the company was present, as well, a silver globe adorned with gold wreaths and the company monogram emblazoned into it.

"May I help you?"

"Rico Gonzales to see Mr. Giménez."

"Do you have an appointment, sir?" the woman asked, eyeing Encizo and Hawkins a little suspiciously. If she'd noticed James break off from the group when they'd entered, she made no sign of it.

"I'm afraid I don't," Encizo replied in an easy tone and gracious smile. "But I'm sure if you tell Mr. Giménez that I'm interested in purchasing some of the high-tech equipment he has, I'm certain he'll see me."

"We are an investment firm, sir. We do not sell high-tech equipment."

"I'm *certain* he'll see me," Encizo repeated.

"So you're not a present client, then?" she said even as she reached for the phone.

"No." Encizo tried another smile. "Not yet, that is."

With one eye still on the pair and the receiver to her ear, the receptionist pushed a button on the vast console. After nearly a full minute of conversation, during which time she kept her voice low, the woman hung up the phone and frowned.

"I've been told that Mr. Giménez is very busy today, but you're in luck. He's willing to give you a few minutes. Please sign in." She placed a badge on the elevated counter. "You will need to wear that at all times while on the property. Also, your friend will have to wait here."

"I'm afraid not, ma'am," Hawkins replied. "Where he goes, I go."

"Well, then, you won't be seeing Mr. Giménez."

"If you please," Encizo interjected quickly. "I'm certain you'll understand when I say that I'm a man of some importance. I receive regular threats against my life. My associate is a professional executive protector. He'll be no trouble, I assure you."

The woman exchanged glances with Encizo and Hawkins. A long, weighty silence followed but eventually she sighed and placed a second badge on the counter. "Are you armed, sir?"

Hawkins nodded. "I am."

"You may accompany your boss, but you are not permitted to carry firearms beyond this point."

A pair of beefy, well-dressed types suddenly made their entrance from a door located near the station and headed for them. By the way the men carried themselves, the Phoenix Force pair could tell they were packing. A split-second decision had to be made and Encizo knew if he made the wrong one it could go hard. The men were intimidating, sure, but they moved with a practiced ease that didn't imply hostile intent.

"That will be acceptable," Encizo said.

Encizo looked at Hawkins, who nodded.

When the men reached him, Hawkins dutifully pulled his sports jacket aside so the men could see his pistol plainly. Keeping his right hand well clear, he reached to the holster and thumbed the quick release. Hawkins then nodded and one of them reached forward to relieve him of his side arm. The man expertly dropped the magazine, jacked the slide to the rear and caught the bullet in one motion. He stepped behind the counter and, using a lockbox key, put the pistol and ammunition inside the box.

"You may retrieve it when you leave, sir," said the second man.

The two donned their badges and the men escorted them to the elevators. James was nowhere in sight, but neither Encizo nor Hawkins was worried about that fact. Calvin James was a consummate professional; he'd be within striking distance if it became necessary and chances were good he'd witnessed them disarming Hawkins. Beside, Encizo had a warbler in his pocket and if anything went down they could have their three friends provide support within a minute.

Encizo just hoped they wouldn't need it.

When they arrived on the top floor of the building and stepped off the elevators, a welcoming sight greeted them.

The entire floor had been converted into an open, airy suite with high ceilings. Morning sunlight streamed through the arched windows but because they faced north it wasn't intense. A three-tier fountain adorned with multicolored glass bulbs occupied the center of the floor. The entire length of the south wall was stepped and water ran freely along it and emptied in a shallow pool at its base. Exotic plants were stationed like sentries throughout, and recessed shelves boasted rare art pieces.

Against the east wall they spotted a massive teak desk carved with ornate designs along its otherwise smooth sides. A pudgy, balding man in his late fifties sat behind the desk. He appeared lost in deep thought but he made no show of their presence. The security men made no attempt to interrupt him or to alert him the guests had arrived. After several minutes the man finally broke away from whatever he'd been looking at, rose from the desk and walked to where they waited near the fountain.

He extended his hand. "Mr. Gonzales, is it?"

Encizo nodded and shook his hand. "Yes, sir."

"I'm Lazario Giménez."

"Thank you for seeing me, sir."

"I must admit that your, ah, offer somewhat intrigued me," Giménez said. His eyes were deeply inset and, given the pudgy skin around them, appeared a bit shifty. Giménez looked at Hawkins. "And you are?"

"Mr. Gonzales's chief of security," Hawkins replied.

Giménez studied Hawkins for some time before returning his attention to Encizo. "I understand that your man here walked into my building wearing a firearm."

"I apologize for that, Mr. Giménez." Encizo offered the little weasel a conciliatory smile. "We meant no disrespect. But I'm in a rather strange set of circumstances of late, and have found it necessary to acquire a man of—oh, how to put it?—special talents."

Giménez made another equally studious appraisal of Enciso before nodding. "I understand. I've been known to use men like this now and again myself. Special Forces?"

"Delta Force, actually," Enciso said. He saw no reason to lie.

If it turned out Giménez tried putting questions about such things, Hawkins would be able to respond with knowledge and proficiency.

"I see. Well, gentlemen, why don't we talk over a drink." Giménez gestured in the direction opposite his office.

The room opened onto a lounge with a full bar of burnished wood. The escorts took position in discreet locations while a young Asian woman appeared from an alcove and waited for their orders. Giménez requested a Tequila Sunrise and Enciso opted for a Johnnie Walker Blue Label neat. In the true form of professionalism, Hawkins declined any alcoholic beverages in favor of a mineral water on the rocks.

While they waited, Giménez and Enciso took a seat in some leather couches just forward of the bar in a sunken area of the room. The accommodations were the finest Enciso had ever seen and he tried to act impressed without overdoing it.

"I see you admire my furnishings."

Enciso nodded. "Very much."

"Although," Giménez continued without missing a beat, "I don't suppose you're here to talk of interior decorating."

"You assume correctly." Enciso offered their host an easy shrug. "I'm informed that you have an interest in other fineries, particularly high-end technologies."

"Indeed I am, but it piques my curiosity to know exactly how you came about this information."

"Come now, Mr. Giménez, I cannot give away *all* of my secrets. Suffice it to say that this is my business and I know it well. And I'm prepared to make a very attractive offer."

"How attractive?"

Encizo cleared his throat as he made a show of inspecting his fingernails. "How would you feel about sixty percent."

"Above markup?" Giménez's bushy eyebrows rose. "That's very generous."

"I work for some very generous people."

"So the interest is not your own."

Encizo smiled. "Very observant, Mr. Giménez."

"I believe I could be persuaded to arrange something for you at that kind of profit margin," Giménez said.

"That's good to hear. There is just one small concession."

"Isn't there always?"

They paused as the woman brought their drinks. When she'd gone, Giménez continued. "And what exactly is this small concession?"

"We need to—"

"Sir, I apologize for interrupting," one of the security men cut in. He bent and whispered in Giménez's ear.

The old man's eyes flashed as he listened, and when the security man finished speaking Giménez looked Encizo in the eye. "You'll have to pardon me, Mr. Gonzales, but it appears we have an intruder in the building."

"Oh?"

"Yes. And I find it much more than coincidental

that this would occur at the precise time you came here unbidden."

Hawkins said, "We didn't have anything to do with it."

"We shall see soon enough," Giménez said, favoring Hawkins with a death's-head smile. He then turned his security officer and said, "Kill him."

CHAPTER EIGHT

While Giménez's men were professionals, and perhaps could be counted as skilled bodyguards, they weren't in the same league as Rafael Encizo or T. J. Hawkins—they weren't truly dangerous men.

Encizo and Hawkins, on the other end, spent nearly every waking hour in a kill-or-be-killed mind-set and when they weren't doing that, they were often training to do it. Moreover, it became immediately apparent that Giménez's closest bodyguard figured he had no reason to work quickly since they had disarmed Hawkins. What the security hardcase hadn't considered as he reached slowly beneath his jacket for his pistol was that both of the men were holding heavy lead-crystal glasses.

The Phoenix Force pair hurled their drinks at the man simultaneously, one glancing off the top of his skull while the other struck him in the chest. Neither of the blows was debilitating but both were painful distractions. It was all the time Hawkins needed to dive in and tackle the man at the waist.

Even as they toppled to the ground, Encizo gained his feet and moved on Giménez, who appeared to be clawing for something at his left hip. Encizo lashed out with his foot and pinned Giménez's arm against the leather cushion of the chair he occupied.

Hawkins landed a rock-solid punch against the jaw

of the bodyguard and then relieved him of his weapon, a SIG-Sauer P-220 Carry pistol. All of this activity had gone down in a matter of seconds and although he'd neutralized one opponent and Encizo obviously had Giménez under control, Hawkins knew that one threat still lurked. The remaining bodyguard had acted with considerably more speed and skill than his cohort, and Hawkins instinctively rolled from his position.

The bullet came a heartbeat later, missing Hawkins by inches as the former Delta Force commando rolled clear and came up on one knee. Hawkins leveled the P-220 and snapped off two rounds. The first .45-caliber slug, hastily fired, grazed the other bodyguard's left arm but his natural movement away from the shooting put him directly in the line of fire. The second round entered his flank just above the kidney and exited his chest, taking a piece of his lung with it. The man let out a surprised shout and then toppled to the ornate tile.

Encizo increased pressure on Giménez's wrist until the man released a cry of pain and the bones in his wrist popped with the escape of gas. Encizo then removed the pressure and frisked Giménez until he found the 9x18 mm PM pistol. The choice surprised Encizo since a man of Giménez's alleged experience would have known that a .38 or 9 mm Parabellum round would be superior for a personal protection weapon. Either way, the pistol would serve a very good purpose.

Encizo pressed the barrel to Giménez's forehead. "Now we'll try this the old-fashioned way. What's your relationship with the Hezbollah operating here?"

"Uh…" Hawkins said, and when Encizo turned in his direction, Hawkins added, "I think we're about to find out."

Their attention shifted to movement near the elevators and suddenly Giménez and his bodyguards posed no threat in consideration of these new arrivals. Five men stepped off the elevator. They wore black fatigues, balaclava-style masks and red berets. Even from that distance Encizo and Hawkins could make out the wicked silhouettes of SMGs and assault rifles. Their uniforms, save for the masks, were identical to the ones worn by the team that had hit Phoenix Force on its way from the airport, as well as matching the description Christopher Harland had given the CIA; these were Hezbollah terrorists.

"Here comes trouble," Hawkins muttered.

The pair threw themselves to the ground, the sunken floor providing them a natural defilade from which to make their stand. Not that it would be much of a stand given they had two semiauto pistols against a quintet of terrorists armed with assault weapons.

"I'd say we're a little outgunned," Encizo remarked.

"Well, at least we'll go out fighting," Hawkins said.

Encizo nodded. "And maybe take a few of the bastards with us!"

"Wait a minute, you fools!" Giménez shouted, leaping from the couch and waving his arms. "You can't—!"

His words were cut down as effectively as he was, the terrorists leveling their weapons and opening fire. They weren't apparently interested in distinguishing allies from foes. They had come with one purpose in mind and they weren't particularly discriminating about it. They probably figured the end justified the means and at that point they were obviously no longer in need of Giménez's services. His body convulsed as more than a dozen high-velocity rounds struck him in every part of his body.

"Let's give 'em hell!" Hawkins cried.

The Phoenix Force pair leveled their pistols and returned fire, diligent to make every shot count. They had precious little ammunition and they weren't about to waste it on less than a sure thing. Both of them took the first one of the terrorists in line simultaneously, Encizo pumping a .45 slug through the man's chest while Hawkins caught the terrorist with a clean headshot that penetrated his chin and blew out the base of his skull.

Before they could take any other targets, however, the muzzle-flashes from another weapon winked from a point behind them. Two more of the enemy were toppled by Calvin James's surprise flanking maneuver. The warrior triggered another 3-round burst from the MP5K machine pistol he'd apparently stashed beneath his suit coat when entering the building and cut down a fourth terrorist. The fifth spun on his heel and tried to find a better vantage point, obviously forgetting that James and Encizo had the only decent cover and they weren't about to give it up.

That didn't leave the terrorist with any options and the pair finished him with four shots, all of which found their marks. The terrorist's body twitched with the impact of slugs to his upper torso before finally toppling prone to the polished tile floors of Giménez's lavish office accommodations.

James trotted to their position and inspected the bodies of the two deceased and one unconscious security man.

As he and Hawkins climbed to their feet, Encizo said, "Any idea what the hell happened?"

James shrugged. "Not sure. I was running around this place trying to figure out which elevator would get me to the top floor when McCarter radioed to say they were watching trouble come straight into the building. I finally located a hidden stairwell. I took it to avoid the terrorists, figuring they'd use the elevator."

"Let's get the hell out of here," Hawkins said.

"Wait," Enciso replied. The Cuban whirled and headed to the unconscious bodyguard, patting him down until he found the key to the lockbox. He tossed it at Hawkins and said, "I'm sure you'll want to get your pistol back."

"Hold up," James said, cocking his head and pointing at his ear to indicate McCarter was trying to raise him. James stood in an attitude of attention and said, "We better make it quick. There's another group of them somewhere in the building."

"You mean there's more?" Hawkins asked in disbelief.

James nodded.

"Obviously, the Hezbollah were watching Giménez," Enciso said.

"It would seem so," James agreed.

Hawkins glanced at Giménez's bloodied corpse. "It looks like the Farm guessed correctly. Giménez had thrown his lot in with the Hezbollah or IRGC or whoever the hell's behind this."

"Come on, let's move out," Enciso said.

The trio rushed to the elevator but James stopped them short. "There's the back stairwell hidden in that recessed area. Maybe we should take it."

"You're thinking the Hezbollah won't know about it," Hawkins ventured.

"They're a lot less likely to know about it than the elevator."

Enciso nodded. "I'm with Cal. Let's do it."

The men took the stairwell and had nearly reached

the ground floor when trouble emerged on the landing below them. They heard the three terrorists before they saw them. James took point since he had the only autopistol. Encizo cursed himself for not thinking ahead and relieving the terrorists of their firepower. Well, they wouldn't have to wait long since he was pretty certain Manning and McCarter were inbound to provide backup. He would've liked to see the look on the snarky receptionist's face when the two Phoenix Force veterans came through the doors geared up with assault-grade weapons and ordnance designed for CQB.

James crouched and waited until the terrorists rounded the corner of the stairs before sweeping the MP-5K muzzle to cut a swathing pattern of autofire across their ranks. The first terrorist took several 9 mm Parabellums in the chest, the force driving him against the wall. He left a streak of blood and flesh as he slid to the ground, his eyes open in a lifeless stare. The second terrorist managed to evade a fatal shot, instead taking one round to the shoulder that twisted him in an upward spiral and slammed him against the outer wall. The third terrorist lost the top of his skull and died on his feet, although he took three more to the chest with James's second pass.

Hawkins delivered a double-tap to the survivor, both headshots, as the three men descended the stairs. Encizo tracked each target with his pistol but held fire, deciding it best to use his ammunition sparingly. They emerged on the third floor and James led them to the main stairwell that spanned all other nine stories, excluding the penthouse offices to which James had found the obscure executive staircase wing.

As they began their descent again, Encizo asked, "Did David indicate how many we were dealing with?"

"He thought a dozen, no more," James replied.

All three of them were panting with exertion by the time they reached the ground floor. They emerged onto a wide hallway that then opened onto an octagonal meeting room, dimly lit. It seemed like an odd place for the stairs to be placed but the architecture in Paraguay seemed to be different from the type favored in other countries. Maybe Giménez had simply wanted it to be different, although it didn't really matter. They were on the ground floor and home free if they could avoid any more encounters with the terrorists.

Their luck held out until they left the meeting room and started to advance down the main hall. Four terrorists were waiting near the bank of elevators close to the reception area, and they were engaged with perhaps three or four of Giménez's armed security specialists—it was difficult to tell from the amount of shots being traded. The security men were armed only with pistols and had grabbed concealment behind whatever proved tough enough to withstand the full-auto hell being directed at them. The terrorists had only mild cover and didn't appear too concerned.

Encizo considered looking for an alternative exit but he knew they couldn't leave the security behind to battle the terrorists themselves. Phoenix Force was in the antiterrorist business, and he wasn't about to slough the work on a poorly armed and insufficiently trained group of security men who were probably just doing their jobs. Encizo couldn't believe that every man working for Giménez knew his boss had been consorting with Hezbollah fanatics.

Encizo noted the timely appearance of McCarter and Manning. As the Cuban suspected, the pair was armed to the teeth and had brought along extras. Even as Encizo holstered his pistol, he reached out for the MP-5 McCarter tossed to him. Manning distributed an M-16 A-4 to Hawkins in equal measure, and now the united Phoenix Force warriors turned their full fury on the remaining terrorist quartet.

Manning brought his FNC to shoulder level and sighted on one of the terrorists. The Phoenix Force reunion had alerted the terrorists to the fact they now had enemies on their flanks, but they couldn't react in time to the new arrivals. Manning got the terrorist dead to rights with a short burst that struck belly, chest and throat. The man's neck exploded in a fountain of flesh and blood, the high-velocity slug nearly decapitating him. His head bobbed in ugly fashion on his partially severed neck and he toppled to the polished tile floor.

McCarter got another terrorist with a full-auto volley to the gut that transformed his target's guts to mush. The terrorist's weapon clattered to the floor and he dropped to his knees, his hands going to the shredded flesh of his stomach and internal organs. A howl of agony was cut short by a follow-up from James, who'd been targeting the man at nearly the exact same moment as McCarter.

Hawkins went prone even as a terrorist brought his weapon to bear, but his timing beat out that of his target by more than a second; it was all the time Hawkins needed. He triggered the M-16 on 3-round-burst mode and the trio of 5.56 mm rounds blew the terrorist's chest wide open. The impact flung him into a potted plant and the weight of his body cracked the rim, eventually collapsing beneath the added force of his fall and coming to rest in a pile of blood mixed with potting soil.

Encizo took the last one with a sustained burst from his MP-5. The 9 mm slugs stitched a spiral pattern in the terrorist's torso and he crumpled to the floor. The echo of weapons reports died in the airy ground floor with its high ceilings. The security guards peered around the corner and realized that their enemies had been neatly dispatched by the formidable-looking team that now dispersed into covering positions where they could deal with any remaining combatants.

Encizo had other ideas and began to shout at the men in Spanish, hopeful his Cuban dialect wouldn't be noticeable. He'd lost much of the islander accent in his Spanish over the years, enough that he could be understood and yet keep others unsure of the exact nature of his origins. Whatever the case, his shouting seemed to work because eventually the three security men emerged from their cover positions. While they didn't holster their pistols, they weren't pointing them in the direction of any of the Phoenix Force warriors.

One of the men, apparently the leader of the group, stepped toward Encizo and gestured with his finger for the Cuban to approach. "Who are you and what is your business here?"

Encizo saw no reason to deceive the man, although there wasn't any time for dillydallying. "We're here on official business of the United States government. These men—" he gestured at the corpses "—are Muslim terrorists. They were sent here to assassinate Mr. Giménez and probably all of you along with him."

The man looked at the bodies with the most dumfounded of expressions. "Terrorists? Why would terrorists want to kill Mr. Giménez? That's preposterous what you're saying."

Encizo cast a frosty eye at the man. "We didn't get far enough to find out why they wanted to kill your boss, friend. All we know is that they're in your country and they've taken a number of American Peace Corps volunteers hostage. All we want to do is find our people and get them out. We have no fight with you."

Wailing sirens wound down and they could hear vehicles pulling up outside.

"You've got about five seconds to decide if you trust us or the terrorists," Encizo told the man.

It didn't take more than a moment for the guy to apparently decide. "We owe you our lives. There's a back exit down that hall and through a cafeteria. It opens onto an alleyway where they get all of the deliveries. Leave here and don't ever come back."

Hawkins suddenly dashed up to them, having retrieved his pistol from the lockbox. "We got municipal fuzz swarming the front doors. There must be at least two dozen of them."

Encizo nodded and turned to McCarter, jerking a thumb at the security lead. "This guy's giving us an out. Follow me."

"Can we trust him?" McCarter asked as they filed in behind Encizo in a hurry.

"Do we have a choice?"

McCarter shook his head. "Nope, I guess we bloody well don't."

CHAPTER NINE

Sulaimaniyah, Iraq

Since the war had officially ended in Iraq, and Saddam Hussein's reign of terror was over, the flooding of the region by civilian contractors had gone practically unchecked. Engineers, technologists, military and political advisers—the list had become almost endless—entered and left the country on a daily basis. There were hundreds if not thousands of foreigners traipsing in and out of Iraq as if it was Disney World, and the three Americans dressed in business casual didn't really look out of place.

The same couldn't be said for Able Team's CIA contact.

The man who introduced himself only as "Zephyr" had a thick salt-and-pepper beard and long hair tied in a ponytail. He wore an OD-green Army field jacket, tan cargo pants and basketball high-tops. While Lyons and his friends realized it took all kinds to move the intelligence community, Zephyr actually looked like a hippy who'd just stepped out of time—a refugee from Haight-Ashbury.

"What's shaking, cats?" he said as he pumped their hands in turn.

"Um..." Schwarz began with a sideways glance at his comrades.

Even Blancanales appeared lost for words. Lyons finally said, "Not much, pal. You know about the arrangements?"

"Oh, sheesh," he replied. "Let me guess. You're all the professional types, right? Strictly business and all?"

"No. We're the mean-and-grouchy types, unsociable and all."

"You'll have to forgive my friend," Blancanales cut in with his usual alacrity. "It was a long flight and we're flying on little sleep."

"Well, why the heck didn't you say so?" Zephyr chuckled and shook his head. "Oh, man, you dudes really had me going there for a minute. Okay, it's going to be a little longer before your plane's ready. How's about I get some eats and hot joe into you. You be down with that?"

Blancanales and Schwarz brightened immediately at talk of a decent meal, but Lyons remained indifferent. His nose wrinkled a bit but he didn't think the smell was coming off Zephyr. In fact, he wasn't even sure if the odor—as rank and strong as it was—could've been produced by a human. It almost smelled as if an animal had recently died and begun to rot.

"Let's just get out of here," the Able Team leader told them.

Within a few minutes they were out of the airport and had climbed aboard a beat-up Toyota Land-cruiser. Blancanales and Schwarz rode in back while Lyons took shotgun. Zephyr made small talk the entire ten-minute trip to a nondescript café at the edge of one of Sulaimaniyah's numerous commercial districts. As Zephyr drove past the storefronts and parked along the street a half block away, Schwarz eyed the café with less enthusiasm than he'd first had when Zephyr mentioned food.

"So what are the eats like in this place?" he asked.

Zephyr laughed. "Don't worry, friend, you'll be impressed. I recommend the *fattoush* as an appetizer accompanied by some Ouzo. Then *shawarma* as the main course. That's a sandwich in pita bread stuffed with shaved goat, lamb and chicken. It's wonderful, trust me. You might be surprised to learn I eat it nearly every day. You'll love it."

"No," Lyons said.

"Sorry?"

"He meant," Blancanales interjected quickly, "no, we're not surprised you eat it every day. Sounds great!"

Lyons didn't contradict Blancanales but he lent his friend a sour eye. The four made their way from the vehicle. All of them felt naked not wearing weapons but they hadn't wanted to risk attracting attention. Lyons couldn't help but be a little jumpy anyway after their encounter in Little Havana, not to mention Harland's betrayal that had nearly gotten all of them killed. He understood Harland's inexperience; hell, the guy was a Peace Corps volunteer not an experienced intelligence agent. Still, he should have trusted his government to at least exercise discretion in such a situation where the lives of Americans were at risk.

Lyons also didn't like the thought they were walking into this new situation in the heart of a country that considered Americans persona non grata. If they were caught or this Hemmati character planned to set a trap for them, something Lyons considered a most likely scenario, Stony Man would see the Able Team commandos returned in a box. It was Lyons's job to make certain that didn't happen and he planned to build every contingency he could into avoiding those ends.

Once they were seated and Zephyr had ordered for them, beginning with strong coffee all around, Lyons asked, "How far to this airfield?"

"About a half hour from here," Zephyr said. "The Army Engineer Corps built it during the heaviest fighting back in '07 and '08. It's seen a lot of use so it's somewhat beat-up, but the dudes I work with are mostly former Navy pilots. Those cats can land on a dime, you know what I mean, dude?"

Blancanales smiled and started to open his mouth when a glint of light on metal flashed in his peripheral vision. He didn't have to turn fully in that direction to catch the profile of an SMG being clutched by an unidentified party masked by a burka. Blancanales shouted at the pair a moment before overturning their table and dragging Schwarz behind it.

Lyons had already noticed his friend's move and managed to get out of the way before the contents of the table landed in his lap. He spun on one foot and went for another unoccupied table nearby—dragging a surprised and much slower Zephyr along with him— even as the first volley from the SMG burned the open space. The flimsy tables were no match for the 9 mm hell being dispatched in their direction, and only the honed reflexes of the Able Team warriors had even saved them from the initial assault.

Zephyr managed to clear a Glock 30 from beneath his coat with an efficiency that could have only come from many hours of training and experience. His hippy ways hadn't obviously extended to his ability to handle himself. Unfortunately he never got off a shot as a pair of 9 mm rounds struck his arm and drove the pistol from his grip. As he cried out Lyons somehow managed to snatch the pistol out of midair and turn it on their aggressor.

Lyons snap-aimed and squeezed the trigger three times. At this distance, with an enemy toting superior position and firepower, Lyons let the natural muzzle rise from the pistol do the work. In this case, it paid off as two of the three rounds struck. The first entered his target's abdomen and the second clipped him at the base of the neck where it met the right clavicle. The gunner spun and his weapon jerked upward, expending a maelstrom of rounds into the ceiling.

The wait staff and other patrons were already shouting or running for cover when the second threat appeared, this one coming through the front door with his SMG held low. Zephyr reached under his pant leg to an ankle holster and came away with a snub-nose, 5-shot revolver that he slid across the floor to Schwarz.

Lyons and Schwarz got the drop on the gunner just as he triggered his first burst, a twin pair of .45 slugs entering his chest while Schwarz got him with a skull-busting .38-caliber slug to the head. The man's brains came out the back and sprayed a nearby window with gore. The terrorist's legs seemed to quiver before he toppled to the wooden floor with enough force to raise a cloud of dust.

As reports from the pistol died out, Schwarz and Lyons tracked the room looking for other threats while Blancanales left cover and rushed toward the first body. He scooped the man's SMG off the floor in a millisecond, inspected it to find it was an AKSU and then he immediately double-checked the action to see if it was still functional.

No other threats appeared so Schwarz and Lyons

turned their attention to Zephyr. One of the wounds looked to have traveled clean through the shoulder muscle but a second lower on the arm looked serious. Schwarz immediately noticed bright red blood spurting from the pulsing buildup of blood beneath Zephyr's arm just below the elbow.

"Just a bite," Zephyr said bravely.

"Bullshit," Lyons snapped. "They got an artery. Gadgets, give me your belt."

Schwarz disconnected the quick-release buckle and cleared the leather belt with one pull. Lyons went to work wrapping the wound, searching around for a dinner utensil. He couldn't find one and finally settled for a pewter candlestick. He twisted the thing between two loops in the belt until Zephyr yelled that it felt as if his arm was being torn off.

"Better than bleeding to death," Schwarz reminded him.

A swarthy type with a long, graying beard and wearing an apron came from the back room and began jabbering and shouting at them, speaking Arabic so fast that even the natives were having a difficult time understanding him. Lyons and Schwarz looked at him and each other helplessly but neither of them could understand what had the man so agitated.

"Cripes, it's not like we came in here shooting up the place or anything," Schwarz said to partly the man and partly to his friends.

"I think he's telling us we've worn out our welcome, gentlemen," Blancanales said.

"Imagine that," Lyons muttered. "Let's get out of here. We need to get Zephyr to a hospital."

Schwarz and Lyons each took an arm while Blancanales moved to the second deceased terrorist and liberated his weapon from him, as well. They managed to get outside and halfway to their vehicle before they heard the crunch of a vehicle's wheels on gravel. They looked toward the street in time to see an older black Mercedes roll alongside them and the back window lower. The barrel of a weapon protruded from it and they all grabbed earth as the weapon opened up. Rounds bit into the flimsy facade of a raw pottery store and the windows caved under the onslaught.

Determined to take the heat off his poorly armed friends, Blancanales rolled a number of times back in the direction they'd come so he could take a flanking position. He came to his feet and extended both SMGs directly at the car. The message he sent was clear, triggering sustained autofire on vehicle. Most of the rounds seemed to bounce off the vehicle and not one of the windows shattered. A few did manage to strike the muzzle of the weapon extended from the back window and that prompted the driver to beat a hasty exit from the scene.

Blancanales rushed back to his friends who were already on their feet and half dragging Zephyr with them. They reached the Land Cruiser without further incident. Once they got Zephyr into the backseat, the Able Team warriors climbed aboard and raced from the scene as quickly as possible, Lyons at the wheel. The Iraqi cops and probably U.S. Army troops would be looking for them soon. They needed to get Zephyr to a hospital and it was better to hit their LZ now and get a chopper to take him than to try to find their way to a medical facility in the heart of the city.

Improviser that he was, Hermann Schwarz carried basic medical supplies with him wherever he went. He broke open an ammonia ampoule and held it under

Zephyr's nose. That brought the guy around enough that they could get directions to the LZ from him. He faded in and out throughout the trip but within twenty minutes they were bouncing their way down a rutted access road that eventually opened onto a makeshift airstrip.

They came within fifty yards of the specialized jet when a dozen armed men in civilian clothes seemed to come out of nowhere and converge on them, pointing assorted pistols and automatic weapons at them. Lyons brought the vehicle to a crunching halt, and Schwarz was out the door before the Land Cruiser had fully stopped.

"Don't shoot!" Schwarz said. "We're friendly!"

"What's the pass phrase?" one of the men demanded.

"November Mike!" Zephyr managed weakly as Lyons and Blancanales helped him out.

"Oh, shit," the man said as he and several others lowered their weapons and rushed to help.

Another man, identifying himself as a team medic, ordered them to lay Zephyr on the ground and elevate his legs. As they did, the medic sent a man to get his medical bag. While the medic inspected the tourniquet, the man who'd demanded the pass phrase ordered several others to get back to their posts and secure the perimeter. Once that was done, he gestured to Lyons and the two engaged in a sidebar while the rest helped prep equipment obtained by the medic's runner.

"You must be Irons," the man said, extending a strong handshake. He had light brown hair and an accent that left Lyons figuring he was from Georgia or Alabama. "I'm Mark Biggert. I'm the XO of this unit."

"Military spec-ops?" Lyons asked.

Biggert nodded. "Seventh Special Forces Group, Airborne. What the hell happened?"

"I wish I knew, chief."

"Our orders were to assist you guys with an AR2 HALO drop over Iran," Biggert said. He jerked a thumb in Zephyr's direction. "Nobody told us we'd be getting casualties from the civilian end."

"You know him?"

"You're kidding, right?" Biggert shook his head and smiled. "Anybody who's anybody knows Zephyr. That old son of a bitch should have been dead by all accounts. Sometimes I think the power of Almighty God's the only thing keeping him alive."

"It would seem that way today," Lyons said. "Look, I can't get into much of what we're here for, but I can tell you I'd consider it a personal favor if you could get Zephyr to a doctor or hospital. We owe the guy our lives, frankly."

"Done," Biggert said with a curt nod. He turned toward the group. "Sergeant Daly, front and center!"

A young, strapping man of about twenty-five immediately broke from the group and came to a casual but alert position in front of them.

"This is Staff Sergeant Daly, our assistant medical NCO." Biggert turned back to Daly. "Sarge, we need get Zephyr out of here on Medevac as quickly as possible. Can you radio HQ and see to it?"

"Yes, sir!"

After Daly saluted, whirled and double-timed for a Quonset hut on the edge of the airfield, one that Lyons hadn't noticed until Daly took off in that direction, Biggert said, "He'll get the best care possible, sir. Is there anything else you need?"

"Well, I understand you'll have all of our gear for

this jump. And that you would be able to supply us with weapons, munitions and ordnance."

"Actually, we can provide some of the weapons and munitions," he said. "We explained it to our CO, Captain Whelan, who took it up the chain of command. It's our understanding that the Company boys assigned to rendezvous with you in the Elburz will take care of the rest."

"I appreciate anything you can help us with," Lyons said.

"Well, we'd best get you guys suited up. We need to get airborne as soon as possible. We'll only have a very small window of time and this little fiasco's going to put us behind as it is. No worries, though. We can make it up in the air."

TWO HOURS LATER, THE special HC130 jet cruised at thirty-two thousand feet. The Able Team warriors had been breathing pure oxygen for the past forty-five minutes and were now suited in special polypropylene-knit undergarments beneath the HALO suits. This wasn't a regular process for the trio, and none of them had minded discussing among themselves how they weren't exactly fond of this kind of operation. Still, they knew it had to be done and there was no other way to get inside Iran.

When the signal came, Lyons went out first and was followed closely by his two friends. The Able Team leader wore a special GPS that would guide them to the coded homing signal. They would get as close as they could to that signal before deploying and then they would deploy together based on a signal from Lyons. This would ensure that they didn't end up too far apart, separating them and losing precious time while they regrouped.

The deployment of the chutes went off without a hitch at about three thousand feet, and within ninety seconds they had reached the ground. The touch-down actually surprised Lyons as the impact didn't end up being nearly as bad as he thought it would. He performed the standard four-point roll when his feet touched the ground, as he'd learned from Biggert only the most experienced parachutists would actually attempt to land directly on their feet. That roll took most of the shock from the landing and Lyons was glad he'd listened to the Special Forces executive officer.

Within another minute, Able Team were cloistered in a copse of trees and invisible to any prying eyes.

"I mark us about half a klick from our rendezvous point," Schwarz said after a quick study of the advanced GPS device.

"Out-freaking-standing," Blancanales said. "We're nearly halfway home, men."

"Yeah, this is some vacation," Lyons grumbled as they set off across the dark, bleak landscape.

"THERE IT IS," ABNEY said, pointing to a small blip on the handheld gizmo.

Poppas leaned over his cohort's shoulder—he assented with a nod and grunt. Their contacts were close now, damn close, and it wouldn't be long before they reached them.

The two CIA agents had been waiting for hours. Although it was summer, the nighttime temperatures in the Elburz Mountains still dropped near freezing. The two had been huddling close together for warmth, determined not to risk building a fire or wasting precious gas by running the engine of the antiquated jeepney. Neither of the men had operated in the field for many years and they weren't used to these kinds of vigils. No amount of training at Langley, Camp Peary or anywhere else could prepare them for the rigors of such a hostile and unyielding countryside.

"I hope these guys aren't a bunch of bureaucrats from the Company," Poppas said.

"My understanding is they did a HALO jump to get into this country," Abney said. "That doesn't sound like a bunch of bureaucrats to me."

"Humph."

"Not to mention that they aren't supposed to be Company at all. These guys are from another page in the book—one even we aren't apparently important enough to know about."

"How many were they sending again?"

"Three males, for the five hundredth time."

"What's got your panties in a bunch?"

Abney produced a scoffing laugh. "I'm tired of sitting out here freezing my dick off, that's what. I can't believe we've had to wait this long."

"Actually, these guys are pretty much on schedule," Poppas said as he pulled the glove away from his wrist enough to expose the luminescent face of his watch.

"Which should be another indicator they're not bureaucrats."

"Yep." Poppas lit a cigarette.

"Do you have to keep smoking out here, Pops?"

"It's keeping me warm."

"That's bullshit. Nicotine thins the blood."

"Well, excuse me, professor," Poppas countered. "Anyway, it makes me happy. And if I got to be stuck out here, unable to feel my ass, the least you can do is not begrudge letting me do something that makes me happy."

"Never mind that they taught us the odor from a cigarette can carry as much as a hundred yards and the glow can be seen from up to four times that distance?"

"I'm covering the cherry with my hand," Poppas said. "I wasn't born yesterday, you know."

"Apparently you haven't learned much," a low, steely voice said behind them.

CHAPTER TEN

The two whirled and clawed for hardware but stopped when they saw the specter-like outlines of three men: their contacts. Lyons flipped on a red-lens flashlight and as they stepped closer, the Able Team leader introduced himself and then his comrades. The expressions of both CIA men implied they knew the names were probably bogus, but in the same minute they didn't really appear to care.

"Damn it," Poppas said through clenched teeth. "You stupid bastards nearly got your heads blown off."

"Well, if we *had* been the bad guys you'd both be dead right now," Lyons said. "We've been standing behind you nearly five minutes now. And put that damn smoke out."

Poppas didn't move to comply. "I'm sorry, but I don't recall anybody saying we answered to you."

"If you get us shot dead out here, answering to us will be the least of your problems, friend," Blancanales said. He smiled. "So I'd advise you to do as Mr. Irons asks."

Poppas felt like challenging the man, but something in Blancanales's warning smile told him these guys were the real deal. Poppas didn't feel like conducting his next tour in the Antarctic so he ground the smoke out against the sole of his boot and then stripped the ashes. He dropped the spent butt in his shirt pocket and then directed the three men to their vehicle parked a short distance from the rendezvous point.

"First time in Iran?" Abney asked as they approached the jeepney.

"Would it make any difference if it were?" Lyons said.

"No…just making small talk."

"Don't mind him," Blancanales said. "He's always grumpy after jumping out of a perfectly good airplane. We got hung up before that. We're surprised to be here at all."

"That's some pretty ballsy stuff you guys did," Poppas remarked. "We don't get too many covert agent types willing perform specialized HALO jumps."

"Ever done it?" Blancanales asked.

"Once or twice, but it's been a really long time."

"So what exactly can we expect as we get closer to Tehran?" Lyons inquired.

"We'll be coming in on a road that leads from the airport," Poppas said. "We have your identification and some local wear. You'll need to put that on. It's in a trunk at the back."

Lyons gestured for his two comrades to make it happen and then returned his attention to Poppas. "What are the chances we'll encounter police?"

"Pretty damn good, so I hope you can be convincing," Poppas said. "They're pretty used to seeing us since we make sure to get out regularly at least two or three times a week. Travel at night's restricted, but it's still less risky than venturing out and back in broad daylight."

"What happens if they make us?" Lyons asked.

"We make them dead. Fast. And then we get the

hell out of there and hope there aren't any witnesses," Poppas stated.

"Yeah, there's little doubt they'd come looking for you and in force."

"That's no lie," Abney said.

The conversation dried up as Blancanales and Schwarz returned attired in local dress. While Lyons went to put on his own duds, Blancanales made an inspection of the local papers in the beam of a penlight clenched between his teeth. After a close inspection he killed the light and grunted with satisfaction.

"Whoever did the job on these is good," he remarked.

"Yeah, and we pay him top dollar, too," Poppas said. "That guy gets more per document than we're allotted in food allowance for a month."

"Ouch," Schwarz said.

Lyons returned. It would be most difficult for him to pass any inspection given his very fair features, the blond hair and blue eyes, but Poppas felt up to the challenge. If they did get stopped, and they stood about a fifty-fifty chance, they already had an explanation that he was a former military adviser to Iraq who defected for religious reasons. While the Muslim constituency wasn't exactly popular among some of the more radical factions in the national police and military ranks, an uneasy peace held as the two tried to coexist.

Ahmadinejad had never been a hard-core member of the Islamic faith but he'd been politically savvy enough to realize that he would need the Pasdaran to hold power. The fact that neither side could seize the advantage lent some stability to the Iranian government. Still, if either faction gained the upper hand it could mean significant shifts that would upset the balance of power. That's just what Hemmati and his contacts planned to do, and it had become Able Team's job to make sure that happened.

Neither Poppas nor Abney had been given all of the details but they'd been told enough that they were to keep their heads if the situation went sour. They'd been instructed to give Able Team one hundred percent and no questions asked. While it was clear that Poppas didn't like it, the Company guys knew the importance of the mission. After all, they were supposed to be on the same side and it wouldn't do much for their professional careers if they blew this job when it might count the most.

Once they were aboard the jeepney, Abney negotiated a tight turn that brought them out of the trees and across a field that eventually led to a crushed-gravel road in significant disrepair. Once Abney made it onto the hardball, he turned on his headlights and soon they were speeding down a two-lane highway—its age and condition practically indeterminate given how they were being jostled around—heading in the direction of Tehran. For the most part, it didn't feel much different to the three men than any country road in the back parts of rural America.

"What can you tell us about this Farzad Hemmati?" Lyons asked.

"There's not much to tell," Abney said, lifting his eyes to the rearview mirror as he spoke. "We met him about a year ago."

"He was a pretty easy turn," Poppas said. "Guy was living on the streets and hungry. That's how we get most of them."

"How do you know you can trust them?" Schwarz asked.

"We don't. But that's not really the point." Poppas lit a cigarette and dropped one of the windows. It came to rest on the bottom at an odd angle, age and disuse having taken its toll on the jeepney. "We don't pay them to be trustworthy—we pay them to give us reliable intelligence. If they can't do that then we drop them as fast as we recruit them and they don't have any information about us."

"Other than they know you're CIA."

"That's not a problem," Abney explained. "Frankly, if we take them off the payroll and then they go blab to the government, it's typically a death sentence."

"For them and their families," Poppas added.

"How so?" Blancanales asked.

"Well, if they tell the Iranian government that they know of CIA operatives working in the country, the first question is usually *how* they know. What are they going to say? They got paid to be an information asset?" Poppas chuckled. "No, it's better for them to take the money and keep their mouths shut. It's a revolving door, really."

"We're coming up on a checkpoint," Abney said quietly.

"Okay, you guys, time to play the role." Poppas said. "I assume none of you speaks Persian."

"We left our English-Persian dictionary at home," Lyons answered.

"Fine. If I turn and scratch my chin before I start talking to you, break out your papers. If we're lucky, they'll think all of you speak the language and they won't bother to engage you in conversation. If anything goes wrong, don't move a muscle. You let us take care of it."

"Just wish I'd brought something to read," Schwarz quipped.

Abney eased the jeepney to a stop, its headlights reflecting off a wide aluminum barricade. A police cruiser sat alongside the road just forward of the barricade. The five occupants could make out two officers. One stood by the front door of their unit with a radio in hand while his partner, a wicked-looking machine pistol slung over his shoulder, approached the jeepney on the passenger side.

"Your permit, please," the officer said.

Poppas nodded, stuck the cigarette between his teeth and reached into the dash compartment. He noticed a tense movement in his peripheral vision—the officer reaching to the stock of the machine pistol—although he tried to act casual. He handed the official paperwork to the officer and after a cursory inspection the man handed it back.

The officer then stuck his head into the window and peered in back.

"Who are these people?"

"Picked them up from the airport," Poppas said in flawless Persian.

"Do they have papers?"

Poppas turned and scratched his chin while asking them to produce their identification. They did exactly as he instructed and Poppas went about collecting all three. The dark interior acted as a point in their favor, since the officer could not really see their features clearly. The man gave each paper a quick glance and then handed the stack to Poppas. He didn't say anything else, simply whirled and gestured to his partner. The two men moved the barricade aside enough to permit Abney to drive around it.

All five of them started breathing again once the headlights of the cruiser faded from view.

"Talk about pucker factor," Blancanales said.

"Well, like they always say, 'It's not just a job…'" Schwarz said.

"So you guys mentioned you got hung up before your jump," Abney said. "What happened?"

"We nearly had our asses shot off by a contingent of nasty terrorist types," Lyons said.

"Not really news in Iraq," Poppas said.

"Five minutes after we made contact with one of your guys there?"

"Who was it?"

"Goes by Zephyr," Blancanales said.

"I know him." Poppas grinned. "Guy's a crackpot but he's a first-rate spy, and one of the most experienced left in the Company. Any chance you were compromised because he stepped on his dick is slim to none."

"That's what we heard on that end, too," Lyons said. "The XO of an A-Team assigned to get us in-country was as surprised as we were."

"Sounds like somebody already knew you were coming," Abney said.

"The thought had occurred to us, as well," Blancanales agreed.

"I have a theory," Lyons said. "But let me ask you guys a question first. How do you suppose Hemmati knew about the IRGC operating a training camp in South America?"

Poppas shrugged his shoulders as he fished in his pocket for another cigarette. "Who the hell knows? We figured it was bogus information until we contacted Mother."

"Mother?" Schwarz interjected.

"That's the code name for our liaison to the States."

"Nice, very original," Schwarz said.

Poppas continued. "Hemmati's been one of our better assets and most of his information pans out. But I have to admit I don't trust him."

"Me neither," Abney said.

"Why not?" Blancanales asked.

"Just instinct, I guess. We found Hemmati on the streets, but there was something right off about the guy I didn't like."

"Such as?"

"Well, for one thing, he spoke almost perfect English with barely a trace of an accent."

"Someone who's been trained," Lyons observed.

"Yeah, exactly. And there's the fact that although the guy was supposedly starving he was in first-rate shape. I don't know about you guys, but most people deprived of adequate food and nutrition for months on end usually look like skeletons. You think bums on skid row don't eat well? They feast like kings in contrast to the impoverished here. Plus, Tehran's got a whole shitload of displaced persons from a bunch of countries. They've come as far as the Sudan and the RDC."

"Probably seeking handouts from the Pasdaran," Blancanales said.

Poppas nodded. "Usually."

"So you think Hemmati's full of it."

"Hell, I don't know," Poppas said in a gust of smoke. "The guy's a piece of work—that much I can tell you. Whatever you're going to do for him here, watch your backs. That's the best advice I can offer you. And we won't be far away if you need our help."

"We appreciate that," Lyons said.

"Where'd you learn to speak Persian?" Schwarz asked.

"Had to be able to read and write it fluently before I got assigned. Jester practically got shipped over here straight from the graduation block."

"I was top of my class in linguistics," Abney said, not without pride.

"You're still a wet-behind-the-ears newb," Poppas countered.

Abney puckered his lips and made a loud kissing noise.

Ten minutes passed before they arrived at their destination. The Able Team men looked at the run-down building to their left. Blackness shrouded every window and as Abney killed the engine the only sound they heard was the distant bark of a dog. The crumbling facade did nothing to boost their confidence, but neither did the climb up the creaky stairs—some of the top steps were so warped the bows were obvious with the naked eye.

The accommodations weren't any better. They included three lumpy mattresses atop a gouged wooden floor. There were three rooms: a common area, kitchen and toilet with no shower stall. The cheap toilet boil was gravity fed and chipped in myriad spots. Compared to the chill outdoors, the interior temperature was downright stifling.

"What a shithole," Lyons remarked.

"Get used to it," Poppas said. "This is home sweet home."

"You guys live in these conditions?"

"Not much better, actually," Abney said. "For this part of town, these are pretty decent quarters actually."

Schwarz managed to offer a deadpan, "Somehow I doubt it."

"The accommodations will be fine," Blancanales cut in, sensitive to the underlying reactions of his team-mates. "What concerns us more is that we still don't have any ordnance. We were told you'd be able to supply that to us."

"That's on order," Poppas said. "Should be able to get what you requested by tomorrow night."

"How soon before we meet Hemmati?"

A soft rap at the door provided an answer. Schwarz and Blancanales took up opposing positions, pistols in play. Lyons looked at Abney and Poppas—the three exchanging curt glances—before Abney glanced at his watch and sauntered to the door. He opened it a crack and then stepped back to admit a short young man with dark hair and light brown eyes.

"Gentlemen," Poppas said as Abney closed and locked the door, "meet Farzad Hemmati."

The man appraised the three Able Team warriors, nodded at each in turn and then fixed his gaze on Poppas. "I'd be happy to make talk with these men later but I'm afraid now we have a bigger problem."

Lyons's senses went into high gear. "What problem?"

"I'm very sure I was followed here."

CHAPTER ELEVEN

All five of the Americans withdrew pistols simultaneously as Lyons ordered a huddle. "Any reason to think they're friendly?" he asked Hemmati.

Hemmati shook his head emphatically.

Lyons queried the rest of the group. "Options?"

"I'd say waiting here for them is bad juju," Schwarz suggested.

"He's right," Blancanales said. "I'd recommend we get some running room."

Lyons nodded. "We're in a multistory building that's dimly lit, so we have that going for us."

"How many you think, Farzad?" Abney asked.

"Two for sure," the young man answered with a shrug. "Perhaps more. It was hard to tell."

"Well, if only two, at least we'll have them outgunned," Poppas said.

"Not likely," Lyons said. "If they bothered to tail him here and there were at least two, there's likely to be a lot more."

"But who?" Hemmati asked. "Who followed me?"

"Uh, I'd say we don't have time to discuss the details right now," Blancanales reminded his friends.

"Right. You and Gadgets take point on the stairs between the first- and second-story landing." Lyons looked at Poppas. "You'll hold here and get stragglers from the window."

"What about me?" Abney asked.

"Stick with Hemmati," Lyons said. "If necessary, it'll be your life for his. You ready to go that far?"

"I'd prefer both of us live," Abney said. "But yeah, I understand."

"Fine. This place has a communal toilet, too, right?" When Abney nodded, Lyons said, "Go there now and wait."

"In the toilet?" Poppas asked with a frown.

"If you were searching for him, or any of us for that matter," Schwarz interjected, "is a public toilet the first spot you'd look in a place like this?"

"Okay, point taken," Poppas said with a grunt.

"What about you?" Blancanales asked Lyons.

"I'm going to look for a back way out, see if I can't flank them and get some sort of count. Sync up our personal communications."

The Able Team trio adjusted their radio sets and donned the ear buds before breaking for their assigned tasks. Lyons waited until his two friends were ahead and down the steps, and then ensured Abney and Hemmati made it to their concealment in the communal toilet, a cramped, nasty and stifling place.

It'd still beat a pine box, Lyons thought.

The blond warrior turned on his heel and headed to the end of the narrow hall. Schwarz and Blancanales would have the worst of it given the cramped conditions. Then again, this would also work to their advantage since the enemy could not come up the narrow, rickety stairs in force, which would narrow the field of fire. Lyons was banking on the fact that skilled marksmen like his friends would compare it to shooting fish in the barrel.

As Lyons found a hall window that opened onto a

narrow ledge, he considered their situation. It seemed a little bit more than coincidence that trouble would find them on their very first meet with Hemmati. Lyons had not liked going into this situation to begin with, and he liked the deal even less now. As far as the members of Able Team were concerned, Hemmati was simply a means to an end, and if he didn't perform exactly as expected, then that made him nothing but a liability. Lyons would deal with that if it came to it. Right now, his attention had to be on the mission at hand: keep Hemmati alive and do what they could to disrupt the Iranian regime's plans for the terrorists in Paraguay.

Lyons gave the ledge a practiced eye a moment before climbing through the open window and gaining a foothold on the treacherous, narrow path. The width of the ledge didn't concern him as much as the age and trustworthiness of the building construction. This wouldn't have been his first choice but he'd noticed the ledge terminated at a thick iron standpipe. He figured that was the easiest way down to the street. The new arrivals wouldn't expect anyone to flank them, instead figuring their targets were being watched.

They didn't really know if they were even dealing with enemy combatants yet, but no point taking risks. Operations within Iran were sensitive—in addition to being precarious and unpredictable—and that meant Able Team had their work cut out for them. In practice, it would've been Phoenix Force tasked to handle a problem like this, but looking on it Lyons saw wisdom in Stony Man's decision to send in his team.

Lyons stepped carefully along the ledge, each placement of his foot weight tested before proceeding to the next. He kept his back to the wall, and despite his caution managed to reach the standpipe shy of thirty seconds. Lyons reached for the standpipe, wrapped his hands around it and moved it back and forth. To his surprise, the thing held well and didn't seem to shift or come loose from its clamps. Lyons exercised diligence, nevertheless, as he wrapped his soft-soled shoes around the standpipe and left the comparative safety of the ledge.

Confident it would hold, Lyons went down the standpipe with arachnid dexterity and reached the ground without incident. He liberated his pistol from the concealed holster, hugged the building and peered around the corner toward the front entrance. As he guessed, four men were just making their entrance and their behavior implied they were doing it covertly. Lyons ducked behind the wall, closed his eyes a moment and formulated a plan.

His teammates would be waiting for the hitters between the first and second floor, hopeful they could bunch them in the stairwell—Lyons knew this because it was a standard tactical procedure they'd drilled on time and again. The narrow confines of a stairwell were a perfect way to overwhelm the enemy whenever taking the high ground, and it had the added effect of countersurprise. His teammates would do their jobs, as usual. And if everything went as planned, it would be a cakewalk to glean Hemmati as an intelligence asset and get him and themselves out of the country unscathed.

Then again, almost nothing went as planned in Able Team's line of business.

HERMANN SCHWARZ AND Rosario Blancanales heard the hit team before they saw it.

For a group determined to make their play stealthy, these men sure as hell were making a lot of racket. Then again, they were counting on surprise being in their favor and that's where the Able Team duo knew their opponents had gone wrong—never assume the enemy doesn't know about a surprise operation. If nothing else, they might have simply seen you coming.

Schwarz thought of Abney and Hemmati concealed in the toilet area just one floor above his head. He tightened his grip on the pistol as he saw the shadows of three men shrunk on the wall, a sure sign they were advancing as they got nearer to where the stairs turned. Schwarz had taken a position crouched behind the inside stairwell wall where it terminated at the landing. He looked at Blancanales, who stood two steps above his friend's position, the muzzle of his own pistol pointed almost straight down.

The men locked glances and Blancanales smiled as reassuringly as possible. Each man knew the other had probably asked the same thing: had Lyons found a way to flank the enemy position? If not, they would have to hit hard and fast, and be accurate as hell with their pistols—no mean feat in the gloom of the dim stairwell lighting.

Schwarz took aim at the first human shape that rounded the corner of the stairs but he held off, not wishing to be hasty. Haste could get a soldier killed fast. For the ambush to be effective they needed more players in the game; the enemy had to bunch up and be proximal enough to get in each other's way. Besides, they had unscrewed the lightbulb on this landing, so crouched in the darkness Schwarz knew his targets wouldn't immediately see him as their eyes would not have yet adjusted.

It turned out just as they'd hoped it would, two of them in full view with a third coming up fast. Schwarz steadied his aim and squeezed the trigger. The report from the 9 mm cartridge of his Beretta 92-DS whip-cracked in the confines of the stairwell as the bullet punched through the first man's skull and scrambled his brains. The corpse teetered a split second before gravity took hold, and the gunshot followed by a falling body took the man's two comrades by surprise.

The second man found himself entangled by his dead counterpart, but the third managed to avoid the logjam and brought a pistol into view. Blancanales cut his counteroffensive short with two .45-caliber slugs from a Glock 30. The bullets entered the top of the man's skull and smashed it like a nutcracker on a peanut, the 900 fps muzzle energy from the Cor Bon 230 jacketed hollowpoints blowing his brains out through both ears and the soft palate of the mouth.

The remaining gunner finally managed to get clear of his deceased associate but not in time to accomplish much. He aimed his pistol at Schwarz and snapped off one round that went high and to the right of the Able Team warrior before his two opponents triggered simultaneous replies that ended his life efficiently and quickly. Schwarz's round entered through the soft point below his throat, and Blancanales directed a shot that entered the man's right temple and exited the left, rear portion of his jaw. His body crumpled to join that of his comrades on the midfloor landing.

WHEN THE DOOR TO THE toilet opened, Ron Abney half expected it to be Poppas or one of the special ops agents. He'd never expected it to be a hunkered old woman in a shawl come to use the can in the middle of a firefight. It was this hesitation that cost the young CIA agent his life, because even as he lowered his pistol, the hall light caught the doddering old woman's profile and revealed she was no doddering old woman at all!

The man rose to full stature, raised his pistol and shot Abney point blank between the eyes, painting the back wall in a gory mess.

Hemmati didn't waste any time bursting from the shadowy alcove of the cramped toilet space to his left and brought the point of his elbow on the cluster of nerves where the forearm met the elbow. The gunman, apparently surprised by Hemmati's presence, yelped and the gun sprang from his fingers. Hemmati came on while he still had his opponent off balance and delivered a palm strike that snapped the man's temple against the doorjamb. Hemmati followed that with a knee to the side of the thigh. The vicious blows were the result of years of training by his master, and given the element of surprise the gunner was ill-prepared. His unconscious form slumped to the dirty floor.

Hemmati reached down and retrieved the man's pistol, then burst from the toilet and went in search of an escape route.

AT THE MOMENT HE HEARD the first shots, Lyons came around the corner with a Beretta 8357 tracking ahead of him. While he would've preferred to have his Colt Anaconda—not being a fan of semiautomatic pistols in a CQB scenario—they hadn't been able to bring their preferred weapons on the civilian flight due to the short notice. This had forced Blancanales and Lyons to settle. Since his only choice in .44 Magnum had been the Desert Eagle, much too large to conceal comfortably, Lyons had opted for a reliable Beretta and the SIG .357 cartridge.

The prudence of his choice became evident as Lyons closed on the crumbling stairs of the building stoop only to find one of the men he'd spotted earlier waiting in the shadows, a cigarette dangling from one corner of his mouth. The guy spotted Lyons and clawed for hardware but his movements almost seemed like slow motion to the Able Team leader—he easily had the guy dead to rights. Lyons triggered three successive rounds and all of them connected. The impact of each round drove the man back a little farther, ash embers glowing as if with anger when the cigarette fell from deadened lips and bounced down the front of the man's body. The third round struck with enough force to slam the gunner's back against the front door. With no other place to go, his body slid to the ground to expose the flesh and blood that had peppered the door from the exit wounds.

A shout raised the hairs on Lyons's neck in time to make him drop prone to the sidewalk. The maneuver saved his life when the air came alive with autofire. Lyons rolled onto his back, pistol up and tracking toward the source of the gunfire across the street. His ice-blue eyes flicked toward the third-floor window from where the shout had come, and he saw Poppas's unmistakable silhouette there with muzzle-flashes present even before Lyons heard the echo of the shots bouncing between the buildings.

Lyons returned his attention to a point across the street where he spotted a pair of men with machine pistols advancing on his position. One made it only halfway before Poppas got his range and brought the man down with a well-placed shot to the chest. Lyons flashed a high sign in way of thanks to Poppas, who returned it with one of his own. Lyons steadied his elbow against the pavement and triggered one round after another, once more driving back a would-be assassin.

Their enemies on the street now neutralized, Lyons got to his feet and rushed to help Schwarz and Blancanales.

So MUCH FOR CONTAINMENT, Poppas thought.

After neutralizing their attackers, and discovering Abney's body, Poppas and the Able Team warriors beat feet from the apartment building.

"What's going to happen to Abney's body?"

Poppas shook his head, puffing at his cigarette like a madman as he drove from the scene. "Dunno. The Company will do what it can to get him back. Probably some sort of trade."

"Didn't think that kind of stuff still went on since the end of the Cold War," Schwarz remarked.

"Yeah, it goes on."

"I think it's safe to say we can't go back to that building," Lyons said.

"It will now be the target of attention by the local cops in the future," Poppas replied. "Which basically means it's now worthless as an alternate location for special ops. I guess you'll have to come back to me and Jester's apartment."

"Does Hemmati know about that location?" Blancanales asked.

"Yeah."

"Then we cannot go there," Blancanales replied.

Poppas didn't look surprised but the tone in his voice betrayed the fact Blancanales's statement disturbed him some. "You think Hemmati blew us purposely?"

"I think we don't really know anything about Hemmati," Blancanales said with as much rationality as he could muster. "He knew people were following him, and he knew he was planning to rendezvous with us, and yet he still came to that location. Who's to say he wouldn't make the same mistake?"

"I say!" Poppas wrapped his knuckles on the steering wheel. "Listen, Rose, my ass is hanging out on the line for this, not yours. Not to mention that Jester's dead 'cause I let you guys call the ball."

"That's enough," Lyons cut in. "Abney's dead because Iranian fanatics killed him. That's nobody's fault but the terrorists. Understand?"

Before Poppas could protest, Lyons continued. "Not to mention we now have an intelligence asset in the wind, an asset who knows we're in the country. That kind of information is damaging and compromises our security."

"To make no mention of the fact Hemmati *was* our mission objective," Schwarz added.

"Any thoughts where he might go?" Blancanales asked Poppas.

"I don't really give a shit where he went," Poppas said. "And I don't give a shit whether he's alive or dead and I sure as hell don't give a shit about your mission."

"You might want to rethink that," Lyons said in a tone so calm it surprised his two comrades. "Hemmati has information critical to our operations. As we speak, there's a bunch of good men out there putting it all on the line. Those are my friends and I very much care what happens to them. And if a lack of cooperation gets them killed, I'm going to hold you personally responsible."

"Besides, you don't want Jester's sacrifice to have been in vain," Blancanales added.

The car fell silent and the Able Team silently agreed

to let Poppas chew on that awhile. Pushing the guy wouldn't get his cooperation—he'd obviously been closer to his partner than he originally let on. Deep beneath the gruff exterior, the guy clearly had a sensitive core that years of hardship had obscured with layers of cynicism and indifference. It was something all of the men understood—each having experienced it in his own right—yet they always came back to getting a grip on those things and finding constructive outlets.

Killing bad guys was one of those ways Lyons dealt with the emotional turmoil of all the violence and death surrounding his life and the lives of his fellow warriors. Guys like Poppas, however, didn't always get such a release of pent-up energy. They lived life on the edge of a knife, knowing too well if they got caught the very government who employed them would deny all firsthand knowledge of them.

"All right," Poppas finally mumbled. "I'll help you bastards. But when we find Hemmati can you do me a favor?"

Lyons nodded. "Sure."

"Get the hell out of here and don't ever come back."

Sure is nice to be wanted, Lyons thought. But he kept his mouth shut.

CHAPTER TWELVE

"First thing we need to do is figure out where the rat might've run off to," Poppas told Able Team.

They were gathered around a small table in the back of a dark, run-down tavern—at least it seemed passable as such—in just one of the many crummy parts of Tehran. The stale odor of tobacco mixed with hashish, and a form of illicit liquor none of them would have even tried sampling on their worst day, threatened to overpower the four men. Lyons tried to remain resolute even as he watched the other three express their desire to gag every couple of minutes.

"Any ideas where he might hide?" Lyons asked.

"It's a good question," Blancanales said. "The guy's sure to be running scared. He'll go where things are most familiar."

Schwarz looked around them and said, "We might want to think about taking our own advice. It's not like we really blend into this place or anything."

"Actually, there are a lot of foreigners in here," Poppas replied. "Mostly reporters and other types who want to avoid attracting attention—a few correspondents from Europe, one or two Americans from CNN or the AP. The rest are from other Middle East and North African countries."

"We're still bound to draw some unwanted attention," Blancanales pointed out.

"Agreed," Lyons said. "The longer we stay here, the more likely we are getting caught."

"Well, if you want to find Hemmati, then this is the right place," Poppas said. "You can leave any time you want, gents, and it won't be any sweat off my balls."

"That's too much information," Schwarz said.

"Wait," Lyons said as he inclined his head toward the door.

It proved difficult for the others to make out the features of the arrival at first glance, but once the small man came closer they could see it was Hemmati. Lyons looked at Poppas in surprise but didn't say anything. What the hell? The veteran spook had been right, after all. Lyons had always held only a cautious measure of respect for a lot of CIA field agents in the past, but this time around he'd been proved wrong not once or even twice, but three times. First there had been Zephyr's heroics—nothing the men of Able Team would have expected from a "crazy old coot" anyway—then Jester giving up his life to protect an intelligence asset. Now Poppas had demonstrated great insight predicting Hemmati's appearance.

Lyons rose and moved quickly into a flanking position while Poppas took his cue and tried for a direct intercept. Hemmati spotted Poppas first, naturally, and whirled to escape. He came face to face with Lyons, who'd produced a pistol and wedged it into Hemmati's gut with enough force to imply his threat. At this point, Lyons knew Hemmati was critical to their mission but he also didn't trust the guy and sure as hell wasn't about to risk his life and those of his teammates without a really good reason.

Lyons wrapped a thick, muscular forearm around Hemmati's neck as if hugging the guy. He whispered,

"Make nice, pal, or I won't hesitate to put a bullet in your gut."

A crew of rowdy and obviously inebriated Europeans suddenly burst into raucous laughter, attracting the attention of most of the other patrons who were keeping it to a steady din. Lyons was thankful for the distraction and managed to get them back to their table without anyone paying more than scant notice. He sat Hemmati in Poppas's seat with a shove and then took his own. The CIA man swung another chair from the table around and took up proximity to Hemmati on the opposite side, effectively wedging the young man between them.

"I have only one question for you," Lyons began. "Why did you run?"

Hemmati let go with an almost scornful laugh. "What kind of question is this? What would you have done?"

"I wouldn't have fucking run, that's for sure," Poppas said as he lit a cigarette and exhaled a plume of smoke. With his reddened complexion enhanced by the candle lighting, he looked like a dragon. "You're a fucking piece of shit coward, Farzad. I ought to kill you."

Hemmati tried to appear shaken but he couldn't quite pull it off. Carl Lyons had spent too long reading faces—he knew a bluff when he saw it. Hemmati knew how to be coy and Lyons's experience had taught him how to cut through such a bluff. Poppas didn't scare Hemmati a bit; the guy had been playing the two CIA men from the beginning. Lyons decided the time had come to change the rules of the game and play them the way Able Team played them best.

"The way I see it, pal, you have two choices," Lyons said. "You either come clean with us now or we turn you over to our friend here and split. How would you like to do it?"

Hemmati looked at Blancanales and Schwarz, gauging if he could win their support, but only got a pair of unreadable faces. The two knew exactly what Lyons was doing and neither could say he minded. Jester had been a pretty good guy, one of their own if nothing else, and they weren't for a moment going to divide their loyalties between an American espionage agent and a weaseling Iranian native—that was no contest, intelligence asset or not.

"I do not understand why you treat me like this," Hemmati finally told Lyons.

"Cut the shit," Lyons said. "The only reason you're still alive is because this is too public a place for more direct interrogation."

"Beside the fact," Schwarz added for good measure, "we don't have that kind of time."

Lyons continued. "I'm pretty sure you're not everything you'd like us to think you are. I believe you've been jerking the CIA's chain for quite a while now. Whether for money or some other reason doesn't make any difference to me. But I'm not buying this hard-luck story about you being off the streets. Your hands are well tended with no brittle nails."

Blancanales tugged at the sleeve of Hemmati's loose-fitting, dirty cotton tunic. "And look at your clothes. They're filthy but underneath your skin is clean and unblemished. No pockmarks and no yellowing or indications of fungi, all clear signs of malnutrition and poor sanitary conditions under normal circumstances. You speak well and clear, and it's obvious you've been educated beyond what could be expected of the average Iranian citizen."

Hemmati shook his head. "I sw-swear, I do not know what you are saying. I'm not a traitor!"

Poppas looked around before saying, "Shut your hole, for crissake. You want to get us all killed?"

"I'm wondering if he is," Lyons said as he pinned Hemmati with an accusatory glare. "In fact, I'm beginning to think he brought those hitters to our location purposely. Maybe he even arranged for them to find him, which is what got one of our men killed. They sure found you easily enough."

"Yeah, I'm having a lot of trouble with that myself," Schwarz said. "Their discovery sure seemed too easy to be coincidence."

Hemmati raised his hands now, the look in his eyes betraying his fear. "Okay, I will tell you the truth."

Blancanales's grin lacked warmth. "That would probably be a very good idea, friend."

Hemmati swallowed hard and looked around. "This is not a story that can be overheard. We should leave this place now, before I am recognized talking with you."

Around the fifth cigarette in a row clenched between his teeth, Poppas said, "Why the hell should anybody care if you're talking to us?"

"Please," Hemmati said, his eyes imploring Lyons as he ignored Poppas's question. "What I must tell you... this is not a private place."

"Fine," Lyons said, moving to rise. "But if this is another sucker play, Hemmati, or you try baiting us for a trap, I swear the only thing it'll buy you is a bullet."

The five men left the table and strolled through the dim club and emerged on a darker street. Somewhere in the distance they heard a siren, its wail fading to let the barks and howls of numerous dogs take over. All

of the Americans were on high alert after their first encounter with the nameless enemy back at the not-so-
safehouse—none of them trusted Hemmati.

When they were at a decent distance and ascertained
nobody observing or following them, they walked the
few blocks to where Poppas had parked an old Volks-
wagen microbus as beat-up and ancient as the jeepney.
Poppas had opted to swap the jeepney in favor of using
the van, trading one for the other at a garage camou-
flaged to look like an abandoned business in one of
Tehran's seediest districts. Blancanales had remarked
how easy it seemed for Poppas to move around the
city but recanted the observation when the CIA agent
pointed out it had taken nearly five years for the Company to get any sort of a secure foothold.

"If nothing else, the Iranians are a suspicious lot,"
he'd said. "Frankly, it's a miracle we haven't already
had our cover exposed. There are a lot of shady goings-
on in this part of the city. It isn't really that the locals
don't know it's going on, it's just they have neither the
time nor resources to take care of it. If we get blown,
we pack it in and move somewhere else and start over
again. All of the intelligence agencies do it, from the
SIS to the GRU."

"Well, then," Schwarz interjected with a shrug, "we
wouldn't want to stray from what's fashionable and
stylish."

Once in the VW they proceeded north to the garage, the one remaining place Poppas deemed safe.
They hadn't gone back to his apartment, concerned
that somebody might follow them. The four Americans had agreed the apartment would be a point of
last resort. If things went wrong, and it appeared as if
the situation was already coming apart at the seams,

the apartment would be the rendezvous point and the place they would make their stand or simply convene before beating a hasty exit from Tehran.

None of the Able Team members had any patience left for dealing with Hemmati, and Poppas clearly had even less. Whatever else they might have thought about their reasons for being in Tehran, Carl Lyons had about all he was going to take from Hemmati and he didn't make any bones showing that.

Once they were out of the VW and in the comparable safety of the garage, Lyons hauled Hemmati by the collar of his shirt and tossed him not so gently into the closest wall. He placed a left muscular forearm against Hemmati's chest and his pistol came up in his right hand, the muzzle coming to rest under Hemmati's nose. Hemmati let out an involuntary snort combined with what sounded like a squeal of terror.

"I've played just about all the games I'm willing to play with you, punk!" Lyons's face took on a dangerous hue. "Now you're going to cut all the bullshit and give me the straight story. And if I even sense you're lying to me, I'm going to kill you where you stand. Got it?"

"Easy, Ironman," Blancanales said, stepping forward to put one hand on his friend's shoulder.

"Easy my ass," Lyons said. He shook the hand off and stared at Hemmati as he added, "This punk's been scamming and lying to us so much. I'm not even sure he knows what to believe anymore. Just one lie after another. Isn't that right?"

"Okay, okay! I will tell you!" Hemmati protested.

"Then tell us."

"I am not raised on the streets, as you say. I was raised by the Pasdaran...a student of Islam. Along with my many brothers, we were trained by our mullah to resist this government."

Lyons looked askance at Poppas.

The CIA guy shrugged. "Kind of like an imam or something similar. Those who are abandoned by their families at a young age usually take to the streets. Only a very select few are considered worthy to be taken under the wing of a mullah."

Lyons turned to Hemmati. "Go on."

"There are members of our kind spread throughout the government, many of them high-ranking officials. We are getting ready to change the fortunes of Iran for our cause and our people."

"So you're just another Islamo-Nazi terrorist scumbag," Lyons said.

"No, no! We are for a free Iran…a peaceful Iran. You see, President Ahmadinejad claims he is Islam but he is not. He uses the soldiers of the country to train terrorists outside of the country while he pretends to do no such thing. He only wants to build his nuclear bombs and to kill all those who are not true to the faith."

"Like Israel," Blancanales said.

Hemmati looked at the Able Team warrior and nodded fiercely. "And others, of course, but they are lies. He does not care for those who are true to the pure faith, only that the other nations fear Iran's abilities."

"So this program, this training that's going on Paraguay…" Lyons said. "What is this really about?"

"I do not know," Hemmati said.

Lyons pressed the barrel with more force against the soft point of Hemmati's nose.

"I swear! I only knew that they had sent men from the royal guards to train a unit of the Hezbollah. There was something about technology there, as well. They were training in trade for some kind of technology I do not understand."

"Technology for what?" Poppas said, clenching a cigarette to light so hard between his teeth he nearly bit off the filter.

"Something that has to do with the nuclear bombs. The problem is not making his bombs, it is the access to the kinds of raw materials he needs, as well as the right technology. That's all I know."

"So you're claiming that the people you work for," Schwarz interjected, "these…Pasdaran, you're saying they plan to overthrow the government."

"Yes."

"For what reason?" Poppas said.

"Yeah, that sounds awfully far-fetched," Lyons added. "What did I tell you about lying to us?"

"I have already said, they want to restore the peace of Muslim law to our country. Many of our people suffer. Look around." He waved his hand with what seemed like dramatic flair but Lyons thought he heard conviction in his voice. "There are not enough schools and food for our children. There are not enough jobs. There is no prosperity except among the elite in our government, and we gain nothing for our labors. We would prefer to live in peace than be molested by those who proclaim to be Islam but are not. It is a foul smell to us, these lies spread by those in power. We want change…real change. And we shall have it, with or without your help!"

"So your saying this other stuff was just a pretense to get us inside of your country," Lyons said. When Hemmati replied with a curt nod, Lyons asked, "For what reason?"

"We cannot do this alone," Hemmati said. "We must

have help. It has been discovered that I am working with my people to remove those who would stand in the way."

"Who?" Poppas asked. "And stand in the way of what?" The CIA agent had obviously heard enough and he reached into his jacket and withdrew his pistol. He pointed it in the direction of Hemmati's head and told Lyons, "Step away, friend. I don't want to get any brains or blood on you. That would be a waste of a good outfit."

"Go easy, Pops," Blancanales said, raising a hand. "You might miss."

"I won't miss."

"You might," Blancanales countered. "In which case you've put my friend in danger here and I can't allow that. Just let us get to the bottom of this. This guy is our problem now and we'll deal with it."

"Listen to him, Pops," Schwarz said.

Lyons hadn't taken his eyes off Hemmati and he didn't plan to. He didn't trust the Iranian—not that he'd had any reason to trust him to begin with—especially in light of this new revelation. It didn't make sense and yet Lyons considered the possibility that what he said was too preposterous to be made up.

Poppas finally lowered his pistol. "All right, we'll do this your way."

Lyons gave Hemmati one last look before instructing him to lie facedown on the floor with his hands behind his head, the crown of his cap touching the wall of the garage. Once he was comfortable that Hemmati couldn't escape quickly in that position, he gestured for Poppas and his friends to conference with him out of earshot.

"So what do you think?" Lyons asked.

"i'm not even sure I understand this yet," Schwarz said. "Is he really saying he made up a cockamamie story about having information related to the events going down in Paraguay to get us here so we could help him overthrow his own government?"

"It would appear that's exactly what he's saying," Blancanales said.

"Well, that's just crazy."

"Maybe so," Lyons said, "but it would explain a whole hell of a lot. This mission's been sideways from the start. And while I'm not much on trusting this clown, I do see how the only way they could get outside assistance would be to manipulate the situation in this fashion."

"Did he ever say anything to you about this before now, Pops?"

Poppas took the last, deep drag from the smoke, then dropped it on the old concrete pad and ground it underfoot. "Nope. And frankly I don't believe the little prick. You should just let me kill him and we can be done with it."

"Much as I'd like to," Lyons said, "we owe it to our highers back in Wonderland to at least check out his story."

"You believe him, Ironman?" Schwarz asked with disbelief.

"No," Lyons said. "But that doesn't mean we don't have a responsibility to verify his story. If there's some way we can help him overthrow Ahmadinejad and his cronies, then I'd be willing to do it."

"That would be going well outside the parameters of the mission," Blancanales said.

"Not to mention this is probably all horseshit," Poppas added.

Ignoring Poppas's verve, Lyons told Blancanales, "It would be going out of the parameters of the mission to just toe whatever line they'd drawn for us when a potential opportunity awaits."

"There's something I don't think you've considered here, Ironman," Schwarz said.

"What?"

"Even if Hemmati's telling the unmitigated truth, something we've already agreed isn't probable, we don't have the manpower or resources to launch any sort of real operation. I mean, you heard what Pops said earlier. It takes them years to get inserted into this country, and then they're looking over their shoulder at every turn."

"What's your point?"

"We don't know this city at all, not to mention we're pretty short in the weapons and ammunition department. We also have no idea where to start looking."

"Even if we knew where to start looking, we still don't have any idea what we're looking for," Blancanales pointed out in support of Schwarz. "It's not like the bad guys have signs painted on them. This group over here? No, they're the *good* Muslim fanatics—these are the bad Muslims you should be shooting at."

Lyons weighed the opinions of the two men. He knew ultimately they would follow his orders without hesitation or question, but only after he heard them out. In a firefight it was an entirely different situation—they operated as a single fluid unit, the tip of the spear, as it were. But when the bullets weren't flying it was only the idiot who didn't listen to those with wisdom and experiences beyond their years.

Lyons finally nodded. "Okay, here's what we do. Let's pump Hemmati for more information and go take a look-see for ourselves. Then we can make a more in-formed decision, maybe try to get in contact with the Farm then and tell them what we know. If they want us to go with it then we do, otherwise we fall back to our original mission objectives and split with the prize. Let the CIA sort it out."

"You down with that, Pops?" Blancanales asked.

Poppas scratch the back of his neck, furrowed his brow and then shook his head. "No...sorry, friends, but I'd be worthless as tits on a bull to you guys at this point. I think he's full of shit and I don't want no part of any more good Americans getting killed. You need supplies or intelligence, even this vehicle, I'm your man. But beyond that I can't get involved. I've already seen one good man fall today. It just suddenly got a bit more important for me to make my pension. Thanks but no thanks."

"We may not agree with your decision," Lyons said, "but we can sure as hell respect it."

Poppas nodded acknowledgment and shook the Able Team warrior's hand when offered to him.

"Well, now that that's settled, what's the game plan?" Schwarz said.

"I'm not sure I've thought quite that far ahead yet," Lyons replied.

Blancanales folded his arms and sighed. "Marvel-ous."

CHAPTER THIRTEEN

Asunción, Paraguay

Whether by luck or divine intervention, the men of Phoenix Force managed to avoid an encounter with law enforcement, get back to their vehicle and get the hell away from what remained of Lazario Giménez's empire.

They returned to their hotel to find an excited Brad Russell just in the process of signing off a conference with Kurtzman.

"What's the word?" David McCarter asked.

"It took us a while but we think we now know what this is all about," Russell said. "You know, that Bear is a genius. One hell of a smart dude you got working for you."

"Yeah, he's a bloody charmer," McCarter said. "Uh, you were saying?"

"Huh? Oh, yeah…about this whole new angle we have. Well, it's no secret that Lazario Giménez trafficked in high-tech goods."

"Yeah, we got that part already."

"But what I bet you didn't know is that this isn't the first time he's been known to deal with terrorists or the Iranians."

"Is that right?" McCarter dropped onto an over-stuffed chair and lit a cigarette.

"Yeah. I don't suppose you fellas are familiar with the yellow-cake uranium mines in Namibia."

All of them froze in their tracks, their full attention on Russell now. Their combined reaction wasn't what he'd expected, but when he saw the warriors all looking at him with equal intensity he felt like shrinking down to the size of a penny. He'd apparently struck an unwanted nerve with these men, and whatever they'd been through it was clear from the looks on their faces that they knew exactly what he referred to.

"Um, okay, apparently not a good subject." He looked nervously at the piece of paper he'd been holding and didn't meet their gaze as he continued. "The Iranians had a fifteen percent interest in the mining operations there but they lost it due to changes in Namibian foreign policy, due in large part to U.S. political pressure on officials there.

"Naturally, this forced the Iranians to look to other external support pipelines. Their focus was on conventional technologies but they weren't unwilling to establish other more proven channels if it could benefit them."

"Well, they obviously found one in Lazario Giménez," Encizo remarked.

"Obviously," Russell continued with a nod. "Giménez wasn't just a pimp for high-tech goods—he actually brokered deals between a number of different suppliers and terrorist organizations. I managed to hack into his accounts. He was making cash hand over fist, this guy, rolling in loot and most of it ill-gotten."

"So what exactly are you saying was this cat's angle?" James asked.

"Giménez's main business was to reach out to high-tech manufacturers and brokers that the terrorists couldn't openly deal with. He was popular because of both his connections and the fact he would often front the funds the terrorists needed to purchase the goods. If any of the terrorists reneged on the deal, it didn't mean anything to Giménez because he could just turn around and sell it someone else."

"Yeah, I'm sure there was no shortage of terrorist buyers for a guy like that," Manning observed.

"It means more than that for you boys, though," Russell said. "The fact is Giménez tried to cover his trail and accounts, but he didn't put in the focus he needed to. It wasn't difficult for me to track these other buyers and that's good news for your team."

"How so?" McCarter asked, sitting forward with a look of intense interest.

"Simple. This didn't end with Giménez's death, it gave us an inroad. The trail you'll have to navigate is murky but I believe if we go down the account pipelines it will eventually lead us to where the Hezbollah's operating, and consequently you'll find the people responsible for snatching the Peace Corps volunteers."

"In other words, we're going to follow the money," James said.

"Right."

"So where do we start?" Hawkins said.

"Ah, that's the best part," Russell replied. "There's a place on the edge of the city, a shipping and warehousing district where a lot of imports end up. They operate so cheaply there due to their use of river power. Giménez was one careful dude on the surface, but as I said before, this caution was also a weakness. Most everything he had imported came through standard shipping lines and then landed at only two very select locations. The first was a waterfront location along the Paraguay

River. The second, and this is the more telling one, is a bonded firm out of Ciudad del Este."

"City of the East," Encizo translated helpfully.

"Hey, I don't get it," McCarter said. "You claim that's more telling. Why?"

"Ciudad del Este has a very large Asian population," Encizo explained. "A lot of the religious dominance was Sunni Muslim but later the Shia Muslims took control."

"The exact same background as this Pasdaran the Farm sent Ironman and friends to investigate," Hawkins pointed out.

Encizo nodded. "*Bueno.* And not only is there a strong Muslim sect present in the city, there are a boat-load of Iranians."

"The city's got bucks, too," Russell said. "Their primary economy comes from the company headquartered there that operates the Itaipu Dam. They sell much of their power grid to the Brazilians. It's also a known smuggling center, with an estimated black market value many times that of Paraguay's GDP. One thing very cheap there is electronics."

"Which makes it a bloody good place for a guy like Giménez to have operated," McCarter concluded. He said to Russell, "That's some damn good detective work, mate. So what's our angle?"

"I've sent all of this to Kurtzman," Russell said. "I wasn't about to go step on any toes in Wonderland. I know you guys are operating from pretty much a page that isn't in the playbook, official or unofficial, so I didn't feel it was my place to hand out the assignments."

"Guess we'll have to wait to hear from the Farm," James said.

The secured satellite uplink terminal in the center of the makeshift operations center buzzed for attention and McCarter said, "Looks like the wait's over."

Russell stabbed a button and the beautiful face of Barbara Price filled the screen. She tendered a brief smile before saying, "We received your report about Lazario Giménez. Nice job avoiding law enforcement—encountering Paraguayan officials right now wouldn't be good for the operations."

"We aim to please," Hawkins interjected with a cheesy grin.

Price offered another smile and then got to business. "We've analyzed the information Mr. Russell sent. I must say I'm impressed."

Russell nodded.

"And we're in complete agreement with his assessment," Price continued. "There are definitely additional operations Giménez had going that will probably lead you to the IRGC and Hezbollah there. The Ciudad del Este angle is particularly intriguing, and as we speak Bear's getting additional intelligence on the exact location of the grounds."

"Any early ideas what we may come up against?" Manning asked.

"Nothing I'd want to guess at."

"Give her a try, luv," McCarter prompted.

Price frowned. "We're certain you'll run up against a standard security force, at minimum. You know about the smuggling and black market operations there?"

Several of the men nodded.

"There's little doubt that the underworld operates with impunity in some parts of the city," Price said. "These people are organized, disciplined and well-armed. They're in it only for the profits and they'll do whatever it takes to protect those profits. They won't hesitate to shoot anyone dead who gets in their way. We also have it on good authority that because of the world commerce crisis, the political infrastructure of Paraguay has suffered and in some ways is outright corrupt."

"Nobody's totally innocent, my dear," Hawkins said.

"Maybe so, but we don't need an international incident," Price said. "Do what you have to but try not to make too much noise."

"We'll walk on eggshells until it's time to shake the trees," McCarter said. "That's all I can promise you."

"I know," Price said with a grin. "And I even knew you'd say that. I just got an email from Bear. He's got the details of your strike point and he's sending it along now. Should be there by the time you're geared up."

"We going to be able to use Eagle for this one?" McCarter asked.

Price nodded. "We've arranged to get you to Ciudad del Este via a chopper on loan from a local rescue organization. Please bring it back in one piece—we don't want to have to buy those folks a new one. It took some strings to get it, as it is. Eagle will meet you at Silvio Pettirossi International."

"What about a resupply?" McCarter said. "We burned up quite a bit at our last soiree."

"We've had you resupplied and the equipment will be delivered directly to the chopper. Eagle's there now overseeing the loading."

McCarter nodded. "Well, we'd best get to it."

"Godspeed, men," Price said.

THE CHOPPER TURNED OUT to be a refitted ASH-3D, a former antisubmarine warfare helicopter sold to a civilian rescue and relief organization by the Brazilian navy. Based on the Sikorsky SH-3 Sea King, the craft had been converted for civilian use because it only required two pilots to operate versus the four required for a military application. This allowed the spare room required to fit all five of the Phoenix Force warriors aboard, along with their needed equipment.

Before long they were airborne and cruising along the flight plan filed with air traffic control, citing their purpose as a medical emergency. Had anyone bothered to make a closer inspection, they would've known it was an entirely different story. Among three weapons bags were enough SMGs, assault rifles and ammunition to start a private war. To keep things simple and streamline the resupply, Stony Man had sent six M-16 A-4s—two equipped with M-203 grenade launchers—along with a dozen each of 40 mm and M-69 HE grenades. For the close-in operations, they had two MP-5s and enough 5.56 x 45 mm NATO rounds and 9 mm Parabellums to go around. A PSG-1 sniper rifle and some C-4 plastique rounded out the cache.

Manning reached for the PSG-1 and studied it admiringly. As the team's most experienced and expert sniper, Manning was more than familiar with the rifle. The brainchild of Heckler & Koch, the PSG-1 had been touted as one of the most accurate semi-automatics in the world. Manning wouldn't dispute the claim. It chambered the 7.62 x 51 mm NATO round, military equivalent of the .308. This one sported the 5-round detachable box magazine and a Hendsoldt 6x42 scope effective to 600 meters.

"Sexy!" Hawkins said over the whap of the rotors.

Manning nodded with a knowing grin.

The remaining team members scooped up the M-16

A-4s, save Enciso, who preferred the MP-5. They didn't know what they would encounter when arriving in Ciudad del Este but they planned to be ready for anything. The 190-mile trip dragged on with agonizing slowness, most likely due to their anticipation of the unknown. The battle-hardened veterans of Phoenix Force had been here many times before, but it always seemed worse when there was an immediate and indeterminate threat to civilians, particularly when they were Americans.

On one thing the Phoenix Force warriors agreed—the terrorists would pay dearly if they killed those Peace Corps volunteers.

At last, Grimaldi set them down at the Guarani International and to complete the ruse they had an unattended ambulance waiting for them at the medical hangar. An airport security unit sat nearby to oversee the operation but Phoenix Force made a good show of transferring their equipment and Hawkins beneath a blanket on a stretcher, accompanied by James and Manning in back, while Encizo and McCarter climbed into the cab. Before long they were leaving the airport with lights and sirens going. The security unit didn't even bother to provide an escort to the airport boundary; they obviously had better things to do.

"That was close," Hawkins said. "I thought we'd been blown."

"We figured something like that might happen," Encizo said. "The Farm had it planned to the letter."

"Where to now, boss?" James asked McCarter as he rechecked the action on his M-16 A-4.

McCarter scratched his chin, not looking up from the small digital phone in his hand as he studied the intel the Farm had sent. "Our ride will take about twenty minutes, according to the information Bear sent along. Once we get there we'll have to give the place a look-see and determine our best offensive. We'll be doing this one by ear, gents, so all of you stay loose. Any one or all of us may have to improvise."

"Hot dog!" Hawkins said in his Texas rodeo voice. He slapped his knee and said, "I love me a good improv."

James cast a sideways glance at his teammate. "You really need to lay off the caffeine, brother."

In contrast to what seemed like a long trip in the chopper, the drive to the warehouse district blew by in no time. Encizo killed the lights and sirens approximately three miles from the area to minimize unwanted attention. To their right they saw the massive skyline of Ciudad del Este's commercial center in the twilight, the lights of the Friendship Bridge twinkling in the foreground. They were actually a considerable distance from the downtown now, and McCarter saw why the smugglers who permeated this area managed to operate with so little interference.

It was said that nearly half the cops were on the take, as well, so the smugglers and black market overlords paid a handsome price to go unnoticed. It wasn't really that unusual anyway. The more money they paid, the more money they stood to make. Keeping the government officials and law at bay were the mainstays of black market operations. It wasn't all that much different from some of the seedier areas in major cities across any other country, including the United States. There were many shady goings-on in the back rooms of bathhouses and on the street corners of America; no community stood to completely isolate itself from them.

That thought bothered McCarter, although not as

much as trying to tread lightly in a foreign land. Phoenix Force was in the business of making noise and it ruffled McCarter's feathers any time he was told to "take it easy" so as to not attract attention. They couldn't do their jobs effectively when they had one hand tied behind their collective backs, but McCarter also understood the need for discretion; they were a covert-operations unit, after all, and whether he bloody well liked it or not, maintaining some semblance of secrecy was just part of the job.

"I'm not terribly sure about this plan here," Hawkins said. "There's no guarantee we're going to find anything to bring us closer to our objective."

"Maybe not. But we're bound to shake a few monkeys out of the trees," Manning pointed out.

"I'd prefer to shake a few Hezbollah terrorists out of hiding," James said.

"I'm down with that," Hawkins replied.

McCarter addressed his teammates in the back. "The best we can do is identify the most viable targets and hope they're in an accommodating mood."

DARKNESS ENCROACHED AS Phoenix Force picked their way through some dense jungle foliage on the approach to the warehouse district.

Unlike a lot of other commercial areas, the boundaries between civilization and nature weren't so well defined. The attitude of many citizens was to disturb as little of Paraguay's precious natural resources as possible, since those resources were the chief framework for their national economy. The clearing of land to build structures was tightly regulated, and although they had segregated the agricultural communities—chopping them into contained areas like old serfdoms—the majority of Paraguayans understood the need for protecting their natural assets.

Surprisingly, tourism accounted for another large chunk of the community, although most people preferred to visit the shorelines of South America rather than travel inland. There were group tours, of course, and some who would come to Paraguay to visit relatives, but mostly the country saw more than its fair share of drug smugglers, fugitives from the law and entrepreneurs of the world criminal underground looking for new enterprises in these wild and untamed lands.

As they made the edge of the jungle patch, McCarter observed what he immediately knew to be a sampling from those enterprises.

While none of them could tell for sure if the ten-foot chain-link with razor wire on top was also electrified, they were quite sure those weren't peashooters the sentries behind the fence carried.

McCarter raised a pair of NVD field glasses to his eyes and made a practiced study of the AO. After a careful perusal, he passed them over to Encizo to look, who would then in turn pass them down the line so every man got an idea of the terrain. It was this kind of cooperation and training that had made Phoenix Force one of the most effective combat teams in the world, and a legend in its own right. Every one of them had been cross-trained in at least one other fighting skill besides their primary, and all were well versed in military tactics and operational strategies.

And they were deadly down to the last man.

Once they'd all had a look, McCarter ordered a retreat to the safety of the shadows to discuss a plan.

"Options," he said when they were huddled.

"I count at least a dozen on sentry duty," Manning

said. "That's a long stretch from the fence to the building, and we don't have any idea what we'll find inside."

McCarter nodded. "Taking a direct route is out of the question, then."

The men nodded in agreement. Hawkins nodded at the munitions bag slung over Manning's shoulder. "We could use some of the ordnance there to create a distraction. A quarter stick of C-4 would be more than adequate to blow a hole in the fence, and we could cover the explosion with a couple well-placed grenades."

"Okay," James said. "But how do we breach the fence?"

"Quarter-stick of C-4 would do the job nicely." Hawkins looked at McCarter. "If we split up and enter from two locations it would at least spread them out some."

"We all seem to be forgetting something," Encizo said. "We don't have any idea if those security patrols are actually enemies."

"They're carrying SMGs and sidearms, Rafe," Hawkins said. "Do you really think they're legit?"

It was McCarter who answered. "Probably not, but we have to entertain the possibility, mate. I'm as skeptical as the next guy, particularly in light of the fact our intelligence came straight from the proverbial horse's mouth. But I'm also not of the mind to go wasting innocent civilians without first having some solid proof they're actually bad guys."

"There is another alternative we haven't discussed," Encizo said.

Manning seemed to brighten. "What's that?"

"Well, we could try to find another way in," Encizo said. "A more covert means of access."

"Such as?" James inquired.

Encizo grinned. "We have an ambulance, right?"

"Well, ain't you as slick as possum snot," Hawkins drawled.

RAFAEL ENCIZO CHURNED up as much dust on the road leading to the compound as he could, lights and sirens blaring. They'd managed to find some spare uniforms in the ambulance, which was not simply a mock unit but actually a fully stocked medical rig. One uniform happened to fit Encizo, while James was the only other one who could get into the jumpsuit-style uniform.

"Don't take any chances," McCarter had instructed the pair. "If they get suspicious or it looks like your ruse won't work, get the hell out of the way because we'll be coming in on full steam."

The pair hoped their luck would hold out long enough to get inside the operation without actually attracting too much attention. Or, as Encizo had pointed out when first broaching the idea, attracting attention was *exactly* what they had wanted to do. The Cuban had actually been surprised nobody had suggested it to begin with; there were less risks doing it this way, not to mention they could maintain much better control if they were conspicuous and up front than if they ended up having to "break in" to a place from which they would only eventually have to break out again.

The wail of the siren caught the attention of not only the gate guards but also a number of the nearby sentries. Encizo killed the sirens when they were close but he kept the lights on for show. Not only were they a good distraction, but the brightness of the lights and strobes would play havoc with the night vision of anyone looking at them. One of the guards, a muscular type with a brush cut and hard eyes, raised his hand and gestured for Encizo to roll down the window.

"What's going on?" the man asked in Spanish, to Encizo's surprise.

"We got a call someone's having a heart attack," Encizo replied.

"What? Nah!" The guard glanced at James then returned his attention to Encizo. "You've made a mistake. Nobody here is having a heart attack. I would know."

"Are you sure?" James said.

"Was I talking to you?" the man replied.

Wow, James thought. Mean *and* prejudiced.

"We have to check it out, either way," Encizo said. "It's the law."

"You can't come in here. It's a restricted area."

"Restricted?" James said, intent on irritating the man and exasperating his patience. "What you got going on here, some secret government operation?"

"We have to at least talk to whoever called us, or someone in charge here," Encizo insisted. "If we don't then we'll have to call the police and they will come out and ask questions."

For the first time the man looked uncertain. "Wait here."

He spun smartly on his heel and entered the guard shack. Encizo and James had kept their hands in view purposefully, not anxious to get blown away by the tired or trigger-happy types for no reason. But they had the MP-5s close at hand, ready to blast their way out of the situation if that's what it took. Encizo had also liberated a couple of M-69s from their cache in the event small arms didn't prove enough.

Frankly, it was obvious there was more to this place than met the eye. This close the Phoenix Force pair could tell the men were toting a plethora of weapons including some AKS-74Us, Uzis and even a couple of Steyr AUG A3s. Some of the guards held their weapons loosely while others seemed a bit more intent, and suspicious, of the Phoenix warriors-turned-EMTs. Encizo kept one eye on the lead man inside the shack. The man's eyes flicked toward the ambulance a couple of times during his conversation on the phone, but Encizo tried to act as if he hadn't noticed, ignoring the beads of sweat that tickled the back of his neck while he drummed his fingers in mock boredom on the steering wheel.

A minute ticked by, then two.

Eventually the man exited the shack and snapped his fingers at a guard to open the massive chain-link gate, which swung on heavy steel hinges. The macabre squeal of the gate, a victim of Paraguay's infamous humidity, ground on Encizo's and James's nerves even more but neither man dared to mention it openly.

The sentry leader pointed to a squat building just forward of the largest of the warehouse buildings within the complex. "Drive straight to that area and a supervisor will meet you out front. If you deviate from your course, we'll be forced to take action."

Encizo looked around and tried to appear as terrified as possible, not difficult considering the incessant hammer in his chest. Only a fool would not have been afraid to pass into the heart of the hornet's nest. "Wouldn't think of it, pal. Thank you."

The man made no reply as Encizo dropped the selector into drive and eased the ambulance through the gateway. He kept his speed moderate so as not to attract attention, but he left the lights on so that the sentries would have something nice and mesmerizing to watch. He could only hope their distraction was enough for the rest of their teammates to execute the other half of the plan.

As soon as the ambulance became visible from their position and the attention of the guards was diverted, McCarter, Hawkins and Manning broke cover of the jungle line and made for the fence. McCarter joined two links together with an insulated field tool that didn't generate noise or sparks. With a nod from him, Manning and Hawkins took up position side by side and began to make short work of the fence with pairs of heavy-duty breaching snips. Their work was no mean feat, considering they had to cut a hole big enough to fit two men at a time—what was their only means of ingress might also have to serve as an exit.

Yeah, they might have to leave in a big hurry.

As soon as they had tops and sides cut, they folded the fencing down and McCarter went through first, M-16 A-4 held at the ready. The Briton set up a covering position while Hawkins and Manning followed, and then the three men broke into a sprint across the field. They aimed for the only point of cover, an outhouse placed midfield probably for the use of the sentries. By the time they reached it, the trio could observe the gate being opened and the ambulance passing through.

"It worked," Hawkins whispered.

"It damn sure did," Manning replied.

"Now what?" Hawkins asked McCarter.

"We wait," McCarter replied.

CHAPTER FOURTEEN

The guy who came outside to greet Encizo and James had a big belly and a shock of red hair and a beard to match. Those features, coupled with his bright blue eyes, pegged him as maybe of Irish or Scottish extraction. His fists were like a pair of junior hams and he sweated profusely. In fact, he had a towel draped around his wide neck—more like a washcloth against that beefy exterior—that he used to mop his forehead and neck.

"Miserable fucking heat!" He looked at the Phoenix Force pair and in English said, "What's this about someone calling an ambulance?"

"We don't have any more details than that," Encizo said.

"Well, there ain't any problem," the guy said. "So you can just turn your asses around and get the hell out of here."

In one smooth motion the two were out of the ambulance and Encizo had his MP-5 pressed deep into the man's gut. "Turn around and gesture for us to follow. And if you make a sound or a wrong move, I'll perform surgery right here on you."

Something went strange in the man's expression, something between shock and anger, but he could see Encizo told the truth. The guy was no fanatic and he obviously didn't feel like getting his hide blown all over the building facade behind him, so he did exactly as Encizo instructed. As soon as they were behind the safety of the door, James removed the medical jump bag he'd slung over his shoulder and withdrew an M-16. Keeping one eye on the narrow hallway to either side, he put his SMG into battery before donning the headset of the portable communications gear.

"Orion Three to Orion Leader, come in."

"Hear you five-by-five, Orion Three."

"We're in."

"Roger that, Orion Three. Give us the high sign as soon as you have confirmation of legit target contact."

"Wilco, out here."

James snapped off and then looked their heavyset prisoner in the eye. "Listen very carefully to this because I'm only going to say it once. We're going to ask you some very simple, straightforward questions. If you lie to us then we're going to hook your ears up to the nearest source of raw power and flip a switch. Got it?"

The man nodded, huffing and puffing and sweating—the red-faced complexion paled some. "Wh-what do you want to know?"

"We'll get to the details in a moment," James said. "First, who are you?"

"Name's Sweeney."

"You packing?" Encizo asked.

"No, too damn hot to wear a gun. Besides, the boss don't allow it."

"So there are no sentries inside, either?"

"None like out there." Sweeney waved in the general direction of the exterior. "Those goons aren't really part of our team."

"Hired help?" James inquired.

"Pretty much."

"Please be specific," Encizo replied with a cool smile, brandishing the MP-5 with an implicit threat. "Yes or no?"

"There are only two guys who're armed, jackoff," he said. "Private security for the boss."

"The team leader for the hired help said you were the boss," James said.

Sweeney looked at James with strained lines in his face. "I'm the boss *here* for the operations. Director of operations is my official title, but I'm not the big boss."

"Oo-oh, he's the director of operations," James said to Encizo. "Very official and all. Quit stalling, Sweeney, and tell us who the real boss is and why him and nobody else is allowed to carry."

"I can't tell you that! I'll get my balls cut off if I blab. Besides, fuckheads, I ain't no squeal and I got a reputation. So you can throw me in the slammer or you can kill me. I've been in jail before and nearly been killed, too. It won't be no sweat off my balls either way, but I'm not going to turn on nobody."

"You keep forgetting that there are other ways to make you talk," James pointed out.

"And they're not very nice ways," Encizo added for effect.

Sweeney shook his head. "Don't freaking matter because ain't no way I'm going to rat on nobody and especially not the boss."

"Have it your way," James said. He decided to play a hunch. "But if it's Lazario Giménez you're protecting, then I suppose we'd better break it to you that he's dead."

Sweeney didn't flinch. "The hell you say."

"The hell we say," Encizo said. "I was standing right next to him when he went down."

"You killed him?"

Encizo shook his head shortly. "The people we're looking for killed him. Look, friend, we don't really give a crap about whatever it is you've got going on here. That's a problem for the Paraguayan officials to deal with. The people we work for would prefer we get our information without drawing attention. Which means if you can supply us that information, we can leave here nice and quiet-like and there doesn't have to be any trouble. But if you screw with us then we're going to have a big problem and it's not going to turn out well for you or whatever it is you got going here."

"Maybe I'd be more inclined to help if you told me who killed Lazario," Sweeney said.

"Maybe you should be more inclined to cooperate in the interests of self-preservation," James said.

"I don't suppose there'd be any harm in telling him who's behind this whole thing," Encizo said.

James shrugged.

"But I think we'd best get out of this hallway before we draw any more unwanted attention." Encizo waved the muzzle of the MP-5 at Sweeney. "Lead the way and don't try taking us into a trap or you're through."

Sweeney gave Encizo an embittered look before whirling on his heel and leading the pair deeper into the bowels of the warehouse. As they went, James and Encizo looked for anything that might give them away—cameras in the corners or recessed into light-filtering bubbles within the ceiling—since they weren't yet entirely sure where this operation would go. Encizo had played a hunch, a hunch that had paid off, but it didn't mean Sweeney's people wouldn't have planned for such an eventuality.

At the same time, the fact they'd found this operation

at all and that it happened to be one in which Giménez
had played a vital role seemed almost so coincidental
that it bordered on storybook cliché. Encizo had never
been one to believe much in coincidence and neither did
his companions. In some regard it almost felt like they'd
been drawn into a trap, and yet Encizo couldn't put his
finger exactly on it. To get drawn into a trap would indicate a very elaborate network and considerable planning—Encizo didn't think Giménez would've had that
kind of foresight, and Sweeney certainly wasn't "in-
the-know" enough to have figured on a covert operations team from the U.S. coming here.

Conversely, he could understand James's reticence
in giving away their hand too soon. They'd more or less
stumbled into this one connection that might actually
point them in the direction of the Hezbollah. If it went
sour now, their chances would decrease dramatically
of finding the Peace Corps volunteers or coming to any
sort of real conclusion about exactly why it was that
the IRGC and Hezbollah were so chummy. Granted, it
was in Iran's best interest to subsidize terrorist cells all
over the world, particularly those with an unchallenged
hatred of the U.S. or her allies, but they wouldn't have
risked exposing themselves like this unless there was
a huge payoff at the end of the line.

Sweeney seemed true to his word because he led
them to the office areas that, at this hour, appeared
all but abandoned. The offices on either side of Sweeney's followed a circumferential path around a cluster
of desks in an open area separated by cubicles that were
dark, with no personnel present.

"Where is everybody?" James asked.

"It's night shift," Sweeney said. "Everybody's gone
home. There are only the guards and a skeleton crew

on, and I think the janitorial service is still here but they're cleaning up another area right now. We should be undisturbed."

He mopped his brow and neck again. "Can I sit down?"

Encizo nodded. "Don't try anything."

Sweeney dropped into an oversize office chair behind his desk. "Just don't get too nervous with the trigger finger, pal."

"No reason there should be any problems at all if you cooperate," James said. "Soon as we learn what we need to know, we'll be out of here."

"Now quit stalling and tell us what exactly is going on," Encizo said.

Sweeney shook his head. "I can't remember how many times I warned Laz something like this might happen. I fucking told him not to get involved with these Arab pricks, that it could only go bad for us. When I used to work for the bosses back in the States, I used to tell them never to cooperate with the Sicilians or Italians because you just couldn't trust those wop pukes any farther than they could throw ya."

James produced a mock smile. "Nice to know that ethnic differences are still strong among organized crime factions in America. But never mind that, Sweeney. What else do you know about this?"

"I know shit, is what I know. Those motherfuckers!" Sweeney slammed his fist on his desk but Encizo and James kept rock-steady aim on him with their SMGs. "Relax. I said I won't give you no trouble and I'm a man of my word."

"Go on," Encizo said.

"The Hezbollah are only interested in themselves and whatever they can get their hands on."

"Which is?"

"Mostly high-tech goods." Sweeney fished a cigarette from the pack on his desk, lit it and then immediately had a coughing fit. He mopped his face before continuing. "They're buying up all the shit they can and I know they're using multiple sources even if they swore they were dealing exclusively with Laz."

"How do you know that?" James asked.

"You're kidding me, right, pal?" Sweeney snorted for effect. "You really think I got to be in this position because I don't know what the fuck's going on around here? The black market in this city is ripe for the taking for anyone who has two things—balls and brains. It's never been so easy…like taking candy from a baby. We smuggle all kinds of shit in here, and I'm saying this to you only because you say you don't care."

"We care," James interjected. "We just don't care right now. Back to the terrorists. How long have you been dealing with them?"

"If you're talking just the ragheads, only about six months," Sweeney said, and he took a deep drag. In a cloud of smoke he said, "But there are others here we've been subsidizing for years. Groups from Europe, the Golden Triangle. Hell, we even done business with the Russians."

It was James's and Encizo's turn not to be all that surprised.

"What do they want all of these high-tech goods for?" Encizo asked.

"I don't know but I got a theory based on my past experiences."

"Which is?"

"They probably want to schedule a series of isolated hits in different areas, and they figure high-tech equipment like senders and receivers, triggers and other such devices can help them do that. Maybe they want to spread a gas or trigger a bomb or whatever. Who gives a shit as long as they don't try it near us and they pay their bills on time."

"Did it ever occur to you that a good many of those attacks might occur in the United States?"

"Oh, boo-hoo," Sweeney said. "What do you want me to do, boyos? Seek a pledge from every crazy bastard that comes into business with us? Besides, I'm not buying or selling direct to them. This place is only a storage area. You can kind of look at us as like a bonded warehouse. We hold the goods here until we get the money and then we arrange the shipments."

"Are there any shipments scheduled for the Hezbollah?" James inquired.

Sweeney's expression was unreadable. "I ain't going to fucking tell you that. Not ever. Even if Laz is dead I still have to do my job or we lose this whole thing."

"Your loyalty is admirable but the fact is you're protecting the same ones who killed your boss," Encizo said.

"Don't matter." Sweeney took another long drag. "We got other customers and I got to protect them. If they think we turned over on them, we'll be out of business."

"You're going to be out of business anyway when we get done with this place," James said.

"You told me you didn't care what was going on here—"

"We lied," Encizo cut in. "And you *are* going to tell us exactly where you plan to ship the goods to the Hezbollah or I swear we'll make you very sorry you ever met us. Now get your fat ass out of that chair and take us to where you have this equipment stored."

"It's too late, boys," Sweeney said, calmly smoking and now grinning ear to ear.

"What are you talking about?"

"You shouldn't have let me get to where I could set off the alarm. Take a look behind you."

The two whirled in time to see a veritable army of the hired help winding their way through the cubicles and into position, weapons held at the ready. They were mere shadows within the darkened and confined spaces, but there were enough of them that Encizo and James could estimate they were outnumbered somewhere between ten and fifteen to one. Those weren't good odds when they didn't have much in the way of running room.

Encizo turned to Sweeney. "There's just one problem. We figured you might pull something like this."

Sweeney looked smug. "And?"

"You made the mistake of bringing the bulk of your force indoors."

"Yeah," James added. "And that's exactly what we hoped for."

EVEN AS MCCARTER'S TEAM watched the activity unfold in front of their eyes, they knew the ruse had worked. It happened with more suddenness than they'd expected, and it happened in such a way that by the time most of the sentries on the ground disappeared inside the building, James and Encizo would've likely acquired the information they needed. As good fortune would have it, the enemy had made a huge tactical blunder and left only two sentries guarding the front gate. This would be child's play for McCarter and his team.

The crackle of the signal beeped in all three of the warriors' headsets a moment later.

Manning held position, prone at the corner of the portable toilet, the PSG-1 set out on a bipod in front of him. McCarter and Hawkins broke cover, fanning out as they made a beeline for the front gate. They were on top of their enemies before either of the sentries even knew they had trouble. The one standing outside the shack scrambled to get his assault rifle into action. The only thing he got for his troubles was a pair of well-placed rounds through his skull courtesy of Hawkins's M-16 A-4.

McCarter dispatched the other terrorist still inside the shack with a sweeping burst from the hip. The 5.56 x 45 mm NATO slugs punched through the Plexiglas window as if it were made of rice paper and shattered the sentry's breast bone and hip. Unfortunately, McCarter didn't get the guy before he managed to pick up a phone and start screaming into it.

McCarter double-checked the man to make sure he was dead and then keyed up his headset, addressing Manning. "Orion Leader to Orion Two. We're going to have company shortly."

"Orion Two copies, Leader," Manning said. "I'm ready."

AS THE GUARDS SNAKED their way through the cubicles, James reached into his bag of tricks and withdrew a pair of M-69s. He tossed one at Encizo while keeping the other for himself. On a nod, the pair yanked the pins and tossed the bombs through the doorway simultaneously at forty-five degrees, angling the grenades from each other to achieve the maximum effect. They dropped behind the shielding of the office walls—the upper portions being made of heavy plate glass wedged between metal frames—as they closed their eyes and plugged their ears.

The grenades did the job neatly, blowing at almost the exact same time and catching about a half dozen of the enemy combatants in the shockwave. The force proved enough to actually blow the glass out of the office windows, clearing the crouched warriors but flying directly at Sweeney. The guy threw up his hands and managed to avoid being completely torn to ribbons by the deadly shards, although some lodged in his forearms and one clipped his ear and nicked a fleshy lobe.

Encizo and James pressed the offensive, rising from concealment long enough to spray several more of their enemies with autofire. Staying on offense only made sense at this point, seeing as they were outgunned and outmanned even in the wake of the effects of their M-69s.

James scored first, punching a 3-round burst through the gut of one aggressor while a second gunman tried to angle out of the line of attack. James led him just enough with the muzzle that the guy stepped right into his line of fire. The slugs cut an ugly swathe up the man's belly but the kill shot was a round through the right lung. The impact spun him and his corpse slammed into a cubicle wall.

Encizo tagged another guard with a 3-round burst through the chest, subsequently lifting the guard off his feet and dumping him on the thin carpet. He crashed close to another gunner who'd been lining up on Encizo for a clean head shot. The shot went low and wide of the Cuban, and Encizo responded with accurate force before the guy could realign his sights for a second pass. The man's skull disappeared in a gory wash of crimson and gray, his head coming apart like a cantaloupe under the pressure of a sledgehammer.

Within less than a minute the Phoenix Force duo had managed to reduce the numbers on the opposition by about half, but still faced at least ten gunners. They only had two more grenades and they didn't want to waste those on a long shot. The guards had learned a newfound respect for the pair and backed off, taking shots wherever they thought they might score a hit without risking exposure.

Over the select staccato of autofire from the enemy, James said, "Any ideas?"

"I was hoping you had some!" Encizo said as he slammed a fresh magazine into the MP-5 and released the bolt with clang.

"Maybe we should call up the rest of the team and see if they can help out."

"Good idea."

James nodded and then signaled for McCarter, who came back with a reply immediately. "Hang loose, mates, we're on our way."

"Hurry, Orion Leader," James replied. "The natives are getting restless."

"MOVE OUT," MCCARTER told Hawkins as he finished disabling the radio and phone communications inside the guard shack. "Orion Two, you hold position."

"Understood," Manning replied.

McCarter and Hawkins dashed in the direction of the ambulance, watchful for any resistance. They hadn't planned for it to be this easy but so far things were going well, much better than McCarter had originally anticipated. With any luck, the information source Encizo had indicated they required was still alive and they might actually make some headway in this thing. So far they'd been on the defensive and this had turned out to be their first big break.

They were within twenty-five yards or so of the ambulance when trouble appeared in the form of a half-dozen sentries. Apparently the operators here had a small army at their disposal and that only stood as more evidence that even if they weren't directly supporting the terrorists they were in collusion with them.

Hawkins got the first one with a short burst through the midsection but realized his mistake a moment too late—in his haste to defend against one he'd missed the threat from another. Hawkins did the only thing he could, and the least predictable at this close distance, dropping prone and rolling away from the direct line of fire. He came around just in time to see the gunner, who'd fired one burst and was already reacquiring, stiffen. The man's back then arched and he flipped prone to the pavement.

From his peripheral vision Hawkins caught the flash coming from the general area where they'd left Manning, and in that split second he realized the Canadian had just saved his life with that uncanny marksmanship. Yeah, Gary Manning was to a hunting or sniper rifle what David McCarter was to a target pistol.

"Damn fine shooting," Hawkins said to Manning.

McCarter had his hands full with two more of the guards; he took a knee and dispatched them with practiced efficiency nonetheless. The first gunner bought it with half a dozen 5.56 mm slugs that dotted him from crotch to chest, the final one blowing out the better part of his throat. The other one got a pair of rounds through the face, the force of the high-velocity impacts nearly decapitating him. At a minimum, there wasn't enough left of his face for even his mother to have recognized him. He staggered back and forth like a drunken bum several seconds before crumpling to the pavement.

THE REMAINING AGGRESSORS went down thanks to the unerring skills of Gary Manning.

Number one fell under a well-placed slug from the PSG-1 that passed clean under the shoulder blade, through the heart and out the chest at a point just below the clavicle. Manning watched the messy eruption through the scope as air and blood mixed in the open, a mark of the bullet's passing.

Manning swung the Hendsoldt scope into position on the remaining target, took a breath, let half out and squeezed the trigger. The enemy guard had been too occupied trading shots with Hawkins and McCarter to realize his comrade had fallen under the sniper code of "one shot, one kill." Unfortunately, Manning made the mistake of overcorrecting for windage and the round grazed the air just above the kneeling guard's head. The man turned and looked wildly in every direction— searching for the source of the shot, no doubt—so Manning waited patiently until the last moment when it seemed as if the guard was looking straight at him. The scope showed every gory detail as Manning delivered a round that penetrated the man's head through his upper lip.

The impact smashed facial bones and the head came apart under the effects of bullet cavitation.

Manning keyed up his mike. "Orion Two to Leader, you're all clear."

"Roger," McCarter said, with a wave of thanks.

The pair scrambled to their feet and were soon out of view.

THE HEAT, SMOKE AND STENCH of blood nearly overpowered James and Encizo as their enemies pressed the attack.

Clearly they were aware of how much the odds were stacked against the Phoenix Force pair, and the enemy planned to take complete advantage of that situation. Without waiting, they had started to hammer the area with heavy suppression fire—they had even employed the strategy of half the team burning rounds through every wall, window and piece of furniture while the other half reloaded.

A miasma of plaster dust and debris from ceiling tiles being chopped to shreds threatened to overcome the two warriors. Whenever they got a lull they directed short, controlled bursts against their enemies in the hope of keeping them at bay at least part of the time. They weren't going to put them down any other way at this stage of the game and it didn't really matter if they could see their enemies or not. At this point, it seemed more important to stay alive while they waited for reinforcements.

It seemed like forever but in reality they didn't have to wait long. The noise being generated by their enemies worked to their advantage by giving McCarter and Hawkins something to key on, and before long the enemy had begun to take more of what they'd been dishing out. Smartly, Hawkins entered the fray with a grenade that smashed the fortifications of three of the ten or so gunners. Arms and legs were separated from torsos as the M-69 did its job without prejudice or regret.

Within a heartbeat the remaining gunners found themselves in a brutal crossfire. They tried to hold their positions but the crisscross of rounds through desks and cubicle walls proved too much. Their leader finally ordered a retreat but with few exits that weren't covered by Phoenix Force their attempted withdrawal turned into little more than a slaughter.

A pair of the gunners fell under a sustained burst from McCarter's M-16 A-4. At least fifteen to twenty rounds were shared between them, and they danced like marionettes under the handiwork of a puppeteer having an epileptic fit. Two more dropped from a controlled series of bursts from James, who happened to be closest. The darkness had allowed James's vision to adjust whereas the continuous autofire and blast from the grenade had all but blinded the two guards. They practically walked right up to James's makeshift defilade and the warrior took them down hard with his M-16.

The trio that remained tried to vacate together but found no quarter when they exposed themselves just right. All four Phoenix Force warriors seized this unparalleled advantage and decimated the enemy force with fields of fire specifically designed to avoid casualties among each other. One took a dual burst to the chest, casting blood and flesh on every solid object within a ten-yard radius. Another lost the back of his head when a round punched through his forehead at the same moment another half dozen transected his spinal column. The last took a belly full of lead, intersecting from three different directions, and by the time he toppled his midsection comprised something about as cohesive as unset gelatin.

For a long time the Phoenix Force team members held position, waiting patiently for more resistance, but after a time it became quite apparent they weren't going to encounter more. Once each man had shouted an all-clear in turn, McCarter and Hawkins advanced on the office and were soon reunited with their friends.

"Thanks for the assist," James said with a broad grin, shaking each of their hands in turn.

With the reunion complete, the clanking and scurrying of something behind them caught their attention. It was Sweeney on his hands and knees, trying to scurry from the scene like the rat he was. With the assistance of McCarter, they hauled the death-dealing jackal to his feet and hurled him onto a nearby sofa—or what was left of the thing.

"Now," Encizo began. "You were going to tell us about the Hezbollah."

CHAPTER FIFTEEN

Stony Man Farm, Virginia

If there was one thing Hal Brognola had to admit he hated most, it was poor intelligence.

Poor intelligence didn't do anyone good in this business. The Farm couldn't make good decisions with poor intelligence; the teams couldn't operate as safely and efficiently as possible with poor intelligence; and the plans of the enemy certainly couldn't be subverted if those charged with frustrating them possessed poor intelligence.

Unfortunately, Brognola thought, this entire mission had been filled with poor intelligence.

Price and Brognola, joined by Aaron Kurtzman, were gathered in the ops center of the Annex. Brad Russell sat in courtesy of the satellite video feed they'd set up between the Farm and Paraguay. Although they weren't accustomed to dealing with outsiders in such operations, Brognola had decided to make an exception where it concerned Russell. First off, the guy had proved his worth several times over already while demonstrating an ability to operate as part of the team, irrespective of the fact he had no real decision-making powers or a direct relationship with Stony Man personnel.

What had most impressed Brognola about Russell,

however, was the fact the guy didn't press them for information. For whatever reason, Russell seemed satisfied with the knowledge he was making a contribution and not whining about jurisdiction or other such nonsense. If Brognola had anything to say about it, and he did, there would be a formal commendation from the President on Russell's record before they were all through.

"Let's consider what we have so far," Barbara Price was saying. "A group of Peace Corps volunteers get snatched by Hezbollah terrorists who are under training from members of the Iranian Revolutionary Guard Corps. Less than twenty-four hours later, Christopher Harland shows up with a wild and cockamamie story about how this has something to do with the IRGC against the imperialistic West, and yet we discover that the Hezbollah is actually involved.

"Now there's high-tech training going on by a business magnate who's actually wrapped up with the black market goings-on in Ciudad del Este, all the while brokering high-tech materials for the highest bidders. Before we can even assess that relationship, though, we get information about an intelligence asset who has information about this situation, only when we send our people to investigate do we actually find out there's a plot to overthrow certain officials, including Ahmadinejad, out of office in the name of Sharia law."

"It's like a bad B movie," Kurtzman remarked.

"In one respect it does make a lot of sense, though," Russell interjected.

The point got Brognola's interest. "Go on."

"Well, if you look at it from the aspect of a lot of nations who've recently started to crack down on terrorist organizations, it makes good sense they'd turn to alternate methods of getting supplied whatever they needed, be it guns, drugs, bombs or technology."

Price nodded. "That's a good point."

"Sure is," Kurtzman added.

Obviously gaining confidence, Russell pressed forward. "Let's suppose that the well starts to dry up for the usual sources of support for the terrorists, be it due to loss of resources or money or just political pressure. Even fanatics have to maintain good business relations and they can't do that unless they establish reputations through alternate pipelines. You take an area like Ciudad del Este, an area already heavily populated by Muslims and other Asian ethnic groups that are more likely to be sympathetic to such causes, and you have all the makings of a huge black market source to which terrorists can turn."

"And because of the Third World agricultural exports and the corrupt government officials within the country, they don't draw world attention as much as countries in the Middle East, Asia and Europe," Brognola concluded.

"Right."

"So if we consider now what we've been told by Sweeney, it starts to make more sense," Price said.

"Well, at least the information Sweeney's providing will be enough to help the team pinpoint the exact location of this Hezbollah camp," Brognola said.

"Indeed." Price looked at Kurtzman. "Bear, what do we know about Sweeney?"

Kurtzman tapped a key on the board in front of him and the hood's picture materialized on the massive screen at the other end of the room. "Glengarry Sweeney, born June 5, 1956, in Dublin. His father was a Red IRA supporter and a longshoreman by trade, his mother a clothes designer on a three-year assignment in Ireland. His father died in a work accident and Sweeney was able to enter the U.S. as an American citizen because his mother was a U.S. citizen."

Brognola grunted. "Raised in the Irish quarter of New York, I notice."

"Yeah," Kurtzman replied. "The guy took to the Irish organized crime routine like stripes to a zebra. His first arrest came when he was only thirteen, caught selling cartons of cigarettes to his classmates out of the trunk of a stolen car. While they couldn't stick him with grand theft auto since they didn't have any proof he actually took the car, they did get him on possession of stolen goods plus the illegal sales of untaxed cigarettes to minors."

"A slap on the wrist for a thirteen-year-old," Price said.

"Twelve months in a juvenile correctional facility, only four months of which he served due to good behavior."

"Three-to-one rule," Russell said, which brought nods from the others. "Got to love that strict New York penal system."

"What can you expect from a liberal state?" Kurtzman remarked.

"Go on about Sweeney," Price said.

"He managed to keep his nose clean after that," Kurtzman said. "Or at least he managed not to get caught again until he was twenty-four. Did a nickel upstate New York for armed robbery. The liquor store clerk died but they managed to pin that on the other guy with Sweeney, because Sweeney was waiting outside in the getaway car. What nobody knew at the time was that Sweeney had recently signed on as wheelman for an underboss in the Durfee crime family."

"Why didn't they get him on a felony murder charge?" Price inquired.

"Apparently he claimed he didn't know there had even been a robbery going down, or that anybody had been shot. He claimed his buddy went inside to buy cigarettes, came out and they drove away. His buddy rolled on him for a reduced sentence so they ended up getting him on the robbery charge. Six months after the guy who rolled on him got out, he disappeared and was never seen or heard from again."

"Probably encased in a block of cement at the bottom of New York Harbor by now," Brognola said.

Price nodded. "Probably. Bear, how did Sweeney end up in Ciudad del Este of all places?"

Kurtzman smiled as he tapped another key. "That's the interesting part. Apparently, Sweeney became associated with this man, Jahanshah Mokri."

The picture displayed on the screen was of a muscular, clean-shaven young man who was actually quite handsome. He had a dark complexion, dark hair and chocolate-brown eyes; his patrician nose and strong jaw contrasted nicely with his exotic looks. He wore the uniform of the IRGC, and a number of unfamiliar medals, probably citations and other meritorious markers of Iranian special forces, adorned his chest.

"Mokri is a decorated member of the Iranian Revolutionary Guard Corps," Kurtzman said. "He's also a known consorter with terrorist groups and has been spotted throughout countries all over Asia, Africa and now South America."

"That seems like a very unlikely match-up, a guy

like Sweeney and an Iranian special forces soldier," Russell remarked.

"Not when you consider it in the context of their meeting," Kurtzman replied. "These two only ended up together because they were assigned to eliminate the same man, a former Italian mobster by the name of Caselio Bracco. Bracco allegedly committed a brutal rape and murder against a young Iranian girl who turned out to be the daughter of Mokri's deceased brother. It was a blood debt to be settled as far as Mokri was concerned, but the atrocity was committed on the turf of the Irish mob, and that's how Sweeney got involved."

"They committed the murder together?" Russell asked.

Kurtzman shook his head. "No. As rumor had it, Sweeney apparently felt that the oath of family sworn by Mokri took precedence over mob honor, so he begged off and let Mokri do the actual deed, even though he took credit. When word got back to the bosses of what actually happened, they ostracized Sweeney for violating truth and honor, and told him never to return to the United States. Mokri felt some bit of loyalty, so we think, and although we don't have proof it seems like the best theory at this point, that Mokri recommended Sweeney for employment with Lazario Giménez."

"That would make sense," Price said. "Has Sweeney confirmed that?"

"Sweeney's apparently not talking at all," Brognola interjected. "Once the team put down his guard force, Sweeney refused to cooperate."

"It's my understanding your team is dealing with that," Russell said. "In fact, they beat feet out of the area and are on their way back to Asunción as we speak. I understand they'll be arriving soon and that they have something very nice in store for Mr. Sweeney."

Price nodded. "They were in contact with us directly after the incident that took place there. Apparently they were going to destroy the high-tech equipment but instead they opted to leave it in place and simply place an anonymous call to the authorities in Ciudad del Este."

"Smart move," Brognola said. "If the underworld is as infused there as we've been led to believe, word of the equipment's destruction would certainly get back to Mokri. What's the team's next move, Barb?"

"I've advised them to take whatever steps are necessary to extract the information from Sweeney, up to and including chemical interrogation. They're a little concerned with that since Sweeney's health isn't apparently that stable, and they think the introduction of conventional pharmaceuticals might cause a stroke or even sudden cardiac death."

"That wouldn't be good," Brognola said. "I'm sure there are plenty of people within the Department of Justice who'd like to speak with Sweeney. Not to mention he'd be a great source of information for interrogators at Guantanamo Bay."

"I can see him fitting right into a nice, comfy cell there," Kurtzman said.

"Okay, that's as far as we can take this conversation with you, Mr. Russell," Brognola said. "We appreciate your assistance on all of this, not to mention your great insights. We're going to keep you on as a support tool for the team there as of right now, if you're okay with that."

"Whatever you need, folks, I'm your man," Russell

said. He grinned and added quickly, "In fact, this is the most fun I've had in a long, long time. Thanks for letting me play. Out here."

Without ceremony there was a brief pause and then Russell's image winked out.

After a glance of confirmation the communication uplink had actually been cut from Kurtzman, Brognola said, "Okay, what's the status on Able Team?"

"They just checked in about a half hour before you got back from your meeting with the Man," Price said. "Apparently there's a lot more to the story with Farzad Hemmati than we were originally told."

"Did the Company know about the details?"

"Not as far as we can tell. Hemmati apparently sprung this on them after he was followed by members of Iranian internal security to the meet location set up by the Company. In the course of the encounter, which Lyons assures me they did everything to avoid, one of the CIA's men fell. I don't think they would have deliberately set up one of their own."

Brognola harrumphed. "Maybe and maybe not. You can't really tell these days what the Company's going to do. Although it does seem really unlikely they'd allow something like this to happen purposefully, especially when all it does is make them look incompetent and embarrass the director."

"It also creates a nightmare for their operations," Price pointed out. "Do you have any idea how it long it takes to train agents to get inside a system like that? There's very little chance they'd compromise their own operations when that much work goes into establishing assets. We spend quite a bit of money to establish foreign agents in these countries."

"Agreed," Brognola said. "Okay, so what's Able

Team's take on Hemmati's story? In fact, what is Hemmati's story? Why did he mislead the CIA to begin with?"

"Hemmati apparently grew up under the tutelage of Muslim clerics. So far, he's refusing to identify exactly who these individuals are, either those to whom he answers or others on his team."

"That seems to be going around," Kurtzman said.

Price nodded. "What we've inferred from Hemmati's claims, however, is that this is definitely the work of the Pasdaran sect. They're allegedly frustrated with the lack of attention paid to Sharia law by the current administration and they're on the verge of a religious coup to seize political control. There are some higher-ups already in place, apparently, and ready to overthrow Ahmadinejad's entire regime in favor of a new religious state, one based on Muslim ideals.

"We're sort of in a catch-22 at this point," Price continued. "None of the boys is really buying Hemmati's story, but Lyons pointed out that this could still be an opportunity."

Brognola's brow furrowed. "How so?"

"Well, he figures if Hemmati can lead them to some of these places where Ahmadinejad's people are operating within the city, they can take them out before they have a chance to hatch whatever plan they have using Mokri's people and their IRGC/Hezbollah contingent. You see, Hemmati's convinced if they seize control of the central government that the leaders of the IRGC, which are relatively weak in the eyes of the Pasdaran, will bow to the new order and that will leave Mokri high and dry. Such a coup would give Phoenix Force the opportunity to move in unmolested."

"It seems they're on the verge of exercising that option now," Brognola replied.

"True." Price smiled. "But Hemmati doesn't have to know that. Lyons has decided to keep Hemmati incommunicado while simultaneously making him believe they've actually fallen for his ruse."

"Assuming it is a ruse," Kurtzman said.

"Even if it isn't, I don't think I need to point out to either of you that it would be doubly useful for Able Team to investigate further, and to take any action they deem necessary based on that information. There are a lot of very dangerous criminal elements inside the Iranian regime, not to mention the psychological impact eliminating some of these persons would have on Ahmadinejad's less loyal supporters."

"I don't know, Barb," Brognola said. "It seems like sending Able Team deep into the heart of Tehran with a carte blanche terminate-on-sight order might not be such a good idea."

"I know it has a lot of uncertainties and pitfalls," Price said. "But I'm not sure having them wait there twiddling their thumbs to babysit a CIA asset while they wait for the best opportunity to get out of the country doesn't put them in *more* danger. Additionally, they've advised that apparently the death of the one CIA agent has left his partner skittish and uncooperative. He's apparently pledged to provide his support per the terms of the original agreement but not beyond that."

"Sounds like interagency squabbling," Brognola said. He drummed his fingers on the table, producing a thrum from his nearby coffee cup. "We were promised complete cooperation by the CIA. I have a good mind to get the President on the phone right at this moment."

Price put a hand of restraint on his arm. "I don't think this is the Company's decision as much as that of the now sole operator in-country, Hal. Carl seems to think this guy's more dangerous if they try to bring him in against his will than if they just let him sit it out while they do their thing. Besides, they need someone to keep an eye on Hemmati while they check out his story."

Brognola emitted a long sigh as he chewed on his lower lip.

Again, they were at the mercy of relatively poor intelligence. What else did Lyons, Schwarz and Blancanales have to go on other than some story from an Iranian foreigner, and a religiously trained Muslim to boot, who could well be a double agent working for Ahmadinejad? The whole situation reeked of bullshit and yet Brognola knew Price's points were cogent: there were a lot of very nasty individuals loyal to Ahmadinejad and his bid for ultimate power through the acquisition of nuclear weapons. Maybe eliminating some of these individuals would weaken the infrastructure and still serve to protect the United States, as well.

Finally, Brognola looked at Price and nodded. "Okay, your argument's sound even if I still have concerns about the parameters of the mission. Able Team's been in tighter spots, so I have no reservations about their ability to bring something good out of a very bad situation. And as you've already pointed out, there's not much more they can do until we can get them extracted. Staying in one place could be worse for them than if they get some movement under their feet."

Brognola shoved an unlit cigar into the corner of his mouth, a nervous habit he'd taken on almost as many years ago as his twice-daily doses of antacids, which he kept in the breast pocket of his shirt like an extra appendage.

"And then there's just the plain, simple fact that I have a policy of noninterference when it comes to mission control," Brognola said. "You're Stony Man's official mission controller and I'm content to let you fill those shoes. You have an unwavering talent for it, in fact."

"So it's a go?" Price said.

Brognola nodded. "Let Able Team know they have a green light for twenty-four hours. After that, they either get out with Hemmati or they'll be on their own. We can't wait any longer to extract them. Especially not with Phoenix Force so close to locating the Peace Corps volunteers and unraveling whatever else this Jahanshah Mokri might have up his sleeve."

"That's the very interesting part," Price said. "We showed Mokri's picture to Christopher Harland and the guy went six shades of green. Apparently he's the one who put Harland up to all of this in the first place."

"Even so, he's still operating under the orders of his Iranian masters," Brognola said. "The sooner Phoenix Force can find the IRGC and these Hezbollah fanatics, the sooner we can all sleep easier. Whatever happens next, we need to be prepared for a full-on response to prevent bigger problems."

Price nodded. "I'll let both teams know what we're up against."

"And tell them we're pulling for them. Get them whatever they need, Barb. Whatever they need."

"I have the sneaking suspicion they already know that, Hal." Price winked at him and added, "But I'll tell them."

WHATEVER ELSE THE THREE hard chargers planned to do with the information from Hemmati, Stephen "Pops" Poppas had his own plans.

For one thing, someone had to pay for Jester's death. Hemmati seemed the most viable candidate, but he was now under the protection of the three unknowns who'd swooped into their territory and Poppas couldn't risk pissing off whomever it was they worked for. At least, that's what Mother had kept telling him on the secure radio call he'd placed.

Then there was Hemmati's ridiculous story about the Pasdaran and being raised by Muslim clerics, acting as if he was some kind of religious prophet. The New Mohammed. Poppas smiled at his own wit as he chewed furiously on the end of a cigarette, his sixth in the past hour. Poppas stared out the window of his apartment, sipping the hot Turkish coffee he'd purchased from a street vendor. It was illegal as hell, this stuff they were peddling, but plenty worth the risk for what Poppas was willing to pay—or any of the other rich white bastards living in the country.

The fact remained that for the most part the Iranian citizens themselves didn't hate Americans, at least not as much as the government wanted the rest of the world to believe. Sure, they didn't agree with the religious beliefs of the West, that great Satan, but they had nothing against capitalism or the concept of the American wealth. Or was that really China's wealth now? Oh, what the hell did it even matter? As far as it concerned Poppas, he had only one official mission and that was to support the three men in their quest to kill Ahmadinejad's cronies. That was something he could live with.

But what he wouldn't allow to happen was for their mission to override his own quest for revenge. He

meant to take whatever he could out of the intelligence
Hemmati gave them and go on a little adventure of his
own. He'd beat the information out of the little prick
if that's what it took, but one way or another Hemmati
was going to talk. Yeah, he was going to talk a lot, that
little bastard.

Poppas would also make sure after he'd dealt out
a good measure of revenge—no, not revenge but justice—for Jester that he'd get some money back to the
guy's young wife. Of course, she'd never really know
where the money came from or even why she was re-
ceiving it, but it would at least help ease the agony of
her husband becoming little more than a star on the
CIA's Memorial Wall at Langley. A guy deserved a
hell of a lot more than that for dying for his country.

Poppas turned his attention back to the task at hand
as he considered his options. It wouldn't be easy to
get this mission done with the three amigos breathing
down his neck. While he'd agreed to watch Hemmati
while they pursued their mission, whatever the hell it
was, he'd only agreed to keep *one* eye on the piece of
shit, and then not even all of the time. What that implied, however, was that he'd only be able to go seek his
own brand of retribution when the other three weren't
present. It also meant he'd have to find a way to stash
Hemmati during the times he was out.

Poppas thought he knew how to do that pretty easily.

Next consideration was where to start, but Poppas
quickly dismissed that as a barrier. He'd return to the
local watering hole where they'd caught up with Hemmati. There was no question he'd find the information he sought inside such a place; maybe he'd agree
to give whomever provided him with the information
he needed some sort of exclusive scoop on a top-secret

story—he could always finagle a deal and then renege on it at the last moment, either claiming the information didn't pan out or that it was ultimately a mission from which he might not return.

What the hell could anyone who agreed to play along actually do to him if he decided to hedge his bets and then back out? It's not as if he planned to come back from this place anyway. Chances were good before the night was through that he'd end up a star on the wall, too, assuming the cheap bastards back at Langley didn't actually discover the circumstances surrounding his death—that he'd broken cover and violated orders on a personal mission of honor to avenge the death of a colleague.

Whoa there, Poppas, he thought. Don't get ahead of yourself.

First things first, and that was to get that special package out to Jester's wife. For the moment, Hemmati was still under the care of the special operators out of Wonderland so this was probably his last chance to do what he needed to. Poppas went to the wall into the bedroom he'd shared with Abney. The young man's twin bed, made neat with the corners still tight, haunted Poppas and caused his vision to blur for a moment.

The CIA agent shook off the emotion and then proceeded to the wall safe secreted behind a pull-out panel in the closet.

Poppas withdrew the tightly wrapped bundle of brown butcher paper, its interior coated with waxed paper. The bundle encircled the equivalent of one hundred thousand dollars in untraceable British bearer bonds. Unlike many other bonds, which were alleged to be untraceable, this particular set had been specifically designed for CIA agents. They were used as an alternate source of currency whenever an agent had to come up with something of value quickly that was difficult if not impossible to trace. It was an unspoken rule among agents that if one died, his partner, or the one who'd been closest, was to send whatever he could to that individual's family. The government's insurance plan for CIA agents who died in the line of duty was hardly worth mentioning. Typically, it totaled one lump-sum payment of one-and-a-half times an agent's salary. The only thing the families got to keep long-term was the medical and dental insurance coverage, but that ended for the children when they reached twenty-two years of age, or upon marriage, or on graduation from an accredited post secondary institution.

Well, whoop-de-do and tra-la-la.

Poppas knew that America could and should have done better than that for its covert operatives, but similar pacts and even official organizations had to be set up for covert military operatives and SOGs because the benefits to families of those fallen were hardly adequate. Poppas was old school and he'd always believed that America should take care of its elderly, widows and orphans before worrying about schooling the children of illegal immigrants or giving jobs to their parents.

After Poppas collected the needed items, he left the apartment in a hurry and pressed toward his goal. First, he'd drop off the package to an outbound courier—only giving the address to the individual and making sure he committed it to memory—then he would go off in search of the information he needed. Maybe the security forces were responsible for Jester's death and maybe they weren't. Whoever had been responsible, Poppas planned to make sure they paid in kind and in full.

The Company man was so intent on his own vengeful thoughts, he failed to notice the tall figure who stepped from the shadows and, keeping a respectful distance, followed him down the sidewalk.

CHAPTER SIXTEEN

Asunción, Paraguay

When Phoenix Force reached the hotel they were using as base of operations, McCarter went to check in with Russell for an update while the remaining members of the team took Sweeney to one of the spare adjoining rooms.

McCarter had agreed with Calvin James's assessment that to use a truth serum or other chemical interrogation techniques on Sweeney would jeopardize the man's health. The last thing McCarter needed was a dead body on his hands to dispose of, even if that dead body was a scum-sucking hoodlum.

McCarter's attitude was more or less one of indifference toward types like Sweeney. He felt the mission came first as it always had, and there was no way such objectives should be compromised for guys who acted like animals to begin with. Sweeney's type had violated the rules for so long, operated with impunity above or below or just outside the society of the civilized that they deserved little more consideration than the animals they emulated. Despite his feelings, however, McCarter just didn't want the hassle of having a body to deal with in a very public place like the hotel. Only the fact it was a moonless, starless night and approaching 0100 hours had spared their team any discretion. It reminded McCarter this was the off season.

"How's our new guest enjoying his accommodations?" Russell asked when McCarter entered the room and dropped into what had become his favorite chair.

The fox-faced Briton smiled tightly. "He'll come around on his own soon enough. And if he doesn't, I'll bloody well kick his arse. What about you—you got word from our people?"

Russell nodded. "We've come up with a working theory."

"Did you just say 'we,' mate?" McCarter said.

"I did. And I'm not taking any liberties. Even your top guy has indicated he welcomes my contributions."

"Well, I've never known him to talk out of both sides of his mouth, so you can bank on the fact it's the bloody truth."

"I'll tell you like I've told him," Russell said. "I'm having the best time of my life."

"You keep that attitude and you might get a job on Bear's team one of these days," McCarter said. "I'll damn sure put in a spot of a good word for you."

"Thanks."

"So what's this working theory?"

"Well, we've identified the leader of the local group. At least, we think we have. Guy's name is Jahanshah Mokri and he's a member of the IRGC...or at least he *was.* There's a strong possibility he's fallen out of favor with his Iranian overlords, although that's more of a personal theory than what we came up with together."

"What makes you think so?"

"It seems Mokri was the one who recommended your new little guest for a job in Giménez's organization. Given the connection between this Mokri and

Sweeney, it's definitely enough that a relationship of some kind could be inferred."

With that, Russell began to explain the entire history of the Italian mob hit, as well as all of the subsequent intelligence, including Sweeney's separation from the Irish mob in New York on sour terms. "Loyalty's a big thing with guys like Sweeney," Russell concluded.

"Which would explain why he's not willing to roll over on Hezbollah now," McCarter said tiredly. "I wonder if it would stir Sweeney to know that it was actually Mokri who sent his own men to shut Giménez up for good."

"What makes you think that's what happened?"

"Simple. First of all, Giménez was the only one who was an actual link between Sweeney and Mokri. Second, it stands to reason that Mokri reached a point he felt he could no longer trust Giménez and yet he was sure he could put his faith in Sweeney."

"He may not feel that way if he finds out that the warehouse in Ciudad del Este's been compromised. He'll send someone to try to kill Sweeney."

"He already may have," McCarter said.

"Huh?"

"Someone's been on to us since we got here, Russell. Not to mention that we were followed to Giménez's place. You don't think the timing on the road from the airport, as well as the attack at Giménez's office suite, were just a little too convenient?"

"If that's the case, we could be under observation right now."

"I don't believe it," McCarter said. "I think we were plenty careful setting up our operations here. As far as anybody knows, we could be in any one of a hundred hotels. Not to mention we've been watching for tails any time we leave or return, and I've got Mr. Gray sweeping all three suites for bugs any time we come in or go out."

"Yeah, I've been using that little doodad of his after every meal is delivered and maid service comes in. I haven't observed anyone acting furtive or out of place. I think we're safe and clean here."

"We can go about our due diligence but we're not completely one hundred percent secure *anywhere,* chum. Don't bloody well forget that when you're on an operation or it could wind up your last."

"Point taken."

"Now," McCarter said, sitting forward, "I think we might just go have a little chat with Sweeney. Maybe it's time we let slip that the warehouse got compromised."

As McCarter rose, Russell said, "Yeah, but won't that put Mokri on the alert? Maybe cause him to send out a team to track Sweeney down and kill him? Or what if Sweeney escapes somehow and gets word to Mokri?"

"Why you just read my blooming mind," McCarter said with a grin. "That was exactly what I was just thinking."

"YOU GUYS CAN GO FUCK yourselves!" Glengarry Sweeney snarled. "I'm not going to tell you anything more."

"No reason you should have to, wise guy," McCarter said as he entered through the door of the adjoining suite. "I just got off the phone with some people who've told me a lot of interesting things about you. They wanted me to pass on a message to you."

"What message?" Sweeney said as he mopped his forehead.

"Apparently a termination order's been issued for

you by someone named Jahanshah Mokri." When Sweeney's hand froze in mid-mop, McCarter continued. "I see that name rings a bell."

Sweeney tried to shrug it off. "No. Why should it?"

"Don't try to bullshit us, pal," James said. "You know damn good and well who he's talking about."

The fact was that not even James knew who McCarter was talking about, but Sweeney didn't know that. He'd only drawn the conclusion by spotting Sweeney's reaction much as McCarter had; in fact, all of them had seen the Irish mobster stiffen at the mention of Mokri's name. Whatever game David McCarter had decided to run with, the rest of the team members had no intention of blowing it.

"Come on, Sweeney," Manning added for effect. "You know we've got you dead to rights. Might as well come out with the truth."

"Listen, mates, let's not put too much pressure on Sweeney," McCarter said, waving his hands at the rest of them as if attempting to quiet a crowd. "From what I understand and have heard of this Mokri bloke, we're looking at a dead man right now. Isn't that right, Sweeney?"

"I'd say it was right," Sweeney said, his mood clearly becoming agitated. "If I knew what the fuck you were talking about it."

"Let's not try to play the innocent," McCarter said. "Maybe we're gullible to fall for it but I can assure you that this Mokri character isn't. And word has also apparently gotten out that the warehouse has been compromised. Cops crawling all over that place right now."

"How did they find out?" Hawkins asked.

McCarter smiled and winked. "I think a little birdie told them. Least, that's what I hear."

"Hmm, tsk, tsk," James said, shaking his head. "You know, it's too bad you didn't want to deal with us, Sweeney. Now you have Mokri out looking for you. We've seen his handiwork firsthand, eh?"

Encizo nodded. "You're not kidding. Mokri's people cut Giménez and his entire security staff to ribbons within just a few seconds. We barely escaped with our own necks intact. I wouldn't want someone like him on my ass."

"I got no reason to worry about this Mokri you keep talking about," Sweeney said. "He doesn't know where you guys are at, and you're not going to let him near this place. You think I'm stupid?"

"Oh, we're not interested in him coming to find us," McCarter said, tightening the noose. "Mokri doesn't know who we are and he doesn't really care, I'm positive. The only one at this point he's going to be worried about is you. That's why he killed Giménez, because poor Lazario could connect you two. Now that the warehouse has been compromised, well…he's got no use for you. It looks like he'll have to get his technology somewhere else."

"True dat," Hawkins said. He looked at Sweeney. "But you can be damn sure that a thorough guy like Mokri will want to tie up all the loose ends, partner. Soon as we cut you loose, you'll have maybe what… twelve hours to ride out of Dodge?"

"If that," Manning added, shaking his head as if troubled by the unfairness of it all.

"You…you can't let me go," Sweeney said. "You got to take me back to the States. I got rights."

"Well, unfortunately there's no extradition treaty between Paraguay and the United States," Encizo said.

"I know my fucking rights. I'll waive extradition, right now!"

"Well," James began, "unfortunately, you're not wanted for any crimes in the United States. All of your criminal activities were actually here in Paraguay. So technically we have no jurisdiction to hold you."

"Besides," McCarter said, "we don't need a dead body on our hands to dispose of in the event Mokri does catch up with you while you're in our custody. Mr. Gold, why not go ahead and cut our friend here loose."

"No! You can't do this!" Sweeney was practically whining now, the tone in his voice pleading, begging the Phoenix Force warriors to change their minds. He looked hopefully at each of them but they simply turned away one by one as Encizo, aka Mr. Gold, stepped forward and used a Cold Steel Tanto fighting knife to cut off the plastic riot cuffs they had used to secure Sweeney's hands.

"There you go, friend," Encizo said. "Good luck out there. Hope you can swim."

"No, wait! I'll tell you whatever you want to know," Sweeney said. "I can help you. I know a lot of stuff. There's all sorts of junk going into America that I helped get into the country."

"Sorry, not interesting enough," McCarter said as the rest of his men vacated the room. "You'll have to do much better than that."

"Okay, okay! I know Jahanshah Mokri...I'll admit it. And I know what he's got planned."

"Too little too late," McCarter said, starting to follow Encizo through the door.

"I know where he's at!"

That stopped David McCarter in his tracks, although his pause was little more than a clever ploy. It was entirely possible that in truth Sweeney had no earthly clue where Mokri happened to be operating. After all, he was directing operations at the warehouse and responsible only for overseeing the shipments to Mokri's base of operations. The actual overlord of the entire plan had been Giménez and they had no evidence that Mokri had dealt directly with Sweeney beyond getting him placed with Lazario Giménez's operations.

Unless…

McCarter reentered the room and one by one the remaining members of Phoenix Force followed suit. McCarter sat on the arm of an easy chair positioned next to the sofa that Sweeney was stretching with his girth.

"You were in on it, weren't you?" McCarter said as he pinned Sweeney with a hard stare.

"What, in on what?"

"You were in on the hit," McCarter said. "You had the whole bloody thing planned from the beginning, didn't you?"

"I think you're right," James said, taking up position with McCarter and favoring Sweeney with an accusatory stare. "He didn't so much as bat an eyelash when we told him Giménez was dead. In fact, he started talking about how he'd warned him not to get involved with the Arabs. We hadn't made any mention of the Arabs or the Hezbollah before he started blathering about it."

"Yes, indeed, Sweeney," Hawkins said with a goofy grin and conspiratorial wink. "You sure stepped in the cattle shit this time."

"What my friend's trying to say is that we know all about your association with Jahanshah Mokri," McCarter said. "We now believe you conspired with him to kill Lazario Giménez so you could deliver the goods he needed and take over Giménez's empire at the same time. With the old man gone, you didn't figure there would be anyone to stand in your way. And you could keep Mokri and his IRGC goons satiated by providing them with whatever technology they needed."

"What was the price for betraying your own countrymen? Huh, Sweeney?" Manning said. He stepped forward and got in Sweeney's face. "What was the price of watching a bunch of innocent members of the U.S. Peace Corps get ravaged all in the name of profit? What would your former bosses back in the States say about your loyalties now?"

"Those pricks wouldn't understand what the fuck loyalty is, any more than you cocksuckers."

With that remark, McCarter reached out and cuffed Sweeney along the side of his head. "That's enough, smart ass. Now you're going to tell us exactly what the plan was and where you were planning to ship the goods. We want precise locations and we want to know exactly how the transfer was supposed to happen."

"It's no good now, you dumb pricks," Sweeney said, ducking reflexively at the possibility McCarter might slap his ears back some more. What the cowardly mobster didn't realize was that McCarter had struck him not out of anger or because of Sweeney's rebellion, but because he had insulted the honor of the Phoenix Force warriors by inferring they knew nothing of honor.

"We haven't told the cops anything yet," McCarter said. "We needed to keep those goings-on in that warehouse intact and not draw anyone's attention until we could get the information we needed from you. We've bought ourselves time and we've bought you your life."

"As long as you cooperate fully," James said. "And don't try any more sucker plays like you did back at the warehouse."

"So speak up, chum!" McCarter said, slapping his own thigh in unabashed glee. "We're all ears."

Paraguay River, 80 km northeast of Asunción

WITH LESS THAN TWELVE hours remaining until their shipment arrived, Jahanshah Mokri could feel the excitement grow in his heart like the stirring of his groin at the thought of the virgin girls back in his country.

He missed Iran so very much but he missed his status there more. According to his masters, President Ahmadinejad was extremely pleased with the progress being made in their training of the Hezbollah. As soon as they had the equipment delivered, they would be able to utilize it to make their intended strikes throughout America. That would be the end of the line for Mokri, since he wasn't going to have the pleasure of actually participating in any of the operations. His job was to train their allies in the Hezbollah and no more.

In some respects, Mokri found it really difficult to respect these trainees. Oh, they worked hard and trained hard; he didn't have any dispute with anyone on those points. Unfortunately, they were used to doing things like a band of cutthroats instead of a well-trained fighting force. Mokri had never really believed in the effectiveness of terrorists or guerrillas like the Hezbollah or the Islamic Jihad. To Mokri's thinking, it took more brains and courage to face the enemy directly in combat rather than to kill innocent people and then run away; Mokri knew it was the military code of conduct instilled in him.

Mokri's entire family had served Iran with distinction, going back all the way to the days of Imam Khomeini, when he first came to power in 1979. Mokri's family had managed to keep its status after they'd sided with Ali Khamenei, which had proved to be the right move when Khamenei somehow managed to garner enough support to override the opposition of a number of grand ayatollahs who opposed Ali Khamenei's appointment as supreme leader. In fact, Mokri had been on one of the teams subsequently ordered to place Grand Ayatollah Hossein-Ali Montazeri under arrest and close the Qom school he'd overseen due to Montazeri's refusal to recognize Khamenei's standing as a *marja*. Unfortunately, where Khamenei had failed was to keep a stronger leash on President Ahmadinejad, and now rumors of a possible revolution were beginning to stir within the country. Mokri knew it would be some time before he'd have to take any real action to protect his status but when he did, he wanted to ensure he backed the right play again. That was just one of the many reasons he'd decided to take this assignment, so that he could watch the events unfold in the relative safety outside his country before deciding his next move.

Politics! It always came down to political machinations even within a unit as elite as the Guard Corps. All Mokri had ever dreamed of being was a soldier; from the first time he could remember his father coming home from work wearing that resplendent uniform with ribbons and medals dangling from his chest. Mokri's father had always done well for the family, taken care of them to ensure they had enough to eat and suitable clothing to wear. Mokri had also noticed the deference paid to his family and the fact he got to sit in the choicest places at school.

Then at age seven his life had changed and his psyche was irrevocably damaged, or so he thought when he lost his father and mother during the Iran-Iraq war. Fortunately his father had made many friends and contacts and this had bought the orphaned Mokri a guaranteed place into the Pasdaran under the tutelage of the Grand Mullah Hooshmand Shahbazi. The encounter had changed his life forever and he'd studied with his new brothers in earnest, excelling in everything he did. Eventually he'd been accepted into the IRGC, where he'd served with honor ever since.

Now his present mission was to train their allies within the Hezbollah who, in return, had arranged for receipt of high-tech equipment destined to assist the government of Iran with completing its bid for nuclear power.

Mokri had received word that the stupid journalists and international news correspondents had focused completely on the capture of the Peace Corps volunteers. While Mokri hadn't yet ordered their termination—an insurance policy would not be a bad idea until such time as they received their needed technology—he would get around to that soon enough. He considered even taking a little of the pleasure himself by raping one or two of their women before he shot them in the head. Mokri would definitely enjoy that, although he thought about perhaps not defiling himself with the females.

His god would not be pleased if he was to do such a thing.

In any case, the hostages were a perfect ruse to divert the world's attention from the real goal. Like the crisis when pirates had taken the commercial freighter of merchant marines hostage a few years earlier, the Americans would exercise every negotiation tactic at their disposal to secure the release of their precious volunteers unharmed. In one respect, Mokri didn't really care about whether they died or were released to their country except that they now had observed too much of the operations there. That was the main reason he'd decided to raze their camp and take them hostage, sending the young American named Harland back to the country with a message regarding their ransom.

Thus far, the Americans had only sent a small contingency force of special operatives to attempt a rescue. The problem was that they'd been led on a wild-goose chase. Mokri's decision to terminate Lazario Giménez earlier than he had planned with Sweeney had been born from necessity to cut the Americans off his trail; they had gotten a little too close that time.

Frankly, it didn't make much difference now since they would receive their equipment in short order and be on their way. Mokri had considered eliminating Sweeney once they had what they needed, but he ultimately decided against it. They would need other things from Sweeney, and the fat American-Irishman could probably be useful in other ways as long as he thought there was a profit to be gained from it. Their relationship, as it was, had proved to be mutually beneficial and Mokri had learned to keep such relationships intact as long as they suited his needs.

Once they were safely out of Paraguay and the teams on their way to America, Mokri would arrange to close that loop. There could be no survivors, nothing that would later come back to stab or shoot Mokri in the back when he wasn't looking. He had enough assassination attempts to worry about in Iran without having to worry about them in this dung hole of a country.

Mokri willed himself to be calm, realizing that it was the humidity and the merciless mosquitoes that agitated him more than anything else. Somewhere nearby he could hear the steady hum of the buried generators, smell the first hints of cook fires as the mess crew prepared the breakfast meal. Occasionally he detected the footfalls of men during the guard switch. He checked his watch and realized he'd been up far too long; he would have to think about getting some rest but not until after their goods were delivered.

The flap to the entrance of his command tent, which doubled as a CP, flipped away to reveal one of Mokri's lieutenants. "I thought perhaps you would be asleep, sir, but when I saw the light on…"

"It's okay, Basram." The man looked a moment at Mokri, who nodded permission for Basram to enter.

Basram came inside and handed his commander a note. "It's an important message that just came through over email, sir. I thought you'd want to see it immediately."

Mokri nodded and as he opened the seal on the message, said, "Do we have any updates yet from our deliverers yet?"

"Not yet, sir," Basram said. "But I think you'd better read this message."

Mokri stopped disengaging the crude wax seal on the message and stared at Basram. "Is this bad news?"

"I would not presume—"

"Yes, you would, Basram," Mokri said. "I've never been one to expect anything less than complete candor from my men, and you know this. If it's bad news then you should tell me up front so that I can prepare myself appropriately."

Basram expressed sheepishness. "Sir, I…I was simply going to say…well…"

"Quit your damn stuttering and spit it out, man!"

Basram said quickly and evenly, "I'm not certain what it means, sir."

This piqued Mokri's interest and after one last, studious glance at his lieutenant he gave the message his full attention.

> Jahanshah,
> Our American business contacts entered the city some time yesterday. The situation is under control but I fear negotiations may break down. Please make the appropriate preparations to receive visitors at your end. We're running out of time on the contract. Don't worry, all is under control here.
> Your brother,
> Farzad

At first, Mokri didn't know how to react, but when he saw Basram standing there with such a foolish and anticipatory expression on his face Mokri began to laugh. He laughed long and hard, and his laughter boomed through the tent like the thunder of a storm. Basram appeared completely horror-struck at first but when he saw the true joy in his master's expression he also began to laugh, a chuckle at first—feeble attempt to see the humor in what had sounded like a somewhat desperate message—although he eventually began to laugh with much the same enthusiasm.

Mokri eventually had to suck down a few deep breaths of air and wipe his eyes for the tears that had welled up. "Oh, Basram, you're so gullible at times. All is well, just as the message said. Although it sounds as if our location may have been compromised. Tell our men to prepare for an assault."

"Y-yes, sir. Of course. Do we know when?"

"The Americans are predictable," Mokri replied. "Tell our men the strike will come at dawn."

CHAPTER SEVENTEEN

Tehran, Iran

Daylight had broken in the city by the time Poppas reached the courier.

It made him a little nervous as he entered the run-down business that acted as a front. The shopkeeper wasn't usually open this time of morning and yet he was actually open twenty-four hours a day. Nothing could physically enter or leave a territory, including human beings, except by arrangement of the courier.

And there was a damn good reason for this.

As Poppas had explained to Irons and his friends, it took the Company a very long time to get its people established inside a foreign nation—especially when the nation was hostile to Americans and the United States. Often agents had to be trained in the customs and roles of a country, even have their physical looks altered by a plastic surgeon on rare occasions to get "boots on the ground" of enemy soil.

During the Cold War years it had been somewhat easier to do this, because at the time they didn't have things like HSROP—high-resolution satellite observation platforms—or facial recognition software built into the supercomputers that monitored camera systems at airports and other transportation facilities. These days, it wasn't so easy to get inside a country and couriers were highly specialized in these areas. They were usually foreign assets and quite often citizens of the respective country, paid very well to bribe customs officials, military, police and anybody else with a vested interest in closely monitoring what came in or out of the country. Of course, when someone decided he or she didn't want to cooperate anymore, it was up to the agent inside the country to do whatever they had to do to make sure the security of courier operations could be maintained.

This typically meant termination.

It wasn't a problem most of the time since couriers didn't want to be discovered by officials within their governments any more than their connections. The system just worked and it worked well. The couriers were usually recruited and trained in pairs so that if one couldn't get something done they had a backup. The guy who usually took care of these things wasn't on this morning, which made Poppas more than a little nervous.

The shopkeeper opened the door to admit him and waved him to the back of the shop while he secured the door. Once they were out of view from the casual bystander passing the window—the back blocked by a dark, heavy curtain—the courier moved aside a large wall hanging to expose a heavy door. Beyond that was a stairwell that led to a subbasement with a low ceiling. Every modern technology adorned the cramped workspace. There were cameras, blank passports from a half-dozen Middle Eastern and European countries, and photography equipment, personal weapons small enough to conceal in a pocket, materials to make driver's licenses or other official local credentials.

The list went on.

Poppas didn't really know the courier on duty this morning, but he'd met him a couple of times before. The primary courier, an older man named Shambat, wasn't present. Poppas figured he could trust this courier to do whatever it was he needed, especially since his only intent in coming here was to get his little package sent to Jester's wife and to solicit some information about who at the watering hole might be able to point him in the right direction.

Poppas held no doubt the courier already knew Ron Abney was dead, and that the courier knew he was the sole agent left operating in Tehran. That meant he'd be aware of the unspoken debt and Poppas's responsibility to Abney's family, which implied he would likely know what was in the package and to whom it needed to go.

"I've been expecting you," the man said.

"I'm sure," Poppas said. "What's your name again?"

"I am Hadiq," he replied.

"That's right, I'd forgotten. Where's Shambat?"

"He is away from the city on another errand."

Poppas nodded, taking a clue from Hadiq that to ask any more questions would be a violation of the confidentiality between couriers. One thing that couriers never did was to discuss their business with the agents. It prevented there being any trouble if the agents or couriers were compromised. All payments and bribes were made through "droppers," and no personal exchanges ever took place other than in the safe location. If a courier locale like this was ever compromised, a failsafe was in place that would incinerate everything and leave little to no evidence of what had been in the place.

To the unpracticed eye, it would look like nothing more than an accidental fire, which generally satisfied any of the more curious law-enforcement officials.

Things only got more difficult if in the wake of a suspicious incident, members from the IRGC were dispatched to investigate. That's when the trouble started and was usually an indicator that it was time for the Company man to get out and get out quickly.

Hadiq noticed the small brown paper package under Poppas's arm. "I believe you'll want that sent home."

Poppas nodded, holding on to it a little bit longer before finally passing it to Hadiq; it felt almost as if he didn't surrender the package that he'd wake up from the nightmare that had been these past twenty-four hours and Abney would come traipsing through the door right then, telling him he was fine and all of this had just been a terrible misunderstanding. That feeling was almost surreal even as Poppas handed the package to Hadiq.

The courier must have sensed Poppas's reticence because he smiled and took the package very gently from the CIA agent's grip. "It is okay."

"I know," Poppas said, a hard lump in his throat as he rattled off the address. "You just make damn sure that thing gets where it's going."

"I will see that it does." Hadiq put the package in a metal lockbox and then folded his hands. "Is there anything else?"

"I need some information," Poppas said. "I need someone who can point me to those responsible for the loss of a good man."

"Revenge is a banal and unworthy goal for someone in your position," Hadiq replied.

"Maybe so, but mantras and lectures are not in your job description," Poppas said.

He reached to his pocket for a cigarette and fished one out with a shaky hand. He began to look for a lighter but before he could find his, Hadiq extended one with the flame ready. Poppas leaned in and let the man light his cigarette, but as he withdrew he noticed something odd beneath the sleeve of Hadiq's loose-fitted shirt tunic. It took Poppas a moment to recognize the symbol tattooed there but he recalled with vivid detail where he'd seen the symbol before. Farzad Hemmati had one just like it in the same location.

Poppas covered his surprise with a nod and a smile. "Thanks."

Hadiq nodded. "I suppose that it cannot do more harm than already done to tell you what I know of such a man who might have this information. I have already heard rumors that it was not members of the internal security police but agents of the Guard Corps."

That sure as hell would fit with what Poppas knew so far about the mission of Irons, Rose and Black. Hemmati had mentioned something about the IRGC and their ties to whatever was going down inside of Paraguay. Poppas had heard the information that came through about the hostages seized by Hezbollah, and he knew there was some relationship between that event and Farzad's claims about the IRGC operating in South America. But he didn't really know what the actual connection was about; he also didn't know what that could possibly have had to do with Jester's death, although he figured he was about to find out.

"Why would they want to off one of our people?"

"Besides the obvious reasons that you are here illegally and you pose a threat to national security?" Hadiq shook his head with a frown. "It is not so difficult to believe they would want to assassinate you both, my friend."

Poppas thought a moment about telling Hadiq that

he wasn't the man's friend but he bit his tongue. No point in alienating the guy who might be the only one who could provide substantive information that would lead him to those behind the death of Ronald Abney.

"Go on."

"There is a man at this address," Hadiq said, and he rattled it off twice for Poppas. "Go there and ask for the Hooshmand. He will tell you what you seek to know."

"Thanks," Poppas said. He turned to go and then stopped and pinned Hadiq with a hard stare. "I know this probably goes without saying, but make sure you get that package to where it needs to go. I don't want to find out later it didn't reach its destination."

"I will worry about doing my tasks just as you should worry only about doing yours."

Poppas couldn't be sure if that was a confirmation or rebuttal—hell, it was probably a combination—so he turned and left with the knowledge he'd made his point.

Once out on the street, Poppas checked both ways before turning and heading west up the sidewalk. The chants of prayers were already sounding in his ears but he didn't really care. Nobody was on the street, most of them either having entered the nearest mosque or doing their prayers from the rooftops or in the privacy of their homes. Within an hour, however, Poppas knew the streets would be packed with vehicles and foot traffic. This part of the neighborhood featured mostly local businesses, although some of the residents here actually worked in the city. A large amount of the downtown employment was government workers, and while most were allowed to own vehicles it was a luxury reserved only for those who could truly afford them.

Poppas considered what Hadiq had told him and what he would learn from this Hooshmand. It occurred to the CIA agent for a moment that he could be walking into a trap although he didn't really know why Hadiq wouldn't send him there. It didn't benefit the couriers to dispatch agents to their deaths, and would only complicate matters if they were to call that kind of attention to themselves. It would also put them on the Company's TOS list. The Terminate On Sight list operated according to an open and executive order of the CIA director. Any name that went on the list was fair game for a CIA case officer, irrespective of the case officer's base of operations. It took a lot to make the list but once on there was only one way off: confirmed death by whatever means necessary. When a case officer eliminated somebody on the TOS, it was affectionately dubbed a "cross-off" and typically earned the agent an unspoken commendation.

Naturally the commendation was not often awarded openly or even by notations within personnel files—even more often they would award it posthumously, making sure the officer got credit only after it would pose no threat to the officer or officer's family, and not compromise any ongoing case. The system was similar to the one used by Golda Meir when she'd ordered Mossad agents to kill the Black September terrorists responsible for the murder of eleven Israeli athletes at the 1972 Olympic games in Munich.

What Poppas failed to notice once more was the man who continued to shadow him.

Poppas had made a critical mistake, allowing himself to be lost in thoughts of discovering the perpetrators behind the death of his friend and seeking his retribution on those responsible. Hadiq had been more right than Poppas was apparently willing to give the

Iranian courier credit for: "Revenge is a banal and unworthy goal for someone in your position."

But Stephen "Pops" Poppas would let history be the
judge of that.

THE STREETS WERE GETTING crowded by the time Poppas reached the address Hadiq had given him, although
this meant little to Poppas since the address wound up
being in one of the worst parts of the city. These were
the slums, actually, poorly maintained dwellings that
could not even be called modest.

The address Hadiq provided was actually nonexis-
tent, but would have been where the alley was between
two legitimate numbers. The odors of urine and animal
feces, along with human garbage, threatened to overtake Poppas as he rapped on a solid wooden door at
the end of the alley. He stood there nearly a full minute and waited, checking the areas above him for any
observers. He didn't see any and it was so dark where
he stood that he doubted anybody could see him from
the street. He was about to knock again when the door
opened just enough that Poppas could see a young,
very well-dressed boy.

"Yes?" the boy said in cultured English.

"I'm—"

"You are expected," the little boy said, and he
stepped aside to admit Poppas.

The CIA man unconsciously felt for the weight of his
pistol nestled in the special hidden pocket of his shirt
before he entered. Again, he couldn't be sure what he
was walking into but there wasn't any reason not to
play this as smart and careful as possible.

His diligence came a moment too late.

Poppas felt the strong hands that grabbed his arms at

the elbows and even as he struggled, something sharp, like the sting of a bee, hit the back of his neck. Poppas resisted at first but before long something foggy and milky came over his vision and, for just a moment, he thought he smelled cracked peppercorn. Then his mouth went completely dry and the world around him went bright white, then gray and finally black.

POPPAS AWOKE TO THE SMELL of something burning.

As his vision cleared and the hazy images came into view, he experienced a sense of great thirst and he realized the odor was that of candle wax. It wasn't strong, the scent overcome by the more powerful odor of what could only be incense, but it lay just beneath the surface of his psyche and it had an almost calming effect. A period of time lapsed—Poppas couldn't be sure exactly how long a period—before his eyes snapped open and he found himself fully awake.

The place was decorated in the rich lush carpets and traditional wood antiques of a long-forgotten era. The Persian tastes were present everywhere, however, and it didn't take a genius to figure out that Poppas had been spirited into the innermost sanctums of the Muslim religious cult known as the Pasdaran. It made complete sense, given he'd learned about this location from Hadiq, who bore a similar tattoo to that of Farzad Hemmati. So the bastards were actually a whole sect with their own influence in every corner. Up until now, he'd been in Tehran thinking he was playing the Iranians for a fool and instead it was him and Jester who'd been played.

Poppas considered the events of the past few hours, and as he sat up he realized—much to his surprise—that his hosts hadn't restrained him in any way. In fact, the bed he'd been lying on was soft and comfortable, and built so low to the floor that it would take some effort for him to get to his feet quickly. That part was probably by design. Once his vision cleared, Poppas noticed two muscular men in loose-fitting pants and blousy tunics adorned with silk vests in a bright array of colors stood guard at the entrance with stoic postures and unreadable expressions.

"I don't suppose either of you guys speak English?" Poppas ventured.

"Both of them speak excellent English, Mr. Poppas," came a deep, calm voice from an area on his left.

The place had been shrouded with dark curtains and woods, an effect Poppas had no doubts was purposeful. The outline of the figure who spoke to him was barely visible in those shadows. There were some sort of oddly shaped objects surrounding the man and after letting his eyes adjust to the gloom another minute or so, Poppas realized they were plush pillows. Well, nobody could say that the Muslim clerics of the day didn't live in considerable luxury. Nobody had looked poorly fed, neither the boy who had answered the door nor the two gorillas posted at the entryway.

Poppas gingerly swung his legs around and self-consciously reached to where he'd felt the sting in his neck before blacking out. They'd obviously injected him with some kind of drug, but whatever it had been only a very tiny bump remained in its place.

"I must apologize for our rash actions but we cannot be too careful," the enigmatic figure said. "There will be no damage or lasting effects, I assure you."

"You'll understand if I don't take your word for it, grandpa," Poppas said.

Poppas didn't want his host getting the idea they

were pals or anything. It was important to keep a professional distance from anyone, friend or enemy, in the espionage world—particularly when stationed in a foreign country. That wasn't something they taught in academies safely ensconced within the United States, but rather something an agent could only learn by operating within the most dangerous and hostile territories in the world for a very long time. If a case officer started getting chummy with potential enemies, the relationship could be manipulated.

"I would think you'd be of a more gracious attitude," the old man said. "Especially considering that it is you who has come to me for information."

"I didn't come to you for information," Poppas said. "I came here at someone's recommendation and instead I got set up but good."

"Ah, yes, you're speaking of Hadiq," the man replied. "He's been working for us much longer than he's been a courier for your CIA. But then, I'm not supposed to really know that any more than I am not supposed to be privy to your real name. Unfortunately, there is no way for my brothers to be effective unless we know everything that goes on in our country. We know most of the real names and those of the families of foreign agents that operate here. Your friends like Mother should really learn to change their tactics. The old ways don't work anymore."

"I'll be sure to pass it on if I leave here alive."

"There's no reason you shouldn't leave here alive, Mr. Poppas," the man replied. "If I wanted to kill I could've ordered it at any time. Yet, you are still alive. I would think that might count for some consideration."

Poppas delivered a scornful laugh. "It doesn't count for shit. Listen, pal, if I'm still alive it's because you think it's more useful to you for me to be that way. When it's no longer convenient I'm sure you'll do me in. Just like you did my partner."

"Oh...you speak of Mr. Abney, although I believe you call him Jester. Is that what you've come to ask me about?"

"I guess that would depend on whether you're Hooshmand."

"I am." A match flared and in the flickering light Poppas got his first look at him. "My name is Hooshmand Shahbazi, Great Mullah of the Pasdaran and Defender of the True Faith."

"That's quite an impressive title," Poppas replied, sarcasm evident in his tone. "But you'll understand if I don't fall all over myself just being in your awesome presence."

"You're a considerably brave man," Shahbazi remarked as he lit an oil lamp. He blew out the match and continued. "It comes from your age and experience. The older agents in your CIA become, the less afraid they are. It's no different than the experiences through which we put our own men."

"You mean like Farzad Hemmati?"

Shahbazi smiled. "I see you've done your homework."

"You may know a whole bunch about me and the others who've been here before me, Shahbazi. That doesn't mean we're entirely stupid or incompetent."

"If you were incompetent, Mr. Poppas, I would have ordered your execution long ago." Something went hard and cold in Shahbazi's expression for a moment before the passive mask returned. "But as I've already intimated, there are plenty of uses for a man of your experience."

"If you think flattery's going to get you somewhere, you don't know me as well as you think."

"Flattery? Perhaps not, Mr. Poppas, but what about bribery? We could make you an extremely wealthy man and take you some place where you could enjoy that wealth for the remainder of your natural life."

"No, thanks," Poppas said. "I'm only here to find out who was responsible for the death of a fellow agent. You don't have that information, then I'll be on my way."

"You'll leave when I decide you can, and not a moment before."

"Fuck you, asshole."

Shahbazi and Poppas stared at each other a long time, and Poppas wasn't about to blink for however long it took. In one respect, Shahbazi had been utterly correct in his assessment that Poppas wasn't afraid.

Poppas had learned to fear nothing through the years. Every day for the past three decades he'd spent his life looking over his shoulder. Even when among his wife and kids during times where he wasn't on mission, his family hadn't asked him any questions or inquired of his furtiveness. They knew better and it wouldn't have done any good to press him anyway, since as a member of the CIA he wasn't permitted to discuss it. On one level he could've read Marcia into his life at any time—the CIA encouraged it. Out of respect to her sensibilities and the safety of his children, however, he'd chosen not to speak of anything he did. He almost wondered if Marcia didn't have more respect for that than she would've respected him being forthcoming about every grisly detail. No…she had too much class for that. Marcia respected the fact that her husband, whatever his faults might be and however

long his job took him away, had done some pretty terrible things for the sake of keeping his country secure.
That's what made him love and respect her the most:
she knew but she didn't pry.

"I would encourage you to forget this," Shahbazi
said. "If I tell you who is responsible for Mr. Abney's
death then I cannot use you and I cannot permit you
to leave. You will be a prisoner here for an indeterminate time."

"I'd escape."

"That also would be a regrettable circumstance,
since any such attempt would have to result in your
immediate extermination. I would think a man of your
will and intelligence might find more productive ways
to serve his country."

"How?" Poppas said with a snort. As he shifted to
get on his feet he heard movement behind him. He
turned to see that the two guards, while they hadn't
moved a muscle, were definitely more alert now in their
posture and expressions. "Relax, boys."

Poppas turned to face Shahbazi once more. "I'm
just talking with the boss here. No reason for anybody
to get nervous."

"We are not nervous, Mr. Poppas." A cold smile
played on Shahbazi's lips. "Of this, I can assure you."

"I guess I haven't been very clear up to this point,"
Poppas said, hoping for a reaction but getting none. He
continued. "If you're not going to tell me what I want
to know, then I guess there's no reason for us to carry
on this conversation. I—"

Poppas reached for his pistol and whipped it into
play in a blinding heartbeat of desperate frustration.

Shahbazi sighed. "Oh, Mr. Poppas, I'd hoped that it
would not come to such as this. You've disappointed

me, not to mention signed your own death warrant. I so wanted us to work together in a cooperative spirit but you've committed an unforgivable act of aggression. My distrust of you can never be reversed now. You pitiful fool."

"You're the only fool, Shahbazi," Poppas said. "You're a fool for thinking that I'd ever work with you or your band of religious fanatics. And you've given me your answer already. It was your people who were responsible for the death of Ronald Abney. A death I mean to avenge." The barely audible sound of a chime rolled through the room and Poppas wondered for a second if it was some sort of crazy music being piped into the room.

Shahbazi's eyes flicked to the two men. "See to that."

Poppas turned and watched as the pair disappeared through the beaded entryway. He'd averted his eyes only for a second but something in his senses told him it was a second too long. He turned back and his eyes widened with horror as he saw Shahbazi, a man who had appeared old and frail, suddenly charge him with a broadsword clutched in his hands.

Poppas squeezed the trigger on his pistol but nothing happened and just before he saw the flash of the blade he realized the clip wasn't present. They had disabled his weapon. Then he felt a burning sensation followed by excruciating pain as the sharp edge of the sword separated his gun and hand from the rest of his body at the wrist. Hot blood spurted from the gaping wound and Poppas managed to avoid a cross-slash meant to decapitate him as he rolled backward over the bed and came to his feet on the opposite side.

Clutching his amputated stump beneath his armpit

to staunch the flow of blood, Poppas waited for the next attack from the devil-eyed Shahbazi, who charged, broadsword held high and ready.

CHAPTER EIGHTEEN

The young boy had proved to be one of Hooshmand Shahbazi's most devoted and brightest students and he sent the signal chime as he'd been ordered to do whenever someone knocked on the door.

But he was still a naive little boy in some respects, and used to visitors of all ages and nationalities—the mullah was a popular and great man, after all. Such visits at all hours were not unusual, and so it didn't really make much difference to the boy that this muscular blond man with the cold blue eyes seemed a little different from the others who had come before. That is until he pushed his way through and shoved the young boy aside with firm but steady force.

What the youngster didn't realize was the man's brusque entry and subsequent treatment were designed to save the young boy's life.

That was a heartbeat before the blond man extended something in his hand, the glint of light revealing it was a pistol at the last moment, and shot the first of the mullah's two bodyguards in the face. The man's head exploded in a crimson-and-gray wash, splattering the eyes of the second bodyguard and disorienting him. Carl Lyons didn't wait for the second guard to recover, instead firing a snap kick that crushed the man's testicles against his pelvic bone. The guy was now completely disoriented, his eyes stinging from the gory remains of his comrade's brains and his groin burning with the trauma to his manhood. Lyons saw no reason to stand on the grounds of ceremony or fair play so he leveled his pistol once more and fired a round that went through the bodyguard's heart.

The Able Team warrior continued forward even before the bodyguard's corpse hit the luxurious carpet runner. He continued down the hall and entered through a doorway covered with tatters of cloth interwoven with beads. The sight wasn't exactly what he'd expected, but then again Lyons hadn't known what he'd stumble onto when he decided to follow Poppas that morning.

He was confronted by a thin, bearded man wielding an ancient sword, slashing and stabbing and shouting at the top of his lungs while he pursued Stephen Poppas through the sparse room. A few times the sword connected with objects that could've been nothing more than trinkets sold by a junk dealer in the streets of Tehran or priceless national artifacts. In either case, Lyons didn't really care. The wounded and bleeding Poppas was the more immediate concern as he tried to evade the crazy bearded assailant swinging a broadsword.

Lyons decided against just killing the wacky old man outright, so he holstered his pistol and made a charge that terminated with a flying body tackle. The pair went crashing into a nearby display of crude pottery that broke on impact and buried a few shards of dusty, jagged pottery into the flesh of both combatants.

Lyons recovered a bit more quickly and managed to knock the sword from the old man's hand. The cleric, despite his age, was lithe and agile and he wriggled from beneath Lyons's weight, springing to his feet with the dexterity of a gymnast. Lyons got to his feet, although not as quickly, and realized that if he underestimated his opponent he might well get his ass kicked.

"You need help?" Poppas asked through heavy breathing.

"No!" Lyons said. "Just make sure he doesn't get hold of that sword again."

"Check."

The cleric didn't wait for any further conversation, instead charging low as if he meant go for Lyons's midsection in a tackle. At the last moment, he spun into a sliding motion and extended his foot so that it connected with Lyons's knee. Only the warrior's years of training and reflexes saved his ligaments from being torn or having the kneecap completely dislocated. Lyons crouched and bent his knee, bringing it far enough off the ground that the cleric's foot instead glanced off his shin.

It hurt like hell but it didn't prove debilitating.

Lyons immediately responded with a merciless counteroffensive that originated with a haymaker against the side of the man's chin. Something cracked beneath the impact, probably the jawbone, and snapped the cleric fanatic's head to one side. Lyons took advantage of the stunning blow to launch a kick into the old man's ribs. A grunt of air whooshed from the cleric's mouth and he spoke something unintelligible. Lyons hauled the guy to his feet by the collar and hurled him into a nearby wall head-first. The cleric's head glanced off the edge of a heavy bureau just over his left eye, breaking the skin and splattering the immediate area with blood, and then he continued forward so that the crown of his head smashed into the wall and left an impression in the Sheetrock.

The man let out a groan and then crumpled to the burnished wood floor in a heap.

Lyons stepped back a bit unsteadily and fought to catch his breath. He turned to see Poppas holding the sword in his left hand while his right was clutched under his left armpit. Great droplets of sweat beaded on the CIA agent's forehead, and Lyons could see he'd been injured pretty seriously. Poppas looked a little disoriented as his eyes first met Lyons's and then he began to look around furiously, searching for something with wild abandon.

"What the hell are you looking for, Pops?" Lyons said.

"My hand," Poppas said, his voice cracking with the strain. "Please help me find my hand…"

"THAT'S THE CRAZIEST story I've ever heard," Herman Schwarz announced.

Rosario Blancanales clapped his friend on the shoulder. "That's because it's true, amigo, and we can all agree that truth is stranger than fiction. Will Poppas be all right?"

Lyons nodded. "I got him to a doctor the CIA uses from time to time. Probably not going to be able to put his hand back on since we couldn't get the thing on ice immediately, but at least they'll pump him full of antibiotics and prevent infection. The nerve damage alone will require special surgery, though, so we're going to have to get him out of here soon. The doctor wants to let him stabilize over the next twelve hours and then says we can haul his ass out of here."

"Do we have an extraction plan?"

"Won't be able to come up with that until I can reconnect with the Farm," Lyons said. "And we're on communications silence until midnight tonight."

Blancanales glanced at his watch. "That's still more than eight hours off."

"What about our new mission objectives?" Schwarz asked.

"There's no change in that," Lyons said. "We'll go forward with the intelligence from Hemmati and to hell with the consequences."

Blancanales shook his head. "I still don't know about trusting Hemmati. You sure his information is good?"

"If it's not, we'll soon know," Lyons said. "As near as I can tell, Hemmati and the courier Poppas used were both trained by this Shahbazi."

"You mean the Shahbazi who won't talk to us," Blancanales interjected.

"Doesn't really matter if he talks to us or not," Lyons said. "When I put him in the same room in that garage with Hemmati, it was obvious they knew each other. They acted as if they didn't but neither of them would get an Emmy for being convincing. They should really train these guys to be less conspicuous."

"Or at least send them to experienced artists for acting lessons," Schwarz joked.

Blancanales inclined his head toward the shop where Lyons originally followed Poppas. "You think the courier's in here?"

"I'm positive of it," Lyons replied. "It's the only other place Poppas stopped before he headed straight to the rat trap where I found Shahbazi holed up. Poppas didn't say anything about this place, but then he probably realized he didn't have to mention it. He knows we can put two and two together well enough."

"So what makes you think Hadiq can tell us anything about the location of these high-profile targets among Ahmadinejad's elite?"

"If Shahbazi's plan was to have Hemmati feed us this information in the hope of overthrowing the present Iranian government, then it stands to reason anybody in the organization would know who and where those targets are. Right?"

"Makes sense."

"So since Hemmati and Shahbazi are going to pretend like they don't know each other, and this courier doesn't have any idea we have both of his friends, the remaining Pasdaran cronies who are scattered throughout the city will think everything's going forward business as usual. And we should hold up our end of the deal by playing the dumb and naive Americans that we are."

"Or at least the dumb and naive Americans we should be," Schwarz said.

Lyons produced a mocking laugh. "You're so funny. Let's go."

The men emerged from the shadows of an abandoned shop and crossed the narrow, unkempt street with as much nonchalance as they could muster. They would've preferred to wait until nightfall but they were running out of time and Hadiq was the only one who could point them in the right direction. The Able Team warriors reached the shop unmolested and after a quick look around Lyons pushed through the door.

The shopkeeper was a short, dark-haired young man about Hemmati's age. He wore the traditional modest garb of the typical Iranian male, nothing that was tightly fitted or would imply carnal tastes. The government had always found it difficult to enforce the traditional dress code among some of its citizens, and with the growing pressure in the country to adopt more modern views—along with the increasing rights of women being touted throughout the global community—less conventional attire was gradually becoming tolerable.

The traditional dress and mannerisms of this man, however, were more in line with those of Farzad Hemmati and it was enough to make Lyons believe they were dealing with Hadiq.

"May I help you?" the man asked.

"Yeah," Lyons said.

The Able Team leader nodded at his friends while he turned and locked the door of the shop. He pulled the shades—the traditional way of letting the outsiders know the shop was closed for business—as Schwarz and Blancanales reached over the counter and pulled Hadiq off his feet. They dragged him over the counter, hustled him through the curtain and pushed him into the darkened back room.

Lyons followed a moment later. "Is your name Hadiq?"

The man's eyes were wide in terror but he remained resolute. Lyons waited only a moment before reaching out and tearing off the right sleeve of the man's tunic at the shoulder seam. Lyons grabbed the man's forearm in his hand and locked his elbow. He then inspected the inside of the man's wrist and saw the tattoo there, the one that was identical to those worn by Hemmati and Shahbazi.

"Yeah," Lyons said. "You're definitely Hadiq."

"Wh-what do you want?"

"A couple of things we want to know," Lyons said. "But let's start with why you sent a particular person this morning to see your master, Hooshmand Shahbazi? Exactly what was your intent?"

"I—I do not know what you are talking about!" Hadiq squealed.

Lyons shook his head and produced a wan smile. "Now you see, Hadiq, that's not really the kind of co-operation we seek. You're being very dishonest."

"Yes, you are," Schwarz said. "And we don't really appreciate that kind of deception."

"You see," Lyons continued, "we're not nearly as gullible as your people might want us to think. We know all about Farzad Hemmati and your mullah, and the intent of the Pasdaran to overthrow the current bureaucracy."

"And we're all good with that, see?" Blancanales said.

"But what we don't like is that one American is dead and another was seriously wounded this morning," Lyons said. "And according to our information, it's the Pasdaran who we currently believe to be responsible for those incidents, not to mention a good many of the others in which we've found ourselves."

"Not to mention it's the Pasdaran who has most likely put our friends in jeopardy." Schwarz added.

"So I guess what we've now come to is a little bit of impatience on our parts," Lyons said. "And we're going to have to ask you to forgive our impatience but we're finding this most inconvenient. We don't like people who try to kill us, or our friends in South America, or any of our fellow Americans."

"What do you want, American?" Hadiq demanded.

Lyons reached out and grabbed Hadiq by one of his ears and pulled him in close. He applied significant pressure to the man's earlobe, squeezing it between the knuckle of his index finger and flat, callused portion of his thumb. The pain produced a sharp outcry from

Hadiq but Lyons didn't flinch. He would just as easily shoot a hole through the man's head and the pistol he made visible clarified his intentions if Hadiq didn't cooperate.

"I want you to start telling us exactly how and when the Pasdaran planned to overthrow the current power seats among Ahmadinejad's associates," Lyons said. "And I also want to know exactly where we can find those of the Iranian government who we know are responsible for crimes against Americans if not all of humanity. And you know what's going to happen to you if we don't get that information?"

Lyons pressed the muzzle of the pistol under Hadiq's chin. "I'm going to hold this pistol right here while my friends tie you down. And then we're going to remove your fingers one at a time until you tell us the truth. So now it's time to decide, Hadiq. How would you like to do this?"

"And make it snappy," Blancanales said.

Schwarz added, "Yeah…we don't have all night, you know."

To nobody's surprise, the Muslim freedom fighter calling himself Hadiq wasn't really as fanatical and loyal as he would've liked to make others think.

As Lyons had so eloquently put it, "He sang like a canary."

Before long Able Team had returned to the garage with a list of names and locations provided by Hadiq. The first thing to do would be to run the list by Hemmati and verify it was legit. Then they'd touch base with Poppas to check on his condition, as well as devise a plan for getting around the city and doing what needed to be done without getting all of them killed in the process. They were pretty well equipped in the vehicles and armament department so there was no reason to worry about that. After they completed their strikes, the warriors planned to swing back around for Poppas and then head out of Iran as quickly as possible.

Hemmati seemed surprisingly friendly and cooperative, although Lyons knew they had no reason to trust the weasel.

Everything about Farzad Hemmati stank, but Lyons was especially surprised to find it was Blancanales who seemed most vociferous and outspoken when it came to that particular subject.

"I don't trust him, I don't trust him, I don't trust him."

Lyons folded his arms, exchanged glances with Schwarz and then studied Blancanales with a smirk. "What are you really trying to say, Pol?"

"I'm saying what I'm saying."

Schwarz sighed. "Well, I'm glad we cleared that up."

"Pol, we have a chance to take care of some really bad guys here," Lyons said. "Hemmati's vetted the list and I'm pretty sure Pops will concur with it."

"Even if they're telling us the gods' honest truth about it, Ironman," Blancanales said. "We're still taking a big risk here. Do we actually *know* beyond any shadow of a doubt that the Pasdaran taking charge of the government's going to be any better than Ahmadinejad's current reign?"

"We're not here to debate that issue," Lyons countered. "Besides the fact, Ahmadinejad has no real power here anyway. Everybody knows that the ayatollah's the real leader in Iran. Ahmadinejad's just Khamenei's little bitch so let's stop pretending that things could be worse under the rule of a religious group. Khamenei's just another Muslim nutcase anyway. Could it possibly get any worse? Maybe this will shake up the Iranian government enough to take their focus off the development of nuclear proliferation, or perhaps even incite rebellion in the country."

"Seriously, Pol," Schwarz said. "I'm actually with Ironman on this one. Do you think they could hate the U.S. any more than they already do?"

"I still don't like it," Blancanales said. "I mean, look what we're doing! We're putting our trust in a band of Muslim fanatics."

"No, we're putting our trust in the Farm," Lyons said. "Look at it like this, buddy. We've already run it by Barb and Hal, and even they think this is an opportunity we shouldn't pass up. And we stand a much better chance of surviving by staying on the move and eliminating the ones who would be hounding our every move if we just sat around and did nothing."

Something changed in Blancanales's expression, a something that softened the heretofore hard lines of his face. Lyons wouldn't have ordinarily worked so hard to sell either of his friends on a plan like this once he'd made his decision and they got their marching orders from Stony Man. But things were a little looser among the three warriors; these men had put their lives in the hands of the others time and again. Lyons needed to feel that everyone was on board one hundred percent, because he'd learned things just operated more efficiently that way.

Finally, Rosario Blancanales rendered a modest smile and let out a deep breath. "Well, I suppose you're right about that last part. But understand, I still don't trust a thing Hemmati says. I'd believe a skunk that stood up and announced he had his scent glands removed before I'd believe a slithering, manipulative snake like Farzad Hemmati."

"Agreed," Lyons said. "Now, let's pack up the VW and go visit Poppas."

THE ROOM WAS COOL AND DARK, the steady beep-beep of a cardiac monitor the only other sound in the room beside the hum of an air conditioner.

Poppas lay on a hard table made soft only by a thin layer of foam and fluid-resistant plastic beneath him. An intravenous line ran vital fluids and sugar water into his arm, accompanied by a bag of high-potency antibiotics. The bulky dressing on the stump where his right hand had been had already been changed twice, but that had been more from the fluids where the doctor had cauterized the wound.

The morphine drip attached to a second IV running through a vein in his lower leg contained just enough medications to make him comfortable but not so much that he would sleep. Losing an appendage was more than likely a horrible and traumatic event from a psychological perspective, one Carl Lyons could hardly imagine having to endure. Yet Poppas seemed to be doing okay with it—at least on the surface— maintaining a brave front like the tough and resolute old bird he was.

"How you doing, friend?" Blancanales asked with one of his disarming grins.

"I've seen better days," Poppas replied in a cracked, groggy voice.

"You feel up to helping out?" Lyons asked.

Poppas nodded.

"I'm going to list off some names for you, see if they ring any bells," Lyons said.

"There's only five so take your time and just tell me whatever you can gather comes to mind," Blancanales explained quiet and gently. "What we're primarily looking to do here is figure out if the names are legit and determine where we might find these scum. Okay?"

"Okay," Poppas replied.

As Lyons read off each name Poppas did his best to put together as many details as he could under his shoddy, drug-addled memory. As it turned out, all five of the names were legitimate targets and undoubtedly from their lengthy list of terror crimes, the elimination of these individuals by Able Team would be a telling blow against the power base in Iran.

"Three of them…" Poppas began to drift.

"Come on, Pops," Schwarz said, snapping his fingers. "Stay with us a little longer. What about three of them?"

Poppas came back around long enough to say, "Three of them will be together. Hit that location first."

Then he went out like a light. As they filed out of the room, the doctor squeezed past them and went about checking vitals. Lyons turned as he went through the doorway and called the doctor. "You take care of this guy, Doc. You hear me? He's put a lot on the line for his friends and his country. He deserves your best."

The Iranian-American doctor nodded. "He'll get my very best, sir. As do all of my patients. I may be Iranian but I'm also an American. I consider it a duty to conserve all life. And while I know what it is you're probably going to do now, and I don't agree with it, that doesn't change what I must do now and that is to save this man's life. It doesn't matter who he is or what he's done. Understand?"

Lyons nodded. "Yeah. I get it. When he wakes up, tell him we'll be back for him."

Once they were back in the VW parked in a dark, disused portion of the city, Schwarz said, "This microbus of ours makes me miss the van all the more. You know?"

None of them could argue with Schwarz's sentiments. They had every modern convenience in the highly customized van Stony Man provided them. The van had a full armory, advanced communications and surveillance and countersurveillance equipment, not to mention—and this was the feature Schwarz always bragged most about—comfortable bucket leather seats. But despite not having such a modern convenience, there was still something almost nostalgic about the three urban commandos decked out in a nondescript VW, cruising the mean streets of a hostile city in search of the worse criminals society had to offer.

"Maybe. But have we ever had so much fun?" Lyons remarked.

"I can think of some other times," Blancanales replied, rubbing his tired eyes.

"Don't be a party pooper," Schwarz said. "You're ruining the jolly mood for the rest of us."

"Sorry. I'll try to be funner about this."

"Funner?" Lyons said. "I'm surprised at you, Politician. That's not even a real word."

"I'm sure it's a real word somewhere," Schwarz said.

"Let's just focus on our list."

"Yes, the list," Lyons said. "So we have an approximate location on our first target."

"Great. You got a plan?" Blancanales asked.

"No. Not really." As he pulled away from the house where they had stashed Poppas, Lyons said, "I was thinking we'd just go there and do a recon, maybe figure out the best way to approach it once we knew what we were dealing with."

"Sounds like as good an idea as any," Schwarz said.

"I suppose the two of you have considered that if there are that many important people crammed into one location, the place will be guarded well. Probably have top security measures in place, electronics and infrared sensors, cameras and so forth."

"You sound a bit pessimistic, Pol," Schwarz said.

"Not being pessimistic, just cautious."

"The fact is we don't have either the equipment or the resources to go up against this thing in any sort of tactical fashion," Lyons said. "That means we're going to have to improvise, come up with a plan of action and then just nut up and do it."

"Agreed. A soft probe will be out of the question."

"So we do this hard-charging-like," Schwarz said. "That's your big plan?"

"I don't see that we have much choice, Gadgets," Lyons countered. "We have a limited amount of time and a big job to do. It's going to have to be a get in, get out thing."

"That's the deal?"

Lyons nodded. "That's the deal."

"Okay, then," Blancanales said. "That works for me."

Schwarz grinned from the back of the microbus. "That's the spirit."

CHAPTER NINETEEN

Paraguay River

"Dawn," David McCarter had said. "We make our move at dawn."

"You sure?" Manning had asked him.

McCarter looked at his friend as they sat in a thicket of dense, gnarled trees less than a quarter-klick from the IRGC-Hezbollah camp. "Something on your mind, Gary?"

"Yeah, as a matter of fact. I think Jahanshah Mokri will be there directing his men. In fact, I'd venture to guess that if he's expecting an attack he'll definitely figure it's going to come at dawn."

"Then what would you have us do?" McCarter said. "We hit the guy now and we'll be completely at a disadvantage. We don't know the lay of the camp and we sure as bloody hell don't have enough night-vision equipment to go around."

"I say we wait."

"For how long?"

"Until late morning."

"That sounds a little bit on the crazy side, Gary," Hawkins cut in. "What's your reasoning?"

"First, we're all exhausted and could use a bit of shut-eye. Second, we've been pushing this thing in the hope of getting to the hostages before Mokri kills them."

"All right, go on," McCarter said. "You've got my interest."

"Let's suppose that grabbing these Peace Corps volunteers for ransom or something else actually holds water," Manning continued. "There's no guarantee the IRGC or Hezbollah will actually turn over the hostages even if they get what they're asking for. Not to mention the U.S. has a non-negotiation policy when it comes to terrorist organizations. We don't deal. Ever."

"That's true," James replied. "That's why they keep dinosaurs like us around."

"Not to mention," Manning elaborated, "that if Mokri has some other goal in mind for grabbing the hostages, he's either already killed them or he'll keep them alive long enough to be a contingency until he actually gets what he wants. I think what he wants is that shipment, and once he has it he'll kill the hostages. In any case, we have nothing to lose waiting a little longer to implement our assault."

"And in broad daylight, it'll be like shooting fish in a barrel," Encizo pointed out.

"Yeah," McCarter said. "For them, too."

"Not necessarily," Encizo replied. "If you think about it, Gary's on to something. They think we'll do the most predictable thing and hit them at dawn. That's when I'd expect an attack from a trained American special ops unit. If we wait, they'll have been up all night, doubled the guard in expectation of an attack. They'll be tired and ill-prepared, and they won't have either the cover or concealment of the jungle. We can come in on the perimeter and hit them fast."

"We'll also be able to get a clear line of sight on

which area they're keeping the hostages in," McCarter said with a nod of agreement. "That'll bloody well enable us to minimize exposing them to live fire. That's a fine piece of thinking, Gary."

Manning turned in the seat of the SUV that had been provided by the embassy. "All right, it's going on 0500 hours now. Sun will be up in the next thirty mikes or so. Everybody grab some sleep. Manning's got first watch."

"Me?"

McCarter grinned as he leaned his head back in the seat and shut his eyes. "Positive. After all, it was your idea."

"Marvelous," Manning muttered.

ALMOST SEVEN HOURS LATER as the sun crawled to high noon, the Phoenix Force warriors closed in on the jungle perimeter surrounding the IRGC-Hezbollah training camp. The call of a dozen jungle birds masked their approach, although the warriors had made this kind of a trek more times than any of them cared to count. They were cautious and with very good reason—to assume this plan was foolproof in outwitting their enemies was exactly the type of misguided thinking that could get even the best teams wasted.

It had happened too many times before, special operations teams that were too cocky and got tricked by an enemy more savvy than originally predicted. The situation in places like Mogadishu during the early nineties was one grisly reminder, not to mention countless others. Every covert operation had experienced its share of pros and cons—even the one carried out against Osama bin Laden hadn't been without problems, although the participants had never chosen to be forthcoming about exactly what the foibles were. Talk outside the group was tantamount to suicide, and it would be a very long time before such operations could come under full public scrutiny.

Maybe ten or even twenty years from now they'll talk about what we did this day, McCarter thought.

To the surprise of the Phoenix Force team, the entire camp was abuzz with activity. It appeared on the surface anyway that Manning had guessed correctly. With the dawn now long past, the Hezbollah troops— marked by their plain olive-drab fatigues—stood out in contrast to the jungle camouflage and black berets worn by their IRGC trainers. The uniforms may have varied but there was one thing abundantly clear: all of these individuals could be counted as enemies and Phoenix Force would give them no corner.

James and Hawkins, who had been sent on a scouting mission, returned within a few minutes.

Hawkins rapped on McCarter's shoulder and then pointed to his eyes before gesturing toward a squat, low structure on the southwest corner of the camp. Several men stood near the building with weapons held a bit casually and somewhat bored expressions. Hawkins then held up five fingers, then one finger and finally a thumb followed by two more fingers. That meant eight hostages in total, two with significant injuries.

McCarter nodded and then turned and signaled the rest of the group to form on him. He nodded at James, who quickly pulled out a map of the camp's general layout, marking each point where there were Hezbollah or IRGC personnel. He then marked the location of the hostages with an H. McCarter nodded after looking it over, then pointed to the H before gesturing to Manning and Encizo. The plan was clear. They would hit the guards overseeing the hostages first, and then break them out and aid their escape while the remaining members provided a covering solution using interlocking fields of fire. Once the hostages were clear, the other two would join the rest of the team and Phoenix Force would complete its business with the terrorists.

There was only one option and they all knew it: total destruction.

PHOENIX FORCE OPENED the ceremonies by launching a pair of 40 mm HE explosive grenades from an M-203 in the capable hands of Thomas Jackson Hawkins.

The former Delta Force officer flipped the leaf sight into acquisition, sighted in at seventy-five meters and let fly with the first grenade. He didn't wait for it to impact, clearing the smoking shell from the breech of the M-203 mounted to the underside of his M-16 A-4. The second grenade he put in proximal distance to the first, and while it didn't really do much in the way of destroying personnel, it had the desired effect of rendering shock and confusion among the terrorists.

As soon as the first grenade went, Manning and Encizo got to work and breached the cyclone fence with the help of a block of C-4 plastique tossed into the center with a trail of detonator cord. Manning flipped the switch on the remote and sent the obstacle, as well as a terrorist sentry, flying through the air with the greatest of ease. The pair swooped into the perimeter through the smoking gap left in the wake of the ordnance and cut the remaining three guards down with sustained bursts from the M-16 A-4s.

A merciless hail of 5.56 x 45 mm rounds shredded the belly of one terrorist sentry. The man's weapon clattered to the soft, damp earth as he abandoned it to clutch at the protruding guts left in their wake. A stray round from Encizo's rifle blew the top of his skull off and put him out of his misery forever. Manning got the other two with strafing blasts, the rounds taking out bone and flesh without prejudice. The terrorists screamed and groaned under the vicious onslaught but Manning ignored their cries. The carnage fell on deaf ears, just as the cries of the innocent hostages had probably fallen on their ears while they'd raped and pillaged and brutalized their captives.

"U.S. Special Forces!" Manning yelled. "Stand away from the door!"

Encizo retrieved his Glock 21 and, standing at an angle he knew to be appropriate for the circumstance, fired a single shot to breach the lock on the door. The men entered the structure and again identified themselves. One of the women jumped to her feet and threw an arm around Encizo's neck in an embrace so tight it nearly choked off his oxygen supply.

"It's okay," Encizo whispered, trying not to be annoyed. "You're going to be okay. Now let go of me and help your friends get out of here."

The girl began to sob but had enough presence of mind to release him and turn to help the others. With the assistance of the six able-bodied members, covered by the Phoenix Force warriors, all eight hostages moved out of what had been a prison of terror and degradation, and moved into the relative safety of the jungle. One terrorist who spotted them escaping made the fatal mistake of trying to stop them. Manning and Encizo saw him at the same time, leveled their assault rifles and triggered simultaneous bursts. A half-dozen rounds ripped through the terrorist's belly and chest, lifted him off his feet and dumped him onto his back with a sickening splat.

Manning and Encizo were already moving away with the hostages before the terrorist's corpse actually hit the ground.

McCARTER HAD INSTRUCTED Hawkins to give James and him five minutes to reach their support positions before launching the assault.

Hawkins had come through in spades.

The Phoenix Force team leader and his able-bodied teammate were settled into position and had their first respective targets in sight before the explosion from the initial 40 mm HE grenade.

James pulled the stock of the M-16 A-4 tight to his shoulder before triggering his first round burst. He barely felt the recoil as both 5.56 mm NATO slugs took the surprised terrorist in the small of the back and slammed him face-first into a warm, steaming mud puddle.

McCarter's target met a similar fate. The Briton's first round glanced the man's shoulder while the second entered a point just beneath the right jaw. The bullet tore out most of the terrorist's throat and spun him into the tightly drawn canvas of the tent alongside of which he'd been standing. A dark smear of blood was left in his wake as the terrorist's lifeless body slumped to the earth.

James was already sighting on another terrorist just as through the sights of his own weapon McCarter saw a striking figure emerge from the tent. The man wore the camouflage of the IRGC but his head was covered by a blocked utility cap with gold wreaths. McCarter knew he was looking at the IRGC terrorist leader and, in that moment, chances were better than good the Phoenix Force leader had none other than Jahanshah Mokri in his sights.

The man stood brazenly in the open and barked orders at the panicked troops, snapping and pointing, his neck veins bulging as he screamed at the frantic Hezbollah troops to get organized. McCarter pulled the stock against his shoulder and resettled his sights, taking a deep breath and willing his body to remain calm. He couldn't risk blowing this opportunity, not when he had the potential mastermind of this sickening nightmare in his sights. McCarter counted down from five, just as he'd been taught while working for Her Majesty's Special Air Service, and then pressed the fat-pad of his index finger firmly against the trigger.

"Steady as she goes, bloke," he coached himself.

McCarter squeezed the trigger with steady, even pressure.

The pair of high-velocity slugs left his assault rifle at a muzzle velocity of 948 meters per second. McCarter involuntarily bit his lip as he steadied the weapon for a follow-up if required. It wasn't. The rounds struck home, the first entering the right chest at an angle that exited out the left shoulder. The impact twisted the IRGC combatant in such a fashion that the second round left a dime-size hole just left of the breastbone, clearly a kill shot in the heart that was obvious even from McCarter's vantage point. The man's body went stiff, completely erect, as his arms shot up in a mixture of pain and surprise. Then he toppled to ground and rolled a short distance before going still.

"From America with love, you murderous bastard," McCarter muttered.

James was being too productive to notice that his

friend and leader had just terminated a VIP. The former Navy SEAL dropped his third target with a well-placed round to the skull. The terrorist, this one a Hezbollah, staggered to and fro with the better part of his head missing. The tearing effect of the 5.56 mm tumbler had ripped away a significant portion of the man's jaw, taking the back of his skull with it and leaving much of that side of his face and jaw exposed. The ghastly sight brought just a tinge of satisfaction to James as he watched the terrorist drop to the ground.

The immediate terrorists eliminated from sight, James and McCarter got to their feet and broke cover to rush the compound. As they moved, watchful for new threats to appear, McCarter keyed his microphone. "Orion Rescue, where away?"

"Clear and secure," came Encizo's immediate reply.

"Good job! Join up as planned and let's do this thing."

"Roger."

T. J. HAWKINS HAD NEVER been one to run from a fight, even from his earliest days as a young boy.

Raised in the heart of the Lone Star State to be fiercely patriotic, the former Delta Force veteran had always loved his country. The ideals of mom, baseball and apple pie were no stronger in a person than Hawkins, and he considered it an honor to fight beside the greatest band of warriors ever assembled.

Hawkins pressed his cheek to the stock of his assault rifle, bracing his forearm against the gnarled trunk of the massive jungle tree, and squeezed off one controlled burst after another. Hawkins's first shots flipped one Hezbollah terrorist onto his back, the rounds turning the man's chest to a mass of goo. A second terrorist, one

of the IRGC members, tried for a flanking position—
the rounds from the man's machine pistol burned the
air near Hawkins so closely he could feel the heat in
their wake. Hawkins flipped the selector to single-shot
mode and dropped the man with a double-tap to the gut.

Hawkins left cover and entered the perimeter of the
camp, holding tight and low as he squeezed off a sustained burst at an octet of terrorists bunched one upon
the other. He made the charge when he heard Encizo's
confirmation to McCarter that they had rescued the
hostages and cleared them from the fire zone. The plan
had been for them to make their assault simultaneously
once they got the signal, and Hawkins wasn't going to
let the cloistered terrorists intimidate him. In fact, these
Hezbollah were demonstrating their lack of understanding when it came to effective combat techniques.

Obviously, they hadn't learned a goll-dern thing
from their IRGC masters.

Hawkins's sustained fire cut a swath of destruction
through the hapless terrorists, tearing out flesh and
bone in a splashing pattern of blood that dispersed in
every direction imaginable. Hawkins realized even as
he swept his muzzle across them for a third time that
James and McCarter were on the move and lending
support. The crisscross patterns of autofire wreaked
havoc on the terrorists, leaving them with no quarter
as round after round hammered their position.

As the Phoenix Force offensive fire died out, the terrorists toppled one over each other in a wet and gory
heap of blood and shredded flesh.

GARY MANNING AND Rafael Encizo hit the perimeter
with guns blazing. Manning had opted for an M-16 A-4

while Encizo tackled his half of the project with an MP-5 in each fist.

After leaving the hostages in a well-concealed and sufficiently distant location, arming two of the men in the group with their pistols, the Phoenix Force duo advanced on the camp to help their comrades deliver the final message.

Encizo spotted two terrorists who broke conceal-ment of a building and tried to outflank him on the left. The Cuban dropped and rolled as rounds from the terrorists' SMGs burned the air where he'd stood a heartbeat earlier. Encizo landed prone and leveled the MP-5s before squeezing both triggers. Twin muzzle-flashes cast an additional measure of ferocity to En-cizo's war face, the MP-5s chattering a 9 mm symphony of destruction. One terrorist caught a burst in the chest that rode to his throat and opened it wide. Pink, frothy sputum erupted from the gaping wound as he tumbled onto his belly.

The second terrorist caught a burst in the pelvis that spun him in a direction facing the perimeter. Even though he was already dead from the remaining rounds that slammed into his side, Manning made sure it was finished by triggering a tri-burst at nearly point-blank range. That impact lifted the terrorist off his feet with such force that Manning had already moved past him by the time the terrorist's body hit the ground.

Manning pressed the attack by taking a knee, an-gling his M-16 A-4 at approximately thirty degrees and triggering a preloaded 40 mm shell from the other M-203 Stony Man had arranged for the team. The weapon may only have had the kick of a 12-gauge shotgun but it felt much worse for the recipients of the rocket-propelled bomb. The HE yield had a maximum effective range of forty meters and it did the job nicely. The shock wave blew some of the terrorists away in parts, while others were lifted off their feet.

Hawkins broke from position at a forty-five-degree angle and delivered a second 40 mm at one of the larger tents. The thing went up as if it had rocket fuel inside of it, surprising the terrorists, as well as the Phoenix Force team members. Hawkins was a bit too close to the blast and the sudden wave of heat knocked him off his feet. He rolled with it, coming to one knee but unbalanced and continued a backward roll. The impetus was enough to send him skidding down a slight decline but he landed without injury at the bottom of the hill near the edge of the jungle.

James saw the results of the blast and noticed Hawkins's subsequent disappearance from line of sight. The team medic immediately keyed his communications set. "Orion Three to Four. You okay?"

For a moment James felt his heart skip a beat as he waited for the reply. A seemingly long moment passed before he heard Hawkins's scratchy reply. "I'm a little cooked but in one piece, buddy."

"You need aid?"

"Negatory! Hold position...I'm all right."

James wasn't convinced but he knew it wasn't time to second-guess his friend.

If Hawkins wasn't all right, he wouldn't have compromised the entire mission for his sake, but neither would he have let James risk getting killed to bring aid for an injury that wasn't life-threatening. James knew good and well if Hawkins wasn't unconscious and didn't have one or more bone fragments protruding through his skin, he would be okay even if an injury took him out of the fight. There was no point in getting himself or other teammates killed for a modest reduction in manpower.

James edged closer to Hawkins's position, however, even as he took down two more terrorists still trying to shake off the effects of Hawkins's handiwork. The badass from Chicago's mean streets made his intentions quite clear as the terrorists tried to respond but didn't quite get there. The first caught a bullet in the chin, the close-in velocity splitting his lower face wide open before it continued through his skull and transected his spine at the neck. The other one took two rounds through the heart, never fully making it to his feet.

With the immediate danger abated to that area, James went off in search of T. J. Hawkins.

DAVID MCCARTER COULDN'T be entirely sure when he'd lost track of Calvin James but somehow it had happened—Hawkins's blast into one of the terrorist tents being the most plausible explanation.

The Phoenix Force leader didn't let it worry him. James could handle himself just fine and even as he heard the exchange between James and Hawkins he knew the guy would do whatever he could to neutralize targets and get to a potentially fallen man. McCarter figured the best way to help his teammates would be to press on with the attack, squeezing their enemies between himself and his comrades.

The terrorist numbers were dwindling fast, and only a few pockets of resistance seemed active. The tent blast had taken down a good many of them and McCarter had little doubt that Phoenix Force had seized the advantage. To let up now could mean handing that advantage back to the enemy and he wasn't about to see that happen. They had come too far and too fast not to press their attack.

McCarter caught two IRGC terrorists completely unaware, nearly stepping on them as he burst through some brush with the intent of using it as a sniping position. The terrorists were actually positioned behind a Yugoslavian-made M-84 general purpose machine gun. The weapon had been hammering out a defensive firing pattern for the past few minutes or so, but McCarter hadn't been able to determine its exact location to that point.

The pair of gunners turned in surprise and McCarter cursed himself for not being prepared. At that distance he couldn't take them both with the M-16 A-4. McCarter managed to shoot the first one through the chest and followed that with a swift kick to the face of the second terrorist. The guy's head snapped to one side and McCarter swung the stock around in a butt-stroke that split the side of the man's face open. McCarter reached for the 9 mm Browning Hi-Power in his holster and fired two rounds before the terrorist could recover. The man slumped backward as a long hiss of death issued from deep in his gut.

McCarter heard the brush behind him rustle but didn't turn in time. A forearm snaked around his neck and yanked backward. The enemy who had surprised him was apparently very big and freakishly strong to have managed to get the drop on someone like McCarter. Fortunately, he wasn't all that experienced and McCarter managed to twist the pistol still in his hand such that the muzzle connected with the man's thigh.

McCarter squeezed the trigger and the hold on his neck abated as the terrorist screamed in agony but the closeness of the shot combined with the slick back-wash of blood jarred the weapon from McCarter's grip.

The Briton spun and delivered a low-heel kick at his opponent's knee. The terrorist dropped to the dirt but before McCarter could do more, Rafael Encizo seemed to appear from nowhere and plunged his Cold Steel Tanto fighting knife into the terrorist's chest, burying the weapon to the hilt. The guy's legs twitched for a moment or two, his torso pinned by Encizo's weight, before going still.

As the ringing of his ears from the brutal reports of weapons fire began to abate, McCarter realized there weren't any more sounds of shooting and that a strange and eerie silence had fallen on the jungle. He listened for the signs of further resistance but didn't hear any. Finally, he looked at Encizo, who was getting to his feet and wiping the Tanto blade against the dead man's shirt before sheathing it.

"Thanks, mate," McCarter said as he located his pistol and grabbed the towel from his neck to wipe the blood from it. "Don't know exactly what bloody happened there."

Encizo grinned and slapped one strong hand on his friend's shoulder. "Even the best of us, David."

"Yeah," McCarter replied wistfully.

The two comrades went off in search of their remaining teammates, first finding Manning and then eventually making their way to where James attended Hawkins. The Texan had his back to a tree but didn't appear any worse for the wear. James was wrapping a bandage around Hawkins's left wrist.

"What happened, bloke?" McCarter inquired. "You get clipped?"

"Nah," Hawkins said.

"Slight sprain, I think," James recited. "Probably happened during his little tumble."

"Yeah, next time you decide to put a grenade up the terrorists' collective arses that close, make sure you don't follow up with the gymnastics routine," McCarter advised.

"Well, thank you, pardner," Hawkins replied. "That's a good tip."

McCarter turned to Manning. "That was a very good call you made, Gary. I owe you a beer."

Manning smiled sheepishly. "Shucks, don't go all soft on me now. But yeah, you owe me a beer."

"Hell, we *all* owe you a beer," Encizo added.

"If you insist," Gary Manning replied.

"All right, mates," McCarter said. "Let's get Hawk on his feet and go retrieve the hostages. We need to get back to the Farm with a report as soon as possible."

As if on cue, McCarter's satellite phone vibrated. "Go, Hal."

"Sitrep," Brognola replied.

"Targets are neutralized and the hostages are safe."

"Nice work, but I'm afraid there's no rest for the wicked. Barb?"

Price's voice came on then. "David, we need Phoenix Force to get the hostages back to Asunción as soon as possible and then get airborne."

"Airborne for where?"

"Tehran," Price replied. "Able Team's in trouble."

CHAPTER TWENTY

Tehran, Iran

If he'd been forced to do it over again, Carl Lyons would've made a different decision. Unfortunately, there weren't many do-overs in Able Team's line of work, and there wasn't any point second-guessing the options.

The compound where three of Iran's most influential terror leaders and power brokers made their home turned out to be a veritable fortress. The place had all of the electronic security measures Blancanales had cited earlier in their discussion, as well as a force of patrols armed with SMGs and attack dogs. Moreover, a roving vehicle patrol of Tehran police officers circled the massive estate every fifteen minutes. The body armor and machine pistols they carried were evident through the detached night-vision scope Lyons had pressed to his eye.

The Able Team leader lowered the scope and passed it to Schwarz. "It looks a wee bit tight."

"You think?" Blancanales replied.

"I don't know, Ironman," Schwarz said. "Are we really sure this is worth all the trouble we're about to make for ourselves?"

"I don't know, Gadgets," Lyons said. "Let's consider for a moment that we've confirmed three of the men inside that house are responsible for the deaths of hundreds of American civilian and military personnel around the globe. Let's also consider that they've oppressed a crazy bunch of religious radicals like the Pasdaran into committing widespread mayhem against allies and enemies alike in this city, all in the name of hating America. If that isn't enough incentive for you to want to blow their brains out, I don't know what is."

"Hey, Carl," Blancanales said easily. "Let us not be testy. We're on your side. Remember?"

"I don't mean to get testy with either of you," Lyons said with a sigh. "I'd just hoped this would be easier. But I guess that's not our lot in life, is it?"

"Maybe we're asking too much of ourselves," Schwarz said.

It was Rosario "Politician" Blancanales who surprised both men with his reply. "No, we're not asking too much of ourselves. This has to get done one way or the other, and we're the only ones here to do it."

"This is one of those times I wish I had McCarter and friends with us."

"Hell, I'd settle for just an endless supply of 40 mm grenades," Schwarz said.

"I'd settle for a grenade launcher," Blancanales added wistfully.

"Well, at least we have that M-72 A-2 we got from Poppas's stock," Lyons said.

Blancanales frowned. "Yeah, a LAW. You sure that thing will even fire?"

"I'm hoping at least once," Lyons replied with a wicked grin.

The three men were positioned on a four-story tenement building two blocks from the veritable palace where members of Ahmadinejad's personal entourage were located. Around them it seemed almost pathetic that the majority of their neighbors were in modest homes. This area was hardly in squalor, though, and by any measure this would have been considered an upscale neighborhood for Tehran. Regardless, Able Team needed a tactical plan and they needed to come up with it quickly.

Without taking the scope from his eye, Schwarz said, "At least that gate doesn't look too strong."

"You think the VW can breach it?"

"Hey, I'll put money on the front end of a VW microbus any day," Schwarz said as he lowered the scope. "We're just lucky they put the engine in back."

"Okay, then," Lyons said. "Let's nut up and do it."

The trio packed up the scope and made their way down the rickety steps to the sidewalk. They checked the dark street in both directions, waiting in the shadows unnoticed for a Tehran squad car to pass by them before they made it safely back to the VW. Once aboard, Lyons started the engine and took a deep breath before putting it in gear while his friends double-checked the actions on their weapons before putting them into battery.

Through a variety of machinations and dealings, Poppas had managed to secure three MP-5 SD-3s along with half a dozen stock M-26 grenades left over from the Desert Storm days. While they weren't exactly modern, Poppas had promised their reliability, having acquired them from the black market weapons system that oddly enough happened to be run by a group of former U.S. veterans turned contractors and advisers for a paramilitary company.

"It may not be what you're used to but it'll do the job," they recalled Jester telling them shortly after arriving in country.

"Ready?" Lyons asked his friends as he put the microbus in gear.

"Tallyho," Schwarz replied.

Lyons eased onto the street at a speed most would have considered ridiculous. The gate was set relatively a far distance off the road, the terminus of the drive up to it at a considerably sharp corner. By security best practices, it should have been much closer to the road, practically on the street, to prevent someone from doing exactly what it was Able Team planned to do now. Lyons continued up the street at a leisurely pace and rolled past the drive without so much as slowing down. He proceeded half a block, timing his turn into an adjoining drive just as a police cruiser rolled past.

Once in the drive, Lyons killed the lights and the men watched as the cruiser proceeded down the street and then turned onto the road that would circle the block on the back perimeter of the drive. Schwarz looked at his watch and then nodded to Lyons.

"We have four minutes from right now. Mark."

Lyons nodded, put the VW in reverse and backed out without ever touching his brakes. At the peak of his turn he put the VW into neutral and let it coast to a stop before putting it in drive and then gradually increasing speed. Lyons barely negotiated the turn into the driveway and then poured on the speed as he cruised up the slight incline toward the gate. When he made the turn he was doing about forty-five miles per hour, not enough to really avoid getting shot at but surely fast enough to clear the gate and make headway to the front doors.

The metal gate was wrenched from its hinges with a screech so loud it would've sent even a clowder of alley cats into a caterwauling fit. The VW gained speed as it dragged the gate along with it, something Lyons feared might happen, but as it turned out was to their advantage. The sparking gate cut out the feet of two guards who leaped aside to avoid being run over by the VW bearing down on them as they were headed down the drive, most likely to relieve the first shift.

As Lyons brought the VW up to the front doors and leaned on the brakes to stop, the gate came free of the VW frame and continued forward at approximately the fifty miles per hour Lyons had managed to achieve. It seemed almost comical, the puttering of the VW engine even as the Able Team warriors watched the wrought-iron missile travel a straight and true course until it slammed into a half-dozen or so guards who were just emerging from the front doors and onto the driveway.

The gate sent them all to the ground and pinned those that it didn't cut practically in two or decapitate.

"Dang, Ironman, a perfect strike!" Schwarz said as they bailed from the VW.

Once EVA, the trio burst through the front doors that had been left wide open. Fate had dealt the enemy a cruel hand and Able Team had no qualms about cashing in on their opposition's misfortune. Only two guards had remained inside the foyer and they were still a bit stunned by watching the majority of their people being cut down by an object that shouldn't have been anywhere near that location.

Lyons and Blancanales leveled their MP-5s and opened on the pair of Iranian gunsels simultaneously. The 9 mm stingers punched through tender flesh, dotting their bellies and chests and leaving exit wounds the size of silver dollars given the proximity of the combatants. Without losing momentum, the trio moved up the steps in leap-frog fashion and proceeded down the second-floor hallway in a fire-and-maneuver drill they'd practiced innumerable times.

Two more guards appeared at the far end of the hallways and split apart, their incredible reactions the apparent product of good training. Still, it did them little good considering the unerring marksmanship of the Able Team warriors who'd managed to get the drop on the pair before they could even bring their weapons to bear. Schwarz and Lyons got one of the guards with several short bursts that slammed the guy with such force into one of the doors he actually broke it down. He disappeared from view save for his twitching feet. Blancanales managed to take the second guy with a short burst to the upper body, one of the rounds a lucky stray that hit him in the face dead-center. The man's brains imploded to mush as the 9 mm Parabellum fragmented and scrambled the inside of his skull.

"Move!" Lyons said, jumping to his feet even as the sound of footfalls below reached their ears.

Chances were good that their intended targets occupied suites on the next and final floor, a sensible assumption given it would make it very easy to protect the men. They reached the third-floor landing and split up, each assigned to find and eliminate one target.

The roof would be their rendezvous point, a move that would've seemed like utter lunacy to their enemies. Again it made perfect sense when they considered the architecture of the building.

Lyons was the first one to find a viable target.

Hamiri Hassani had been the bane of existence for many a covert operative the better part of the past twenty years. Not only had Hassani, head of the National Directorate for Internal Security, arranged the assassination of many agents of both U.S. intelligence agencies, as well as those of her allies, but also the leader of the Iranian secret police had terrorized and tortured American-Iranian citizens who had come into the country with the intent of renouncing their heritage for one that embraced Muslim practice. Hassani was a fanatic who had long believed these individuals proclaiming religious freedom as their grounds for being in the country were actually part of an elaborate front by the American CIA to penetrate the ranks of "true" Iranian patriots.

It was Lyons's distinct pleasure to blow away the groggy face of Hassani as the blinding lights flooding the room shocked him from his sleep. Lyons made certain of his aim so as not to hit the young, impressionable girl—impressionable because she couldn't have been more than fifteen years old—lying next to Hassani. He regretted that some of Hassani's blood splashed her but at least he wouldn't be degrading her any further, and that was a fact in which Lyons could rejoice.

The girl rolled from the bed, not bothering to even cover her naked body as she ran from the room and into the bathroom, slamming the door shut behind her. Lyons made doubly sure the first bullet he put through Hassani's head had done a complete job and, once confirmed, silently thanked the Heckler & Koch company for their excellent craftsmanship. He then moved to the glass doors, unlocked them and stepped onto the balcony protruding off the back of the house.

A stiff but warm breeze attacked the beads of sweat on his face as Lyons leaped onto the rail of the balcony without hesitation and gained a handhold on the roof. The lights of the city seemed to twinkle peacefully, serene, almost as if enfolding Lyons in an uncanny embrace. Of course the Able Team leader knew there was nothing peaceful or serene about Tehran. This was a city filled with people who hated men like him, and he couldn't really say he blamed them. After all, he'd just broken into the home of one of their most revered diplomats and killed the guy in cold blood. Well, not really cold blood—Hassani had done plenty to Lyons's countrymen and scores of innocent people and Lyons considered it a privilege to have been able to end his reign of terror.

If nothing else came of tonight, if his friends lost their lives or he even lost his own, Carl Lyons would have considered it a worthwhile sacrifice.

HERMANN SCHWARZ FOUND Nasim al-Zardooz in, of all places, his bathtub.

The radio was blaring so loud that al-Zardooz hadn't even heard the commotion taking place right outside his window. Neither had he heard the shots being traded with his security force and Able Team on the floor immediately beneath him. That's why it came as quite a shock when Schwarz kicked in the door of the bathroom and found al-Zardooz luxuriating in the mass of strong bath salts and bubbles that reeked of dozens of exotic scents. The miasma of perfume riding on a heavy cloud of steam that spread throughout the room, in fact, practically made Schwarz want to vomit.

"Well," Schwarz said as he moved into the bathroom and slammed the door behind him. "Caught with your proverbial pants down, I see."

Schwarz moved over to where al-Zardooz could get a good look at the MP-5 in the Able Team warrior's grip. Al-Zardooz should've had some inkling of how it felt, being the military religious liaison to the IRGC and representative supreme of the Ayatollah Khamenei. It disgusted Schwarz when he thought of how al-Zardooz had acted so pious and friendly toward Ahmadinejad and the rest of the presidential staff while he sharpened the knife that he would eventually run into the man's back. Not that Schwarz cared at all—it couldn't have happened to a nicer guy than Mahmoud Ahmadinejad.

Unfortunately it would have to be someone else who did the Iranian president in because al-Zardooz had reached the end of the line. The maniac who now sat in his birthday suit covered in sudsy bath bubbles had been responsible for the brainwashing of hundreds, maybe even thousands of the IRGC. It was al-Zardooz who had insisted the IRGC go out and train the terrorist organizations of the world, from the New Islamic Front to the Hezbollah to spin-offs of al Qaeda, in the hopes of undermining U.S. efforts in Iraq, the Sudan, Pakistan and Afghanistan. Still, al-Zardooz hadn't been able to protect every single one of his cronies and now here he was, even unable to protect himself.

Not that he wasn't going to try, a fact made evident by his sudden move for a towel that he pulled away to reveal the outline of a Soviet-made Makarov.

A whining and droning from the radio perched at the end of the tub was producing a foul, native sound that ground on Schwarz's nerves and in the context of this murderous leach now trying to gun him down, Schwarz saw no reason to work too hard here. Better he could kill two birds with one stone, a thought that brought him just a flicker of amusement as he kicked the radio into the water.

Sparks lit up the surface of the water and al-Zardooz's body made herky-jerky movements under the steady crackling of the electrically powered radio. Unfortu-

nately it was the 220-volt system in this country that
proved to be much more of an inconvenience to Nasim
al-Zardooz but the lights only flickered slightly before the radio finally succumbed to water-logging and
shorted out. As did its master.

"No, don't get up," Schwarz said to al-Zardooz's
corpse as he slid deeper into the water. "I'll find my
own way out."

I KNEW THIS WAS A CRAZY plan, thought Rosario Blancanales.

Of course, it hadn't been any crazier than coming
all the way to Tehran for a piece of scum like Farzad Hemmati. Blancanales had already promised he
would deliver a good thrashing to Hemmati when all
of this business was finished. Blancanales had never
been much for the game of hide-and-go-seek-the-fa-
natic whenever he found himself on enemy soil. He
wondered for a moment what had happened to the good
old days where their biggest troubles were American
criminals who committed crimes in America. At one
point, they'd had it made acting like FBI or BATF
agents, even occasionally U.S. Marshals, able to boss
people around and claim jurisdiction on the nastiest
of the nasty.

Then they would quietly slip away and let others
take the credit while they basked in their own self-
aggrandizement.

But no...this time they had to stick their collective
noses where they didn't belong, in a country like Iran
no less, and take on America's most dangerous enemies
on their home turf. It didn't seem fair to Blancanales
but then those were the breaks. Nobody had promised
this job would be fair, neither had anyone made guaran-

tees about where the missions would lead them. Yeah, theirs was not to reason why, theirs was but to do or die and...well, all that other malarkey.

In a way, Blancanales couldn't really complain since he ended up lucky enough to get the worst of the three they'd come to eliminate. While he wouldn't have changed this fact for the world, he had hoped this wouldn't be so anticlimactic. Lyons had argued that destroying the worst of America's enemies couldn't be a bad thing, and on this point he had to admit no flaw in the logic. But the least Rakhoum Rakiim could've done was put up some sort of resistance.

Rakiim had a reputation as being a fighter, a feisty little bastard who would get his mug on Iranian television or in front of the cameras whenever he could to run down the United States and her allies. Rakiim was a diplomat of the slimiest sort, constantly petitioning the United Nations with resolutions while he schmoozed everyone from the Chinese to the Turkish with promises of wealth and oil from the enriched and blossoming Iranian economy. Not that most of the countries were buying it. The Chinese had responded much the same way they did to most of the Middle Eastern countries—pat their behinds if only gently and scold them into playing nice with others, then infiltrate their economies with funds they could then use to buy Chinese products.

Others were more interested in seeing Iran establish a power base within the Middle East that could be manipulated into controlling the entire region and disposing of Israel's independence and recognition as a nation among the world community once and for all. What Rakiim hadn't bothered to mention was that diplomats sent to Iran who subsequently disappeared or met with some unfortunate accident were completely unexplainable. On more than one occasion, Rakiim had spoken words to console those who had sent representatives, assuring them that those individuals had come and left unmolested or were seen safely out of Iranian territory.

Rakhoum Rakiim had, in fact, been responsible for the deaths of at least a dozen American citizens— mostly important business people or other government officials—while they were in foreign countries. Witnesses who defected to America had presented sworn testimony before closed committees regarding the atrocities of Rakiim but they had never been able to get close enough to deal with the scum-sucking lowlife.

But Rosario Blancanales now had that opportunity and while he'd wished Rakiim would show the same kind of alleged courage now that he'd done so many times before on camera, he could see that the puny, unshaved pig—who obviously hadn't shaved or showered in days—simply stared at Blancanales with the glassy haze of an opioid-induced state. In fact, the entire bedroom stunk of opium and there were hookahs and bongs everywhere.

Blancanales could not find it in his gut to end the man's life by a simple bullet through the brain, even though such an end would've been simple and deserving. No, Rakiim's atrocities belied a more fitting end and Blancanales knew what that was even as he yanked the man from bed by his silk pajamas, dragged him to the balcony and wrapped him in one of the thick cords from the drapes.

It was at this point the Iranian death monger began to fight his opponent, realizing the full magnitude of his precarious situation.

Unfortunately for Rakiim, he was no match for the strength and fierce resolve of Blancanales, something that became evident to Rakiim even as Blancanales tossed him over the balcony with the drape cord tied securely to the balcony. There was a shout of surprise and then nothing, and Blancanales didn't wait for further response because he knew there wouldn't be any.

Instead, Blancanales vaulted the balcony rail and jumped to get a handhold on the roof, hoping he would emerge to find his two friends alive and well.

He did.

"Welcome to the party," Lyons said. "You ready to get out of here?"

Blancanales nodded. "Who did you get?"

"Hassani," Lyons replied.

"Which means you probably got Rakiim?" Schwarz inquired.

Blancanales nodded. "You found al-Zardooz?"

"Of course. It was a real shocker," Schwarz said.

"Huh?"

"Never mind. Where did you leave Rakiim?"

"Oh, he's hanging around," Blancanales replied with a smile.

Just as Lyons had predicted, a fire department engine and ladder truck rolled onto the grounds and were escorted to the front doors. The three men were completely obscured along the flat, adobe roof of the palatial home and as yet undetected by the forces that were most probably searching the house at that very moment and probably only now discovering the bodies of the three men.

A large tree overhung the front area, its massive limbs reaching to the very parapet of the roof. As soon as the ladder truck stopped in front of the house, Lyons swung onto the branch and wrapped his body around the thick limb. He crawled to a safe point and after having tested it with his weight, gave a thumbs-up signal to his two compatriots. Schwarz and Blancanales followed suit, dropping from the tree to the edge of the overhang and eventually into the hose bed of the truck where they pressed themselves flat.

It took almost a half hour but eventually the engine left, the firefighters no longer required since they didn't need to stand by and there were obviously no fires to put out. Lyons had reasoned that with the destruction of the gate and penetration of the home that the dispatch of the fire-rescue system, even in Iran, would go without saying. There would be injuries and deaths to catalog and with the discharge of firearms there was always the chance of fire or explosion.

When they were a few blocks from the scene, the three dropped from the back of the truck and made their way to the garage, leaving the weapons behind. Nobody would be out at this time of night in that part of the neighborhood and they were able to move along the back streets and sidewalks without being observed— at least by anyone who could tell they weren't natives of the area.

Once they arrived at the garage, Blancanales confessed to how he'd left things with Rakiim.

"So what are you saying?" Lyons asked in disbelief. "Are you telling me you didn't nix that scumbag?"

"There wasn't any reason to nix him, Ironman," Blancanales replied. "The guy was so gorked out of his mind on opiates that I sincerely doubt if he'll even remember what happened. Not to mention that when it's discovered he was so wasted he let three American assassins get away, I can guarantee you the ayatollah himself will do the job for us. Trust me…Rakhoum Rakiim's as good as dead."

Schwarz shook his head with a chuckle and then glanced at Lyons. "He's got a good point, Ironman. There's no way a guy in Rakiim's position will live that down. His goose is cooked."

Lyons scratched his chin, looked at Blancanales and Schwarz, then couldn't help but laugh himself. "Yeah, I suppose you're right."

"What's next on the agenda, boss?" Schwarz said.

Lyons checked the list. "We have two more and they're on opposites sides of the city."

"That won't make it easy for us," Blancanales said.

"Well, Hemmati claims he has a government sedan stashed we can use, which will probably help us to avoid any questions."

"Oh, yeah, sure," Schwarz said. "Three Americans cruising around town in a car in the middle of the night with government markings? Nothing suspicious about that."

"I don't see as we have much choice."

"There's always a choice," Blancanales said. "We just need to figure out what other option we have available that hasn't yet presented itself."

"Hemmati's offered to drive and I'm inclined to let him," Lyons said.

"Bad idea, Ironman. Very bad idea."

"You just said there's always another option," Lyons replied. "I'm giving it to you."

"Have I mentioned how very much I mistrust that weasel?"

"On more than one occasion. But I have an idea."

"Oh, joy," Blancanales replied.

CHAPTER TWENTY-ONE

Over the Atlantic Ocean

"Okay, you want to explain this to me one more time?" David McCarter said. "Because I still don't get it."

"What's so hard to understand?" Brognola said. "Able Team was tasked with a termination order of several coconspirators in this case, including some high-ranking officials within the Iranian government with known ties to terrorists."

"Well, you'll forgive me if I'm getting out of line here but I don't bloody well agree with your decision, guv," McCarter snapped. "Able Team isn't some personal hit squad the Man can wield as a political assassination tool whenever it suits him. See? I wouldn't have allowed you to send us on any such mission like this and I don't see why it should be any different for them."

"That's not your call, David," Price said.

"And for your information," Brognola added, the intensity in his voice evident even without his face filling the screen aboard the Gulfstream C-21, "the Oval Office had nothing to do with this. It was my choice and I made it."

"You made it," McCarter said. "And now it's gone south and we may well not only lose a good bunch of men, but I'm putting my entire team at risk heading into a situation we know absolutely nothing about."

"Wait a minute," Encizo said. "Let's all just try to be calm about this. With all due respect, I feel it will be more productive for us to put our heads together cooperatively—" he tapped McCarter gently "—and come up with a plan to get all of us home in one piece. Yes?"

"Fine." McCarter grunted with a nod of assent.

"That's very levelheaded thinking, Rafe," Price said coolly. "Thank you."

"No worries," Encizo said as he stood and folded his arms, keeping an ever-watchful presence to ensure McCarter played nice.

"I'm sorry, David," Price said. "We sometimes forget you guys aren't machines."

"No worries, luv," McCarter said. "I apologize, too. I'm not even sure why I let it eat at me like that."

"Let's forget it," Brognola said. "For now, suffice it to say that this idea was actually Ironman's."

"Leave it to that big lug to get himself into a pickle," Hawkins said from a nearby chair where he was icing his wrist.

"So what's the situation as we know it?" Manning asked.

Price frowned. "Able Team's original mission was to get into the country and pull out a CIA intelligence asset by the name of Farzad Hemmati. As you're aware, Hemmati had intelligence that originally impressed us to believe he could assist with helping you track down the IRGC-Hezbollah contingent in South America. It's only recently that we discovered Hemmati isn't just a member of the Pasdaran, but that he had closer ties with the IRGC than originally suspected."

"So he's been playing us," McCarter replied.

"Somewhat," Brognola said.

"What we didn't know," Price continued, "was that

Hemmati was actually raised by the Pasdaran with Jahanshah Mokri. They were practically foster brothers, and, in fact, it was a man by the name of Hoosmand Shahbazi who orchestrated this entire ruse."

"So it's Shahbazi who's behind all this?" Encizo asked.

"Exactly."

"And Able Team doesn't know it," McCarter concluded.

"Right again," Price said. "They missed their original check-in so we have no idea of what progress they've made or even if they're still alive. We do know one of the two CIA agents assigned to Tehran is dead, and we recently received intelligence from our Company contacts that the other's been injured. We don't yet know how serious but we do know he's under the care of an American-Iranian doctor the CIA uses from time to time."

"What's this bloke's name?"

"Stephen R. Poppas," Price replied. "Bear's sent all the data to your onboard systems so you can review his file for further details. Suffice it to say that Poppas has been in the field a long time and he's very experienced. We have no reason to believe he's a traitor or that he's sold out to the Iranians. We've asked the Company to get a message to this doctor, because supposedly they've received one report the doctor has seen all three of them and confirmed they're alive and well."

"But if Hemmati ends up betraying them, there's a better than offside chance they won't stay that way for long," Brognola pointed out.

"Especially if he finds out we're responsible for the death of his brother," Price added.

"Shahbazi and Hemmati would stand to gain a significant foothold on things in Iran if they've managed to manipulate Able Team into rallying for their cause," Encizo said. "What is it you want us to do?"

"First off, we need to get you into the country. Able Team did it by a HALO jump arranged through our military presence inside of Iraq, but we don't believe we have the luxury of that much time."

"Alternative?" McCarter asked, all of the Phoenix Force warriors now gathered around and alert.

"If and when Able Team completes their mission, we have it on pretty good authority their plans are to retrieve Poppas and extricate themselves from the country by the original plan."

"Which is?"

"They were supposed to meet up with an independent smuggling team operating in the port city of Chaloos," Price elaborated. "They were to get Able Team far enough out in the Caspian Sea that contacts in Azerbaijan could get them out."

"We think those people are trustworthy?" McCarter returned.

"As much as any established government authority in the area," Price conceded. "We agreed to recognize Azerbaijan and their independence as a country, not to mention they've made great strides to cooperate in the fight against international terrorism. Our diplomatic relationship has improved dramatically with them over the years, and we've even gone as far as to endorse their bid for one day making application to NATO. Stony Man has contacts in Baku and there are some pretty high-end military choppers refitted for civilian use with oil companies subsidized by American investments."

"Some of those choppers are piloted by Americans,

too," Brognola added. "In fact, Jack knows one of them personally."

"If we can confirm they're alive and ready for extraction," Price said, "we can get them out. But chances are good they'll be coming out hot and that means they're going to need some support. I can't think of a more fitting mission for Phoenix Force under the circumstances. It's going to be tough enough considering they'll be bringing one of our own out, and he'll be wounded."

"Then I guess it's off to Azerbaijan we go," McCarter replied.

"Don't worry about a thing," James said. "We'll do you proud."

"We know you will," Price replied.

"David, don't take any chances," Brognola added. "Use whatever force is required to ensure the safe extraction of our people. I mean *whatever* force required. I'll take any heat from the Man, come what may."

"You realize that if they've made enough noise and attracted the attention of internal security forces that we'll most likely be going up against a contingent of IRGC," McCarter said.

"The thought had occurred to us," Brognola said with a sigh.

"It's not going to be easy to avoid having our mugs splashed all over the international news circuits if we go toe to toe with Iranian military forces."

"That's why we've opted to use civilian means to secure their extraction."

"Still," Manning said. "The IRGC is going to be crawling up and down those shores in patrol boats."

"Yeah, buddy," Hawkins added. "Able Team's not

going to have an easy time of it no matter how you slice this."

"Are we sure that sitting on the sidelines while waiting for them to come barging out of there is such a good plan?" McCarter finally asked. "Not looking to start anything here. Just saying."

"Under no circumstances can we authorize you to enter the border waters of Iran," Price said. She held her hands up in quotation signs and added, "Not *officially* anyway. If IRGC troops pass beyond the boundary lines of the Caspian Sea as established by treaty, then a modicum of forceful response might be warranted. But again, we aren't looking to start an international incident or make CNN headlines. Let's just cross our fingers and hope our boys can get to where you can make a quiet and uncomplicated extraction."

"Understood," McCarter replied. "We'll be in touch as soon as we know something. Out here."

The Briton turned to his teammates. "Was it me or did you blokes get the exact same impression I did from what Barb said just before we signed off."

"You mean the part about official authorization to enter Iranian territory?" Encizo asked.

"Yeah," McCarter replied. "That part."

"I thought it was pretty clear," James said. "She couldn't officially authorize us to do it. Which implies the only way we could do it is *unofficially,* and I for one have no problem with doing things in such a fashion. How about the rest of you fellows?"

"Well, at least we're in agreement on this one," Hawkins said.

"Yeah," McCarter said. "Isn't it just bloody amazing?"

Tehran, Iran

"You understand, Farzad," Carl Lyons told the Iranian, "that if you abandon us, we're going to survive."

"And when we finish our business with these folks, we'll come back and throw you to the wolves," Blancanales added.

"Why would I do this?" Hemmati said as he negotiated the streets of his home city.

They were heading northwest into the district known unofficially as Tiran. It wasn't as flashy as the first neighborhood they had trawled but parts were still moderately fashionable. From the outset, Tehran was much like any other modern city. It had large buildings and a downtown commercial area; there were signs of prosperity everywhere and as many modern structures as more traditional buildings.

Hemmati continued. "It does not benefit either me or my cause to betray you. You are helping me to transform my country into a new Iran, a place where religious freedom and tolerance are the most important tenets. All I want is for my government to give the same freedom to our people that you have in your own country."

"Religious mandate and Sharia law are hardly fair and equitable terms," Blancanales pointed out.

"Maybe to your way of thinking," Hemmati said. "But we do not think like you Westerners."

"Why not save your patriotic speeches for the elections once you've overthrown Ahmadinejad?"

"I'd like to ask a question," Schwarz said. "What the heck makes you think that overthrowing Ahmadinejad's going to buy you any favors within the seat of power? He's nothing but an errand boy for the Ayatollah Khamenei anyway. You don't honestly think that Khamenei's going to share his absolute power with you?"

"The point is not to gain absolute power," Hemmati said, shaking his head. "You see, it is like I say, we think completely different about our countries. You have your beliefs about your country and I could never change those because you live there. This is also true of my country and me, and there is nothing you can say that will change my mind about this because I live here."

"You didn't answer my question," Schwarz said. "What makes you think things will be any better once Ahmadinejad has been removed from office?"

"This you will see once it is done. We are here."

They entered a quiet neighborhood with a row of pretty decent homes. The drives were well kept and many of them had vehicles parked in front of the homes. The sun had just begun to peek over the horizon, signaling the fact Able Team was running out of time. It didn't make much sense for them to keep up with their plans, especially since they still had a chance to make their rendezvous in Chaloos. What they hadn't mentioned was their intentions where it regarded Hemmati.

"TAKING THAT GUY WITH us won't be an option any longer," Blancanales told Lyons after hearing the Able Team leader's plan to involve the young cleric.

"That goes without saying," Lyons said.

"Look, I think this is actually a pretty good plan Ironman's put together," Schwarz told Blancanales. "And besides, once we split, we're going to take Poppas with us. That's not something we'd planned to do when we came into this hellhole."

"Right," Lyons said. "That means there won't be any room for Hemmati or Shahbazi."

"So what do we do with them?"

"Maybe we should let their own people decide," Lyons said.

"What are you talking about?"

"It was something Poppas said to me earlier," Lyons replied. "This name here, the one I want to go after next. Poppas told me that this guy was a staunch member of the Pasdaran. Said he'd given the cause hundreds of thousands of dollars. There's no way Hemmati and Shahbazi would want to terminate this guy unless they planned to turn the tables on us."

"Or if their goal wasn't really the elimination of Ahmadinejad's regime," Blancanales said.

"Up to this point, we've been reacting to everything these turkeys have laid out for us," Lyons said. "This time I want to turn the tables on them. Give them a taste of their own medicine."

"And how exactly do you plan to do that?"

"I'm going to do to Hemmati what he's been doing to us," Lyons said. "I'm going to lead the little bastard around by the nose."

NOW THE MEN OF ABLE TEAM were about to spring their trap, a trap that Farzad Hemmati thought he was setting for them, when, in fact, the young cleric was about to be the victim of his own smug overconfidence. Yeah, maybe Able Team would have to fight their way through a bad situation as they tried to get out of Iran with their hides intact and one disabled man tagging along. But that was a small price to pay when they considered the alternative. And this very morning they had rid the world of three bad men.

It was time to rid it of two more: Hemmati and Shahbazi.

"That house there?" Lyons said, pointing to the residence earlier identified.

Hemmati nodded. "That's the one."

"This should be child's play in comparison to that last place," Schwarz remarked.

"I won't argue with that," Lyons said. He turned to Hemmati. "All right, you remember the plan."

Hemmati nodded. "You have told me many times now and made me repeat back each time."

"Good, then it shouldn't be hard for you to repeat it back without my first reciting it for you." Lyons grinned. "Should it?"

Hemmati sighed. "I am to circle the area three times, first going out one block and then two and then three. If I see police I am to drive away and then return to that point down the road. If you are waiting there, I pick you up."

"And if we're not?" Lyons said.

"I drive back to the garage and wait one hour."

"And if we don't show up?"

"Then I am free to go."

"Perfect," Lyons said. "Let's go, boys."

The Able Team trio left the car and moved nonchalantly up the sidewalk. A couple of times Lyons turned to see Hemmati still sitting there, engine idling, and after a few gestures—including one rather obscene— the Muslim religious fighter eased from the curb and passed the men. He proceeded to the end of the block and as soon as he'd turned and was gone from the sight, the three Able Team warriors broke into a jog.

Lyons went over the seven-foot-high decorative wall first, and then assisted Schwarz from above while Blan-

canales provided base support. At last, the two helped
Blancanales up and within thirty seconds all three of
them were on the grounds near the wall. The nondescript house belonged to Suhrab Ziya, a midlevel clerk
who allegedly had direct access to important government documents. Such access didn't make his death
of any value to the Pasdaran, which was why the Able
Team warriors knew that to terminate him was an
utterly bogus and unworthy goal. There was also no
evidence he'd committed any atrocities against citizens
of America, either in Iran or abroad, or done anything
to subvert American aims or those of its allies.

In fact, Ziya hadn't done anything for which he
should be condemned and this was what had led Lyons
to believe they could turn the tables on Hemmati.

The trio reached the house and moved inside after
picking the lock to the door, mere child's play for the
skills of Hermann Schwarz. Thankfully the house
wasn't sophisticated enough to have an alarm system.
A clock in the kitchen ticked steadily as the second
hand moved with precision, the sound becoming almost
deafening in the eerie silence. It was still early and it
didn't sound as if anybody was up yet.

"Stop!" Blancanales whispered suddenly.

The three froze in their tracks and listened. Lyons
and Schwarz didn't hear anything at first but Blancanales had obviously keyed into something. Then they
heard it, the sound of a flush toilet somewhere above.
There was the padding of feet and within a minute a
young man with rumpled hair and dark skin appeared
at the bottom of the steps and proceeded to a kettle. The
man put water on to boil and then turned to advance
back up the stairs, only to find three men blocking
his path.

Lyons had his pistol out but he wasn't pointing it at the man. "Are you Suhrab Ziya?"

"Who are you?" the man demanded.

"Shh!" Blancanales said. "Don't wake your family. We mean you no harm."

"How do I know this, American?"

"Because although we were sent here to kill you," Lyons interjected, "we've got more brains than that."

"We also know that you support the Pasdaran with money and other things," Schwarz said. "Like information."

Ziya looked puzzled now. "How do you know this?"

"Because the CIA's been watching you for some time now," Lyons said. "Exactly what is it you do for the Iranian government?"

"I cannot talk of my work," Ziya snapped. "Especially not to foreigners. Who are you? Members of the European Common Union? Patriots for the suppression of Islam?"

"Don't be so dramatic," Blancanales said.

"Yes, you could look at us more as concerned citizens on matters of world security," Lyons said. "In other words, we're the good guys."

Ziya expressed defiance by folding his arms and canting his head. "I could hardly believe this."

"We don't really give a shit if you believe it or not," Lyons rebutted.

Blancanales said, "Would it come as a surprise at all that we were sent here to kill you by a man named Farzad Hemmati?"

"Farzad? I cannot believe this. Farzad is my friend."

"Hemmati's not your friend," Blancanales said. "Hemmati's no friend of anybody but himself and his mullah, Hoosmand Shahbazi. The same Shahbazi who heads the Pasdaran organization and is working to overthrow the very government you work for. The incidents of late in South America, the kidnapping of U.S. Peace Corps volunteers. Did you hear about it?"

"Yes."

"Those crimes were perpetrated by members of the IRGC who are sympathetic to the Pasdaran's cause. We've already terminated two high-ranking officials and caused the soon summary execution of a third, bitter enemies of the U.S. who have killed hundreds of our own. But you, we know all about you and you've never been responsible for the death of a single individual. Have you?"

"Islam is a religion of peace, not war. I do not believe in the acts of these terrorists."

"Well, then hold on to your hat," Schwarz said, "because that's exactly what the Pasdaran's doing. These individuals are responsible for the death of a CIA agent, not to mention the squalor and punitive conditions suffered by a good number of your fellow citizens. They hired their enemies to assassinate members of their own government. Why is it so difficult to believe they would issue a contract to drop the hammer on you next?"

"Do you have any proof?"

"Oh, for the love of—" Lyons began.

It was Blancanales who held up one hand while reaching into his shirt with the other and handing his pistol toward Ziya butt first. "You don't believe us? Fine. Take this and point it at me. I'll wait here while you call the police."

"You're mad!"

"Am I? It seems to me that believing we're here to kill you even after we've said we won't is much crazier than letting you believe we're some whack jobs who broke into your house for no reason. Why is this concept so hard for you to get through your thick skull? The facts are what they are, and we have neither the time nor inclination to argue with you."

The entire conversation seemed utterly ridiculous but Able Team had decided to play a hunch and this was their trump card. If Ziya didn't go for it then their entire plan would unravel…and quickly. Such an eventuality would reduce their chances of escaping from Tehran alive, never mind making their rendezvous in Chaloos and getting out of the country alive. On the other hand, Ziya had access to information that could blow the Pasdaran movement wide-open, a movement that obviously posed a much bigger threat to a feckless and impotent leader who liked to spend a lot of time making threats even while he allowed himself to be manipulated like a puppet on a string.

"Anyway, it's not our job to straighten out your country," Lyons concluded. "We got enough problems."

"Yeah, like getting out of here alive," Schwarz said.

Seeing that Ziya did not have the verve or courage to take the pistol, Blancanales put it away and smiled. "I think we've made our point. Now it's time for you to open the nest on these terrorist scumbags and do the right thing. If you won't do it for your country or yourself, do it for your family. You'll be a better man for it."

The three warriors turned to leave and then Schwarz turned back and said, "Oh, and one other thing. We're going to need the keys to your car."

GIVEN THE STRONG TINT of the windows designed to keep out the merciless Persian sunlight, Farzad Hemmati could not discern the fact there were three men in the sedan that rolled past him while he was making his third pass on Suhrab Ziya's home. Neither did he know that even as they drove past him, Ziya was placing a call to officials in downtown Tehran and telling them about a suspicious vehicle that kept driving past, a vehicle with government markings.

It would be less than an hour later when Tehran police would track said vehicle to a garage in one of the seedier districts of the city, a garage where witnesses would later claim they saw a certain VW bus leave and return multiple times with men inside of it. A garage where Tehran police would find two members of the Pasdaran secreted, and in possession of weapons used in the assassination of high-ranking government officials. And while it wouldn't necessarily take the heat completely off of the Able Team warriors, it would damn sure go a long way toward buying them the time they needed to get free and clear.

CHAPTER TWENTY-TWO

Baku, Azerbaijan

Besides the regular contacts Stony Man maintained inside of Azerbaijan, the city of Baku also happened to be home of the United States Embassy to the country.

Operating beneath the recent presidential appointment of the ambassador to the area was the deputy chief of mission. While it wasn't unusual for his office to receive calls at all hours of the day and night, this one turned out to be special because it came from the White House at a time when realistically the majority of the staff should have been nestled snug in their beds, including the President.

Not so on this bright morning as the Man himself was on the phone and leaving very specific instructions in the ears of the deputy chief's first assistant. These instructions, which were quite explicit, were in turn forwarded directly to the deputy chief of mission, who just so happened to be having lunch with an official from the Azerbaijan office of foreign service. It was with a somewhat embarrassed grin and formal apology that he had to cut his luncheon short and return to his office.

"Important matters of state. I'm sure you understand."

When he arrived at his office, the deputy chief reviewed the information that had been directed to his desk and he barely had time to process the gravity of the situation as it was laid out in front of him when he was told the plane carrying the special visitors had landed and they were to be accorded every courtesy, up to and including the use of the Embassy chopper.

U.S. Marine Guards were contacted and told of the impending arrival of these five important dignitaries, but when the deputy chief went down to the gates to greet them upon being advised they were waiting, the deputy chief was surprised that these men did not appear to be bureaucrats at all. Nonetheless, he greeted each of them enthusiastically and showed them to a comfortable briefing area on the second floor of the ambassadorial suites.

"Can I get you gentlemen anything?"

"We could use a place to clean up soon enough, Deputy," said the proclaimed leader of the delegation. He was a straight-laced type with a strong jaw and British accent.

"I'm certain something can be arranged."

"Right now it's my official duty to inform you that we're here under instructions from the man to whom your boss reports, if you catch my drift."

The deputy chief tried for his most cordial smile. "You can say the President, sir. I mean, after all, we are at the U.S. Embassy."

"I got that, thanks," McCarter replied.

"What we're trying to say is that we're here in an official capacity," Encizo cut in, "but our particular mission parameters may be a little, well…unorthodox. This probably isn't something you get much on the Azerbaijan post."

"That's an understatement," Hawkins added.

"Truth be told, this is strictly a need-to-know operation," Manning said. "We were told to expect your full cooperation, so I'm sure you'll understand there are limits to the details we can give you."

McCarter said, "Suffice it to say that the lives of four Americans are at risk, and it's our job to make sure they come through their current situation with their, um, necks intact. You savvy, guv'nor?"

"Um, yes…absolutely, of course. The safety of American citizens is always of primary interest at the Embassy to Azerbaijan. Where exactly did you say these individuals are located in the country?"

"Oh, they're not in the country of Azerbaijan," Mc-Carter said. "At least not yet."

The deputy chief of mission emitted another nervous chuckle. "Okay, I'm sorry but I guess perhaps I've misunderstood. You just said that you're here to rescue four Americans who are in grave danger, but you're telling me they are nowhere within the territorial borders of this country?"

"Right."

"Well, gentlemen, I'm not sure then of how much help the Embassy can be. We've limited resources here and no authority to operate outside the confines of our jurisdictional purview. I'm sure you can appreciate our position."

"And I'm sure the deputy chief and ambassador can appreciate that while your jurisdictional boundaries are severely limited, we have a much broader palette in which to paint our own pictures."

"Come again?"

"What Mr. Brown's trying to say, Deputy Chief," James said, "is that we're going to need the use of the Embassy chopper in short order, and probably a detachment of Marine guards to assist us with our little operation."

"And what kind of operation would that be?"

"The extraction of four American citizens from a precarious diplomatic situation."

"And where exactly might this diplomatic situation be occurring if not within Azerbaijan?"

"That would be one of those niggley details you're probably better off not knowing," McCarter said.

"Well, I'm not sure I can authorize such an operation if it's not in this country, gentlemen. We have very strict rules about these things. And about the unauthorized use of United States Marines for such an operation."

"Which is precisely why we're here," McCarter replied icily. "It's our job to break the rules."

THE JEEPNEY BOUNCED and jounced its way along the road to Chaloos, causing Poppas to grumble and moan with every bump.

"Holy crap, is it necessary for you to hit every bump?"

"Aw, quit your bellyaching!" Lyons said. "It could be worse."

"I think it's worse," Blancanales said, looking at his rearview mirror as they passed the sign indicating they were entering the city limits of Chaloos.

"What's up?" Lyons asked, peering over his shoulder.

"Police cruiser coming up on our six with its lights on."

"You speeding?"

"Nope."

"Okay, Pops, we're going to need your expertise

here," Schwarz said to the CIA guy. "What are our options?"

"Well, you could stop," Poppas said with a grin. "But I don't suppose that really sounds all that appealing at the moment."

"Even with his hand missing he's an ornery son of a bitch," Lyons muttered. "Let's skip the comedy-and-dance routine for some real answers. What else?"

"I'd go ahead and pull over," Poppas said as he started to sit upright.

"Whoa, whoa!" Schwarz exclaimed. "What the hell you trying to do?"

Poppas looked at the Able Team warrior with a scowl. "You want my help or not?"

"Of course."

"Then give me your pistol and get me as close to the back of this thing as possible."

Even as Blancanales eased on the brake and started to pull to the narrow shoulder, Poppas was making his way along the floorboards to the rear of the jeepney, intent on keeping his head below the level of the windows. It was probable the officer would come to the side of the jeepney where passengers embarked and debarked, which would mean Poppas wouldn't be visible at first. He only had to buy a few seconds.

"Okay, now that we've stopped, get ready," Poppas said. "As soon as he climbs onto the first step, I'll give the signal and you knock him on his ass. Then put this thing in gear and go."

"What's the signal?" Lyons asked.

"You'll know it when you hear it."

"Of course we will," Schwarz replied enthusiastically, but he looked at Lyons and shrugged to indicate he didn't have a clue what the agent was up to.

As the cop came to the door and Blancanales opened it, Poppas flipped a latch recessed in the floor and the bottom panel swung up and out. With a steady aim, the CIA agent put three rounds into the police vehicle just as the officer took his first stride into the bus.

Lyons took the signal and came around the corner, planting a solid boot heel flat against the cop's chest and driving him off the step. The surprised officer landed on his ass, at which point Blancanales closed the door, put the jeepney in gear and smoothly accelerated from the scene.

"Nice work!" Schwarz said as he assisted Poppas to his feet and relieved him of the gun. He helped the CIA agent back to his seat and then took position on the seat opposite Poppas. "I didn't have a clue those kinds of panels were even available in these things."

"They aren't," Poppas replied with a broad grin. "That's a special little modification I made to this thing right after we got it for just such a situation as this."

"I guess experience and ingenuity go hand in hand," Schwarz said. He looked at Lyons. "You see that, Ironman? If you live as long as Pops here you might actually turn out to be useful like him."

"Yeah, ha, ha, you're a riot." Lyons turned his attention to Poppas. "How long do think that's going to buy us? We can't outrun a radio, you know."

"We can outrun that radio."

"Come again?"

"The first two rounds I put in his radiator. But the third I put in the transmitter of his car. They mount their radios on the center of their dashboards. Makes for great target shooting but it's hell on the cops."

"You never cease to amaze, Poppas," Lyons said. Within ten minutes the jeepney had made the aban-

doned dock where the boat awaited them. Schwarz
helped to get Poppas aboard the smuggler's boat first
while Blancanales and Lyons covered their retreat, and
then the remaining two Able Team warriors followed.
They climbed into the boat and once all were aboard
the two men manning the small cruiser began to prepare to depart, untying the ropes from the moorings.

"Um, I think we might have trouble," Blancanales
said, pointing at the approach of two large boats with
official markings.

"Blast it!" Lyons said. "That's IRGC, no doubt. I was
hoping we could at least put some distance between us
and the coastline before they figured out where we'd
gone."

"Any way you look at it, it's a long swim to Azerbaijan," Schwarz said. "And cold. Much colder than
Alaska."

"Quit your squawking and get ready," Lyons barked.

The three Able Team warriors brought their weapons to bear, which were only standard M-9 pistols and
the LAW. Lyons watched as the boat got closer, hearing the echo of a bullhorn even they made a fast approach to intercept. He started to yell at the two men
to get their boat in gear but realized in the distraction
that they were already off the boat and running down
the docks, completely abandoning ship and leaving the
four Americans to their fate.

Lyons cursed them and then instructed Schwarz to
get things going.

"What, you think because I'm the technical guy I'm
automatically some kind of marine expert, too?"

"Gadgets!"

"I'm working on it!"

As Blancanales saw the two boats move closer, the

outlines of heavily armed IRGC now evident as they stood on the respective prows, he said simply, "Please work faster."

Upon that statement the boat motor chugged to life and Schwarz put it in gear, slapping the mixture lever into wide open. He couldn't know how far it would take them but with a full tank chances were good they'd pack some distance. The boat was considerably smaller and built for agility, as well as speed. While it probably was no match for the IRGC cutters they might be able to lose their pursuers in shallow reefs or at least get into an area where they could conceal themselves without running aground.

Chances were better than good this wouldn't end well, but the men of Able Team were bound and determined to try. The boat zipped from the launch, the wind on the Caspian Sea warm and smelling of fish as the boat raced across the choppy waters. The speed managed to surprise all four of the men, and as the wind tossed his graying hair to and fro, Poppas let out a shout of glee then broke into song with a practically tuneless rendition of "America the Beautiful."

WHEN WORD CAME THROUGH of the attempted escape by probable Americans a general alert went off through Chaloos.

The Iranian officials had long suspected smuggling operations dealing in contraband such as liquor and designer wear from the West. They had opted to turn a blind eye to these things since the items were typically purchased only by the wealthiest of Iranian citizens, a matter of practicality since those citizens were the only ones who could afford it. Hence, it came as quite a surprise when officers of the IRGC contingent tasked with patrolling the waters were notified of the escape of subversives from the shores of the country.

While they could've been leaving from almost any point in the city, perhaps even waiting until cover of night, the pair of IRGC boats immediately left their port and embarked on a patrol down the shores of Chaloos in desperate search for any activity. Their good fortune came with the appearance of the lone boat moored along the westernmost area of the city, a place otherwise abandoned, and the sighting of the massive jeepney vehicle that was said to have blasted its way out from police custody. Of course, propagandists had advised officials that the officer had been killed even though he wasn't harmed at all, save for a moderate bruise on his abdomen.

But it made the story sound better when the IRGC caught up with the subversives described as probably spies and most definitely Americans.

What the entire contingency of reporters, police officials and members of the IRGC failed to anticipate was that signal was exactly what a group of five very special men had been waiting for, and when the information came through the men of Phoenix Force went into action. A little black spray paint did the trick in covering the markings of the chopper, disguising it as an Embassy asset.

And as Hawkins had so studiously pointed out, "Hey, it's definitely not official now."

None of the men of Phoenix Force could argue with that kind of Texan logic, neither would they have wanted to. Without concern for their own welfare, the warriors piled aboard the chopper, accompanied by a marine crew of three wearing unmarked camouflage fatigues and plain beige helmets. Whitecaps swirled across the surface of the Caspian Sea as the chopper left the roof of the Embassy and made its way out to a horizon of blue and brown.

A slight haze, the result of a muggy day and a low cloud cover, helped to disguise any low-flying aircraft from observation by higher planes or satellite relays, allowing their chopper to literally "fly under the radar" as they went off in search of their friends. They had no idea in what condition they would find Able Team but whatever happened they were certain to encounter military forces under the direction of the Iranian government.

Even if they did, there wouldn't be any way for the Iranians to identify the rescue operation as being conducted by American forces, special operations, regular military or otherwise, so David McCarter saw no reason to concern himself with that point. It was purely a manner of honor this time, and despite whatever sentiments might have been expressed by the loudmouth naysayers like Glengarry Sweeney, McCarter planned to make sure this was their finest hour.

The chopper dipped closer to the sea and at first McCarter got concerned. A quick glance through the forward windscreen, however, helped explain the reason for the maneuver. The pilot had dropped and diverted the chopper to avoid a small, dark cumulus cloud that had formed over the coast of southern Azerbaijan, pointing the nose in a more southeasterly direction that McCarter knew would take them into Iranian airspace before too long. He could only hope once they entered no-man's land that it wouldn't take long to locate their friends.

Somehow he figured Lyons would devise a way to

make them easy to spot, and that thought brought a smile to David McCarter's lips.

"I THINK THEY'RE GAINING!" Blancanales said, shouting to be heard above the whine of the boat's engine as they sped across the open, choppy sea.

"I think you're right!" Lyons replied. He turned in Schwarz's direction. "Gadgets, see if you can get us closer to the shoreline!"

The electronics wizard tossed a wave of acknowledgment without taking his eyes off the dangerous waters ahead. The sea had grown choppier and the temperature was dropping at a significant rate. To add to the difficulties, the whitecaps and wave patterns were disruptive to the small boat, taking them airborne on more than one occasion and threatening to dump all of them out of the boat.

"Damn it to hell," Schwarz muttered under his breath.

He tried to follow Lyons's direction but he knew the situation was unpredictable enough that they could well smash into the rocks or run aground on a sharp reef if they got too much closer to the shore. There were as many treacherous and natural traps along the shores of the world's largest body of water as there were on the open waters, IRGC boats or no IRGC boats.

In one sense, maintaining an open throttle was buying them a small advantage in that they didn't have to worry about the strain of displacing as much water as the cutters pursuing them. Unfortunately, what the IRGC boats lacked in speed they made up for in power and they were gaining an advantage at a considerable rate. That advantage was only heightened by the sudden, thunderous sound of something booming through the air and the flash of smoke and heat that came off the bow of the cruiser.

A moment later, an explosive blast erupted less than fifty yards off the port bow of Able Team's boat.

"I think we have a very serious problem," Lyons said through gritted teeth.

Nothing they had aboard could repel the giant weaponry now in range and being leveled at them, a fact that was evident as another blast, this one considerably closer, blew a geyser of water fifty feet into the air. The blast was close enough to drench the boat's occupants. It wouldn't be long before they got close enough to score a lucky hit.

"Gadgets," Blancanales said, "turn her around. Head toward them!"

"What? Are you crazy?" Lyons demanded of his friend.

"Those guns are built for range, Ironman," Blancanales explained. "Maybe we can get close enough with a LAW to take one of them out."

"And what if we can?" Lyons said. "There are two boats, Gadgets—and we only have one rocket!"

"We'll survive a lot longer against one boat with small arms than we will against those heavy guns, buddy!"

Lyons tried to think of a way to rebut his friend's logic but he realized he had none. Not that it mattered, since Schwarz had already turned the boat and was now on a collision course with the two IRGC cutters. Even from that distance they could see the occupants scrambling as they tried to adjust for the range of the rapidly closing cruiser. Only one of the two boats managed to get off a shot that was well away from its intended target.

As they came close, Lyons readied the M-72 A-2 light antitank weapon and brought it to his shoulder.

Blancanales said, "Are you sure you wouldn't like me to do that, Ironman?"

"Shush!" he told his comrade. "Don't distract me."

Blancanales turned to look at the pair of rapidly approaching cutters and squeezed his eyes shut, certain that Lyons would miss the target either by firing too soon or too late. A moment after he heard the whoosh of the rocket and the roar of propellant as it left the tube, Blancanales opened his eyes in time to see the forward bow of one IRGC boat erupt in a belching column of red-orange flame. The subsequent blast ignited the fuel canisters and depth charges secured along the port side of the IRGC cutter and a moment later bodies flew in all directions as the boat blew sky-high.

"Nice job, Ironman!" Blancanales said, clapping his palm on the Able Team leader's shoulder.

"Thanks," Lyons said. "But now what the hell are we supposed to do?"

"I don't know," Blancanales replied. "You're supposed to be in charge. That makes you the brains of the operation. I'm just the brawn."

"Lovely."

IF THERE HAD BEEN ANY doubt in McCarter's mind that Lyons wouldn't make their location known, it disappeared entirely when the navigator reported a massive heat signature on the sonar that could have only come from an explosion.

"How far?" McCarter shouted at the navigator.

"Exactly eight nautical miles."

"That'll be our people!" McCarter replied.

"Sir, you do realize that we are now well inside of

Iranian airspace. It won't be long before they put jet fighters in the air. We won't be any match for them."

"Then we'd best get in, get our people and get the hell out," McCarter replied. "Hadn't we, Lieutenant?"

"Aye, sir!"

"Carry on, Marine."

The flames from the IRGC cutter were still evident as soon as they were in visual range. McCarter breathed a sigh of relief because he knew the boat was just too damn big to be the escape craft of smugglers. Besides, the flash of muzzles from small-arms fire was pretty evident as they got closer, and with each passing minute the Phoenix Force leader's gut tipped in wondering if they would make it to the scene before it ended badly for his friends.

McCarter signaled for his men to gather in close. When they were within earshot he said, "There aren't any rocket pods or other offensive armament aboard this thing or I'd simply order the Marines to blow that IRGC cutter out of the bloody water. That means we're going to have to do this the old-fashioned way. Get ready for an air assault on the IRGC boat, standard formation!"

The men of Phoenix Force nodded and immediately geared up, clipping carabiners and other equipment to their belts in preparation for an encounter with the Iranian Republican Guard Corps. McCarter stepped forward so he could engage the pilot in conversation; the Marine navigator eagerly stepped aside to let the intent-looking Briton past him, something he wouldn't have ordinarily done for anybody else.

"We're going to have to board that craft!" McCarter told the pilot.

"No way, sir!" the Marine replied. "We don't have

any weaponry and that's a military vessel of a sovereign nation. They'll shoot the belly out of this bird before you can get off a single shot!"

"Listen, mate, you need to give my friends down there a little credit," McCarter said. "We know exactly what we're doing and so do they. There's no doubt they'll provide us with cover fire while we mount an assault against it. Not to mention, there's only a half-dozen armed IRGC aboard that boat minus the crew."

The pilot's slow nod was all the answer McCarter needed. The Briton returned to the rear fuselage and readied his own equipment. The pilot swung the chopper in a wide circle, trying to gauge the best approach that would expose his ship to the least chance of getting dropped in the drink. McCarter left him to it, confident that as a Marine pilot for a U.S. Embassy he had some reasonable level of experience in how to keep his crew safe and his bird out of sticky situations. While McCarter wished he had Grimaldi at the stick, beggars couldn't be choosers.

They would bloody well get this done and get everyone home alive, just as he'd promised. There was no question about it.

The pilot finally settled on an approach directly toward the stern of the cutter but came to a hover directly over the roof. As soon as he swung the chopper into position and had matched speed with the boat, McCarter signaled his team and the five Phoenix Force warriors bailed out of the chopper and descended a pair of cables opposite of each other and hooked to either side of the chopper.

They dropped to the roof of the boat with the practiced ease of professionals and McCarter smiled with pride as he saw Lyons and Blancanales, who didn't look too much worse for the wear, laying down covering fire from pistols that he knew were wholly inadequate for such a task. Well, his friends no longer had to hold their own and go it alone for this mission.

Phoenix Force had joined the fray!

CHAPTER TWENTY-THREE

The half-dozen Iranian Republican Guard Corps troops would've expected many things while attempting to apprehend the American fugitives. But nothing could prepare them for the sudden appearance of a large unmarked chopper as it parked itself directly above their boat, followed by the descent of five human forms clad in combat black.

The first IRGC gunner responded with admirable enthusiasm but completely ineffective tactics. David McCarter immediately seized on that advantage as the first one off the chopper on the port side of the boat. The Phoenix Force leader leveled his MP-5 9 mm and triggered a 3-round burst that dumped the IRGC guard over the side. The man's body hit the water with a splat and floated lazily from sight in the wake of the powerful cutter's engines.

Realizing that they were being boarded, the pilot smartly cut the boat engine in an attempt to give the IRGC commandos every advantage—it was much more difficult to get an accurate bead on an air-assault team if the boat they were boarding was in motion. Even as the cutter slowed, however, it only served to help the Phoenix Force warriors. McCarter and Calvin James were the first to touch down, their boot-shod feet hitting the roof of the cutter with a solid clunk.

The pair set up covering fire as Encizo and Manning followed suit a moment later.

With the quartet now aboard the IRGC cutter, the pilot swung quickly out of range and circled so that Hawkins could get the attention of the smaller boat crew from the side door. The IRGC cutter even with her engines powered down and her screws no longer turning zipped past the boat she had been pursuing just minutes before as Schwarz dropped the throttle switch to full closed and killed the engine.

Even over this part, the seas were still choppy and the smaller boat didn't fair as well. Hawkins didn't let that bother him in the least, simply grateful they had managed to find their friends alive and still kicking. With his injured wrist, Hawkins had been the obvious choice to stay aboard the chopper and monitor the winch operations.

Blancanales was the first to come aboard so he could assist Hawkins with Poppas, who came up next. Schwarz followed and Carl Lyons was the final one to board the chopper. The operations took a total of ten minutes and once they were all safely aboard, Hawkins gave the all-clear signal and ordered the pilot to swing back and pick up his friends. It looked damn sure like they were going to come through this, after all.

McCARTER'S SEA LEGS weren't completely under him, and he lost his balance as a rough wake shifted the boat sharply. He twisted his body and took the impact on his side, grabbing the lip of the roof so as not to slide overboard.

James jumped from the roof just before the change and landed solidly on the foredeck. He whirled and caught an IRGC gunner square in the chest with a burst

from an MP-5. The man staggered backward, his numb
fingers spread wide as he let go of his weapon and it
clatter noisily to the deck. The impact drove him backward, tangling him up with his comrade who'd taken
up a position to cover his flank.

The IRGC guard recovered with surprising speed
and triggered a 3-round burst at James from his SMG.
Two rounds buzzed past James's left cheek but a third
took a small bite out of his shoulder. James dropped
and rolled to escape further injury, and Encizo took up
the fight in his place, moving in on the guard's flank
from above. The man looked toward Encizo in surprise
just a heartbeat before the Cuban shot him through the
face at point-blank range. The man's head exploded in
a gory spray and his nearly headless corpse staggered
with the impact before tipping over the railing and disappearing from Encizo's vantage point.

Manning was in the process of helping McCarter to
his feet when an enemy gunner popped over the rear
end of the roof and tried to draw a bead on him. With
one arm encircling McCarter's waist, Manning had to
direct the fire of his MP-5 single-handed. The weapon
bucked in his grasp as Manning delivered a steady, sustained burst of better than six rounds. Two of the 9 mm
Parabellums entered the IRGC soldier's chest and the
remainder turned his face to pulp from his neck to the
top of his skull.

McCarter finally managed to get his legs back under
him and nodded in thanks to Manning.

Encizo cleared the last gunner aboard the cutter with
a rising corkscrew burst that caught the man in the abdomen. His body did an odd pirouette as his assault
rifle sprang from his fingers and then tumbled to the

deck and down a small flight of steps that landed on a side deck leading astern.

Two of the boat crew had armed themselves, apparently bent on repelling the boarders. Their pistols proved no match for the SMGs and unerring accuracy of the Stony Man commandos. McCarter, Encizo and Manning caught the pair in a brutal crossfire, ripping their tender flesh to shreds under the onslaught of more than three dozen rounds. By the time the last of the autofire died out, the better part of that area of the deck was slick with blood. In minutes they had the officer and three of the remaining crew members secured on deck. McCarter managed to communicate to the men that they would emerge from their situation unharmed as long as they made no attempts to resist their captives.

One of the men, most likely the captain, spit at his feet and shouted what probably amounted to a rash of obscenities at them, though none of the Phoenix Force warriors took it personally. They had good reason to hate the American dogs who had just wiped out their entire contingency and decimated their elite forces in what had amounted to a pretty evenly matched fair fight—at least that's how the members of Phoenix Force would look at it. Historians would make the decision.

Again, in fifty or a hundred years when tales of their exploits could finally be revealed, McCarter mused.

While they waited for the chopper to extract them one at a time, Encizo took the time to bandage James's arm with the team medic's own field pouch.

"While I sure appreciate this, isn't this usually the other way around?" James observed.

Encizo stopped bandaging long enough to say, "Bite your tongue."

James was surprised at first but then he blushed as he thought about the implication behind the words, even if his comment had been entirely innocent and he hadn't meant it that way. With that thought, it triggered a bubble of laughter from somewhere deep inside and Encizo grinned, sharing in the lighter moment.

They were finally all aboard and turning to leave when the pilot gestured McCarter to come forward.

"What is it?" the Briton asked.

"Exactly what I was afraid of," the Marine captain replied. "We just got word that long-range satellites show Iranians are scrambling a pair of jet fighters to investigate."

"Any way we can outrun them?"

"You're kidding. Right, sir?"

"Okay, hold on a minute." McCarter retreated to the back and said, "I don't think we're out of the woods yet. We got Iranian jet fighters on the way and the pilot says there's no way we can get clear of their airspace before they're on us."

A gaggle of tired, muted faces stared back at the Phoenix Force leader, who finally sighed in exasperation. "Oh, for bloody hell, don't at least *one* of you geniuses have an idea?"

"Why not give them something else to look at?" Poppas finally suggested.

"Such as?" Lyons inquired.

"They're fighter pilots, right?"

McCarter nodded. "What's your point, mate?"

"All they probably know is that there's trouble out here and they've been ordered to investigate. They won't necessarily know what they're looking for and they sure as hell won't know that an unmarked chopper's been operating in the area. We're still below radar and the IRGC communication equipment's been disabled. They'll be searching with infrared. You paint a big enough target for them and beat feet, they're not even likely to notice you. And even if they do, it'll be too late because while they investigate whatever you leave behind for them here we're making serious distance, baby."

"I think he's on to something," Hawkins said brightly.

"Me, too." McCarter looked at each man in turn. "Okay, I know at least one of you all brought a grenade or two. Cough 'em up!"

They started fishing through their fatigues and came up with a total of five grenades. McCarter studied Poppas's face. "Now what?"

"Why you looking at me?"

"It was your idea."

"Oh, for the love o'— Stick the crew into a dinghy with a signal flare and then drop the grenades onto the boats."

McCarter grinned. "Now that's the best idea I've heard all day."

"Wonderful, glad you like it," Poppas said with more than a little sarcasm. "I love how I have to think of everything around here. Sheesh, I thought you guys were pros."

"We are," Schwarz said. "But mostly we only do this on a part-time basis. During the day we have regular jobs. We're sort of like a special covert ops reserve, I guess…."

POPPAS'S PLAN WORKED perfectly and in what seemed like an endless drag of time and effort they were soon safely out of Iranian airspace and bound for Azerbaijan.

If they'd had to do it over again, the warriors probably wouldn't have made the same choices. The incidents were splattered all over the news by that evening but the references were pretty vague and most of it sounded like rhetoric by the Iranian government aimed at disclaiming the West. News of the Pasdaran's attempted coup and overthrow of the government never made even local headlines, oddly enough, neither did the disappearances of two Muslim clerics.

A young midlevel clerk in the Iranian government was credited with uncovering a plot to assassinate high-ranking officials, but the actual source of the story was never identified and neither was the clerk. In another strange twist, the highly publicized and controversial diplomat, Rakhoum Rakiim, had voluntarily tendered his resignation to the ayatollah, subsequently fading into political obscurity in no time flat. His family reported his disappearance a few weeks later to officials but the investigation uncovered no leads and it was assumed he'd wandered away from his home, despondent over resigning his tenure in government, and probably went off into the desert to commit suicide.

To the chagrin of the deputy chief of mission, the ambassador to Azerbaijan delivered an official reprimand to the entire staff for the fragrant lapse in security that permitted someone to deface Embassy property, specifically the ambassadorial chopper. Interestingly, there was never an "official" inquiry, and not one personnel file actually listed anything regarding that particular incident.

Stony Man Farm, Virginia

THE MEMBERS OF ABLE TEAM and Phoenix Force gathered around the conference table in the War Room, all with postures somewhere between haggard and just plain beat up. They had been through a lot, yeah, although Brognola surmised Able Team had taken much more of the brunt than their Phoenix Force counterparts.

Carl Lyons in particular usually thrived on action but the Stony Man head fed could see the weary, worn look in Lyons's expression this morning. He needed a rest. Hell, they all did, and Brognola planned to see they got it. These debriefings were not only traditional but necessary, however, and there would be time enough for America's warriors to soon take respite. They had run through most of the preliminaries and much of the air of post-combat tensions had resolved with the passage of time.

"Okay, we've completed our agenda so let me take the opportunity to congratulate you on another fine job," Brognola said.

"And under very tough circumstances," Price added, her face beaming like a proud mother's.

"Yeah, but special kudos to Phoenix Force," Schwarz said. "That's another notch for you guys pulling our bacon out of the fire."

"Any time, chum," McCarter replied.

"We received word from the President last night that the situation in Iran is no better for all of your efforts," Brognola said. "Ahmadinejad is still in power and the threat from Iran's continued nuclear proliferation program, as well as their support of groups like Hezbollah, is ongoing. This was one of those situations forced on us and, unfortunately, you boys got caught in the middle."

Lyons waved off the comment. "The fact is we did what had to be done, Hal. Shahbazi's attempted coup was really as much of a sham as Hemmati leading us around by the nose doing the Pasdaran's dirty work."

"Maybe true. But your actions also led to the termination of a number of very dangerous terrorist leaders. That's no small feat considering you were closely quartered with long-time enemies of America."

Lyons nodded his acknowledgment.

"What about the situation in Paraguay?" Manning asked. "Any plans on the part of the government to tighten up their homeland security efforts?"

"Officials are cooperating with our embassy personnel there," Price said. She winked and added, "I think the move to keep Brad Russell on board will certainly prove to their benefit in the end."

"Okay, that's a wrap," Brognola said. "Get out of here and take some R & R."

"Hey, Ironman?" Schwarz said, nudging Blancanales with an elbow. "How about we take that trip to Alaska?"

EPILOGUE

Stephen R. Poppas stepped out of the sedan and walked slowly but steadily up the rain-slick sidewalk leading to the front door of a modest single-story home in Winchester-Frederick County, Virginia. There were so many things he wanted to say to the young lady whose picture he'd seen maybe a half-dozen times, but even as he reached the front door the words failed him.

Poppas stood there, a number of times turning to leave, then turning back to stare at the door. He raised his hand again but then finally chickened out and went back to his car. As he climbed behind the wheel and reached to engage the push-start ignition, the glint of light on his prosthetic caused his stomach to turn. This gave him pause to consider his actions, his futile attempt to drive all the way out here to console a man's widow, only to chicken out at the last moment.

What the hell kind of courage is that, Poppas? he asked himself.

After his return to his home with an amputated right hand, he'd broken down and told his wife everything about his work—rather his *former* work—as a CIA case officer. Then he'd cried in her arms as she'd rocked and shushed him, and told him it was all going to be okay. No, it wasn't ever going to be okay. The nightmare wouldn't go away until he did this one final task. Only a coward would come this far and then turn back without completing the mission.

Poppas considered that tenet and realized he was right. The three guys he'd encountered in Tehran, and the friends who crossed more than a thousand miles of ocean to their sorry hides, they were the model of courage—they knew what it took to be men because they lived and breathed courage every single day of their lives. That didn't leave any doubt in Poppas's mind that he had an obligation to speak the truth, stand up for the little guy whenever it had to be done and whatever the cost.

Cost? To hell with the costs. Ronald Abney had paid the ultimate cost and his wife deserved to understand just what the benefit of that cost had been.

Poppas climbed from behind the wheel, closed the door and straightened his tie in the speckled window before taking one last walk up the sidewalk. This was the time he'd dreamed of most and while he knew the nightmares wouldn't stop, neither would the sense of something being not quite done until he could perform this one last act of courage. It was an act of courage that Ronald "Jester" Abney would have strongly approved of.

Poppas rapped on the door and a minute later a pert, pretty blonde answered it.

"Yes?" she said. "Can I help you?"

"Mrs. Abney?"

"Yes."

"My name is Stephen Poppas. I worked with your

husband and there's something I think you should know. May I come in?"

Without hesitation, the young woman smiled. "Of course, Pops. I've been waiting for you."

* * * * *